TURTLE COAST

by Betty Anholt

Betty Anholt (signature)

Front cover image: A remnant of earlier times—An abandoned fish-house in Pine Island Sound, Southwest Florida—*Photograph by the author.*

Back cover images: Top; loggerhead sea turtle. *Photograph by Patrick D. Hagan and courtesy of Caretta Research, Inc.* Bottom: Author Betty Anholt. *Photograph from the Anholt family collection.*

AMBER
PUBLISHING

To my family

Jim, Morganna, and Cameron

1

Captain Murdock left the dock office for the boat as the last three-hundred-pound blocks of ice were loaded on board.

Mullet Jim stowed supplies and groceries next. The captain watched his deckhand, his eyes following the man's movements, but disengaged. The Negro occasionally glanced up at the captain as he worked, quick darting glances, trying to gauge the boss-man's mood.

They had worked together for several years. The captain was tough. He expected the best and then some. Jim didn't mind. Captain Murdock demanded more of himself than he ever asked of Jim. Just the same, the deckhand felt a nervous flutter at the beginning of each run. The run boat was much too small a place to be confined when one of the captain's bitter moods descended on him. Jim saw the captain as a body surrounding a gnawing hole. He could be vicious and generous by turns, changing personality like summer storm-clouds. He was not always able to contain the problem that ate at him. Sometimes he was trapped in it.

"Where's our first stop, Jim?"

Mullet Jim looked up, startled. The man knew his route blindfolded, fogged in. This south Florida frontier held less mystery for the run boat captain than it did for the commercial fishermen scattered along the nearly unpopulated coast, fishermen who had lived here since the Cubans had given up their fish ranchos at the turn of the century nearly three decades ago.

"Cap'n, you knows it's Bull Bay fish-house."

"That mail-order package, the one from Sears. The one you packed in first, covered over with the rest of this. Who's it for?"

Mullet Jim scratched his head and started to explain."Well, Cap'n, it's for Jake over to Bull . . ."

"Exactly. You sure as hell haven't gone so stupid on me you're fixing to put all the first stops on the bottom, are you? Pull that mess apart and pack it proper!"

"Yessir, boss."

Jim bent his head down to hide the grin he felt coming. The old man seemed in a pretty good temper today. As he pulled the packages out to adjust them, he felt the deck rock as the captain came on board. Jim knew no matter how violent the captain's mood, its worst fury was directed within. That made Jim tolerant of the bad times. The skipper was a cast-iron woodstove on a bitter winter night, glowing red with fury, rattling its lids, even exploding. Once the fire went out, though, it still stood, black and cold. Inside were ashes.

A pile of groceries and merchandise still waited on the dock for families and fishermen down route. The captain tallied supplies they received against fish they delivered to the fish-houses, fish which filled his ice hold on the return. He usually brought whatever the fishermen needed on his next run. Unless it wasn't in stock in town. When people depended on you it was necessary to be reliable, regular, and good with accounts. A captain did not last long otherwise. Seamanship was only part of his job. People were scattered for seventy-five miles down the coast, isolated by choice—and their job—fishing. Independent people who were able to survive what was thrown at them. Still, they were dependent on the run boat's periodic appearance, which brought a piece of town life to them. The run boat served as a pickup, delivery, post-office, and newspaper. A touchstone for people who for months sometimes didn't see anyone but other fishermen.

Murdock's was an important job. The run boat was the belt, the timing chain, that coordinated all those isolated gears, so they worked in concert with the packing company and even the rail-lines north. And Murdock was captain, the man in charge of the run boat. He enjoyed being essential, especially for the fishermen down-line. They were as necessary for him. Their spare, focused life centered in tidal rhythms confirmed his suspicion that the universe held concerns of greater importance than humankind's.

He knew people alone weren't necessarily lonely, but they still needed to look into other human eyes occasionally, to be reassured of their humanness. He needed reassurance too, when unhappy memories assailed him.

Detail work, organizing, kept his mind busy while his body piloted the boat through the water. It was an ideal spot for him, not dealing with anyone for long, and everyone for a while. His work done well guaranteed a good opinion from everyone. Everyone who knew him. Except the one who knew him best. The only one who really knew him. Himself.

Murdock took his tally books into the wheelhouse and checked the boat contents. A half dozen battered fuel drums were battened down, stained with differing amounts of rust and paint. The captain thumped a pair of drums at random.

"Don' worry none, Cap'n. They all filled. And our tank too. Plenny a fuel aboard."

"I worry." The captain shot Jim a look."You do the forgetting and I catch the hell."

Jim laughed. "Now Cap'n, you know you only adds interest and passes it on ta me!"

"Listen here, you insolent black buzzard, you'd be smart to get hopping so we can leave this damn dock before the sun goes down and I have to throw your worthless bones to the jewfish under that dock."

"Naw, boss. You sure wouldn't wanna be doing that with all them fish to be loading. That be awful hard work for a captain to be doing. Don't forget Bill ain't along today. Not that the engineer would load fish either!" Mullet Jim screeched with laughter as he brought his arms over his head to cower in mock fear of retaliation.

Captain Murdock grinned. "Get moving, you sorry clown. We can't let Bill know he's needed on this ice-bucket. Be a long trip, doing without him."

He picked up a package from the deck and squeezed it.

"Mrs. Pratt's wool yarn doesn't need to be iced down. I'm putting it in the cabin. She'd probably not want it shrinking up to nothing, even if it's going to be for her new baby's clothes."

"Won't be long and we'll be seeing the little one, I 'spect."

"You ever seen a baby born, Jim?"

"Not actually. Been nearby when Mama birthed some of her babies, though."

"You'd have been a baby too, then," the captain said.

"I reckon. But she still midwifes some."

He squeezed the package of yarn again. "Well, anyone, man or woman, ever tries to convince you that a woman isn't as tough as any two men if she has to be, has never seen a woman give birth, away from all those damn doctors and preachers and what all." He paused a moment as he reached the wheelhouse door.

"You know, maybe that's why we're so anxious to keep them contained in four walls. We're afraid of them."

"'Fraid? Of women? Cap'n, you ain't cast off yet and you got too much sun already!"

"Go ahead and laugh, Jim. But you think about Mrs. Pratt, raising a pile of kids on that little island. Or Miz Lewellen down the way. She fishes rings around the old man and then goes home and tends her garden and house. I know for a fact she brings in three-quarters of their catch. That time he was laid up and couldn't do anything, she still brought in damn near as many fish and took care of him to boot." The captain shook his head in admiration.

"Ain't many women fishing for a living," Jim observed.

"God help the men if they decided all at once that they'd rather."

"Cain't imagine you wiping noses while some woman's running this boat, Cap'n." Jim giggled.

"I knew a woman who ran a lot bigger boat than this. She knew how to do it, too. Anybody thought it was funny, changed their tune after watching her work. She took it over from her daddy. Happens sometimes. A husband dies or takes off, and the woman starts to do his job. Because she has to. And decides, by golly, she likes it, too."

"I ain't never seen the woman's gonna take my job, boss."

"Maybe you don't want to, Jim. Probably no woman's gonna want your job, but Heaven help you if you run into the right one. You can laugh. That's only because you haven't met your match yet. You'll see. When it happens, you remember I told you."

The mooring lines cast off, Murdock eased the ice-filled boat through the channel across the wide flats. The town, small enough to start with, shrunk rapidly as the heavy-laden boat lifted her bow to meet the waves, crashing through to their troughs. A southwest wind funneled through the pass fifteen miles west. It opened the expansive harbor to washboard rollers. The boat bucked rhythmically as she headed for the islands on the north side of the harbor.

"Be a bracing ride, Cap'n."

"Think you can find your way?"

Captain Murdock turned the wheel over to Mullet Jim with the comment. Then, going forward, he found a comfortable spot where he could settle and watch the faint mist of islands and shore separate from the horizon, delineating the grey-blue sky from grey-green sea. That dividing line merged in the pass. One color ran into the other so smoothly that it looked like the boat might ride into the sky, except for the solid thumping the rollers made. The crash of the white spray as the bow smartly met the green sea, to rise and crash again, made it clear this was no ethereal sky ride.

Jim kept the bow pointed just north of the pass. The first stop, Bull Bay fish-house, usually had a variety of fish to dump in the hold on the return. Calm weather would mean the boats could venture out into the Gulf. The captain had seen times when the fish-house overflowed with kings and off-shore snapper instead of mullet and seatrout.

Further south, especially when the shark factory had gone full steam, the fish-houses had been full of cobia caught almost as a by-product of the sharks, a bonus, according to George at Carlos Pass. If anyone were an expert on sharks and the job of skinning them for their leather, it was George. He lived sharks for many years, netting them with heavy tarred rope nets, and skinning them at the shark factory, where he'd lost most of his hand to a shark that wasn't quite as dead as he'd thought. Murdock was not too sure he'd stay on the water in any capacity if he'd been in George's shoes.

But George, like a number of solitary men along this coast, preferred to live on one of the fish-houses or a small lighter—houseboat-barge— nearby. An occasional netter peddling his fish was all the company he desired. Over the last few years of running the route, the captain had become friendly with George. He believed George stayed on the water because he genuinely enjoyed it. But men stayed in this watery wilderness for other reasons. Murdock had learned not to ask too many questions. Lawmen asked too many questions. It did not pay to be thought a lawman, or to show too much interest in anyone's comings and goings.

Captain Murdock pulled his pipe from his pocket, tamped in the tobacco, and lit up. The pass was more defined now. A horizon showed where the lighter-colored sky touched the sea. The rhythm of the waves hadn't changed, but it wouldn't be long before they would be able to round the cape and run behind some fringe islands. That back way was no shorter, but it smoothed the ride when the harbor turned windy. The harbor was one big stretch of water. Taking it lightly was not wise.

He could see the eroding bank of Cape Haze where Indians had built their mounds centuries ago. Now gnawed by wind and water, those elevations must have been the perfect observation point in their time. If scrub growth were cleared away, the breeze would deter the mosquitoes and gnats. The view on a clear day extended for miles inland, upriver, beyond the pass into the Gulf, and south along the sound. He had climbed to the mound crest once. The view was what he imagined the silently soaring man-o-war bird sees as it drifts placidly high.

Mounds were scattered throughout the entire waterway. Murdock could envisage silent Indian watchers prepared, like owls in the night, to pounce on unsuspecting prey if their blood thirst demanded. Or to allow passage with the impassive lack of concern any powerful man or beast possesses. It must have been unnerving for Spanish scouting parties to wonder if or when a savage Indian attack might come.

Nothing was left of them now but their mounds—and maybe ghosts. Good thing, too. He was sure storms and skeeters wouldn't get much attention if those cannibals were still around.

The engine cavitated as Jim swung the boat stern 180 degrees to round the cape. The sharp turn to avoid running broadside to the chop brought Murdock upright.

"Screw runs better in the water."

"Yassir." Jim gave him a saucy grin."But, sir, you think about it, it runs a lot faster outta the water."

Murdock glared at him.

"That's the way you want to run that prop, that's fine. I expect you'll enjoy poling this tub from here to the Ten Thousand Islands and back."

"Maybe I'll just keep it in the water, Cap'n."

"Sounds like an idea to me."

They shared another grin and paid attention to the boat. The rhythm of the swells, approaching now from astern, made a markedly different ride.

Instead of crashing into each wave, the boat was lifted by the swell, and the bow slid down into a trough. When they looked forward toward the bow, they saw green water as they slid toward the wave trough. It receded to sky as the boat bottomed out and began to climb the face of the next wave. The crashing was gone. But this following sea produced a feeling in the gut that made few people prefer its smoother ride.

Neither Jim nor the captain wasted time watching forward anyway. They scrutinized each wave catching up to the stern. As the boat lifted to allow it passage they momentarily relaxed and started to eye the next swell. The prop's growl accented the swell rhythm as it cavitated, exposed then submerged.

In less than a quarter mile the water smoothed. They had moved within the lee of the islands, out of direct line with the pass. Simultaneously, both men sighed. With a hold full of ice, it would not take much of a swamping wave to put a boat on the bottom. And parts of this harbor had bottom sixty or eighty feet below. While this was no storm sea, not paying attention always meant trouble.

"Looks like we don't have to swim today, Jim."

"Good thing. I ain't never tried that."

"I imagine you'd learn pretty quick, if you noticed one of those big old sharks come up to see what you're doing in their water."

Jim shuddered. "That ain't even funny, Cap'n."

"Right enough, Jim."

The water was almost smooth now, and the boat moved well. They would soon reach Bull Bay.

Off to the north, in a protected bay, some netters were working a flat. They were too distant to raise a hand to, let alone recognize. Tomorrow on the return he would pick up their catch. Those fish didn't know it yet, but they would soon be on the ice that now filled the run boat hold.

2

Sam's boat had been blue, once. Also green. And black. But now the wood was mostly bare, weathered, driftwood grey. It was sound, and that was the important thing. Deep down sound. Other than paint flecks the wood was velvet soft, napped by thousands of encounters with oysters and trees, sun and waves. Sam's calloused fingers unconsciously caressed the boat's side as he arranged its contents—a half dozen cane poles, a throw net for bait, another for mullet, a jug of water. A square of canvas was lumped forward, next to a gas can. The can, almost as innocent of paint as the boat, flaunted its assorted dents and rust more dramatically.

Sam's beard, or stubble, was more brown than gray, and the hat hid the sun creases around his brown eyes. His pant legs were rolled to the knee, futilely. The waves, though small, were enough to wet his trousers. His feet were bare, and more calloused than his fingers.

Getting into the boat, Sam lowered the motor and pulled the cord. On the second pull the popping of the stink pot sounded reassuringly.

The bay was hazy—the sun not yet above the horizon. Small islands were faint shadows where water blended into sky. It was possible to believe nothing existed a few feet from the boat surrounded by its patch of oiled water. Powering the boat, he pulled the rudder right, and arced smoothly left into the unseen bay. After a few moments, he nosed left again; arbitrarily, it seemed. Then he turned off the motor, allowing the tide to nuzzle the craft forward.

He stood, prepared to throw the net. Smudges of mangrove loomed to either side. The boat was being pushed into a wide tidal creek. Sam threw left as the current carried the craft on a right sweep. The channel edge yielded some baitfish—even a few shrimp that hadn't yet buried into the mud.

He threw a few more times, emptying the net on the deck and transferring bait into the well after each throw. Spider crabs clambered through masses of seaweed. Occasionally a portion of the weed moved, a flash of silver that revealed a missed baitfish, or a darker, more ominous-looking dogfish or sea-robin.

With sufficient bait, he rinsed the net and threw the seaweed debris over the side, scraping his boat clean. Re-entering the bay, he pointed the boat west and baited the poles, positioning them like spider legs around the body of the boat. With the motor again shut down, the unruffled tide eased him smoothly along the bay.

Haze was now pink from the rising sun. It seemed to push the tide forward, hurrying toward midday. Though it had thinned, it held stubbornly to the bay water, unwilling to allow the sun to penetrate.

A cork twitched. Before his hand touched the pole, a second one was also dancing. His drift was across grass flats, full of hungry spotted seatrout. They faced into the tide and obscure sun, and snapped up the shadowed offerings. Action was quick. He boated the fish and rehooked in the same smooth motion. Sam played the poles as dexterously as a church pipe organist would perform on his instrument—constantly reaching and replacing poles, baiting and unhooking, untwisting a small tangle of seaweed, securing a cork.

From a distance the little boat looked like a frantic water beetle, stuck in some mystery sap. It would pull a leg free, only to be caught once again until another leg came loose in its turn.

Suddenly, the sky was blue. In an instant, it seemed the haze had gone. The grass flats were varicolored, sand patches bright and barren-looking. Action slowed.

The little boat floated alone on the water. A couple of miles east, where he'd started, his small house shone white as the sun touched it. An osprey called as it volplaned across a nearby island.

Sam secured the live well and generally neatened the craft as the boat neared a small point. He moved casually around the boat, aware of any movement in all directions. Stillness was complete. Even the fishhawk in the distance had disappeared.

He turned the rudder and the boat slipped quietly behind the point. Then he reached for the push-pole and moved smoothly along the point, finally turning into the mangroves. To anyone watching, he had disappeared as completely as a ghost through a brick wall.

He now poled along a nearly reclaimed tidal channel which twisted left and right as if to imitate the roots of the mangroves it hurried through. At extreme low tide its mouth appeared to be a small, blind, indentation among the mangrove stilt roots. Any higher tide masked even that.

Sporadically the mangrove wall thinned, and the bay became apparent as a brightness beyond the arched tunnel which he moved through. The water, clouded green from the rising Gulf tide, hurried him along. A fallen limb, partly under water, filtered sea grasses from the channel, their streamers pointing his way. A little green heron guarded a turn, caught in a position of suspicious immobility as Sam passed. Mangrove crabs hitched along the branches, their scratching movements loud in the silence.

Presently, one more bend, and light intensified. He gave a final push on the shelly creek bed and the boat slid out into a nearly circular small lake. His emergence lifted some wading birds off their perches, to squawk desultorily and finally resettle on the lake's green walls. From its center Sam looked at the little lake's edge. The birds, the white-stained leaves below their roosts, the dead trees, all punctuated the green. The lake bottom about three feet below the keel was a rich, soft peat brown, clearly visible. When he placed the pole and pushed, a cloud of particles stirred behind him, glinting and rotating as they fell stately to the seabed again.

He headed for a clump of silvered, long-dead, fallen timber near the entrance. Close to, he picked his way cautiously. The soft, polished look of the wood belied its real cast-iron character.

He snugged in the boat, tied it, and climbed over a large limb to a low, but solid, patch of shelly sand. One step higher was a sun-lit patch of tough grass, and beyond that shrubs and trees crowded a low elevation. Its green was brighter and more varied than the surrounding mangrove. The eroded remains of this ancient mound extended perhaps thirty feet inland.

Sam reached back into the boat, lifted the canvas and his water jug free, and laid them on the bank. Then, sitting on the grass with his bare feet on the shell, he unwrapped a breakfast. He ate leisurely, watching the sun paint shadows as the water lapped at his feet. Some fiddlers had cautiously reappeared in the black mud margin dividing the mound from the lake. He wiggled his toes, precipitating a mass dive of the crabs for their holes.

It was nearly mid-morning. Sam rose and gathered the canvas. Stepping up on the mound, he walked back through the brush into a clearing.

The site was relatively flat. A log seat furnished a good view across the boat to the lake. The lake entry, though hidden to the right, would reveal any visitors well before they would detect the mound. The Indians, as usual, had planned their location well.

It suited Sam's purpose too. He looked approvingly at the high haze now whitening the sky, and turned to set his load down beside the bricks of his still.

In the several days since he'd last been here, not even a raccoon had explored the hammock. No disturbances marked the palm-brushed sand—not even a snake track. No rain had fallen for weeks, though it soon would start. In a short time he'd be setting up some tin to funnel rainwater into a storage barrel. It was easier than hauling fresh water the way dry season demanded. Less noticeable too. The only creatures to heed were the birds, and they didn't tell. They were better than guard dogs, sure to raise a ruckus if someone should sneak up the channel.

Sam had considerable respect for his lake birds. He never bothered them unnecessarily. Any curlew for his dinner pot he'd shoot out on the flats. He didn't plan to upset his guard birds in any way.

The copper pot, set up on its brick base, was ready to be fired up. A quick check with his nose over the pot confirmed that fermenting was well along. Replacing the lid, he checked the ends of the copper tubing coil for stray bugs. He didn't need any repeats of the time a mud dauber wasp had sealed the worm coil.

That time he had left hurriedly without checking to see that the worm dripped properly into the crock. No emergency, just a careless certainty that everything was fine.

When he came back, he thought Carrie Nation herself, or the Charlotte County Sheriff, had somehow gotten past him. The pot was dented and spilled, the fire extinguished by the mash. The worm split along its seam as it exploded. The worst casualty was the crockery jug. The kick of the explosion had lifted it to smash on the bricks he used to support his equipment. Some of the bricks had even been cracked or chipped.

And the mud dauber? Sam didn't know where the wasp was, but his little house was still secure in the bitter end of the coil—snug as a tick in a hound's ear.

He learned from that experience. Never again did he set up his equipment without first blowing through the worm, making sure no obstructions blocked it. He always checked the drip, checked everything. Most of all, he appreciated the power he dealt with. Any bang that could peel open a copper coil the way he'd seen made him grateful he hadn't been sitting alongside the still when it exploded.

He kept that plugged up, ripped open, piece of plumbing to remind him of how easy it is to make a mistake.

Today everything was to his satisfaction. Dough sealed every crack along the lid, the fire burned right, the slow drip had started at the end of the worm. Only a distorted smokeless column of air emanated from the fire, making it impossible to spot from a distance.

He arranged a heavy log so that it would fall when the fire burned low. It would be his signal to wake and restoke. Until then, it was time for a nap.

When the run was over, Sam meticulously finished his housecleaning. Carefully he hid the batch and wiped down his equipment. Tomorrow he would distill it one more time. Two distillations made a quality product he took pride in. Not every maker of moonshine would do that.

The tide was nearly high. He decided to try his luck throwing the mullet net along the margins of the upper flats. The big fish deserted them for deeper channels at low tide. The spot he contemplated wouldn't be far out of the way as he headed for the fish-house. Murdock's run boat, the *Jeanette*, was due in later today, and Sam had a standing order with the captain. Murdock re-distributed his product before the boat finished its run up the sound. Except, of course, for the captain's cut. Sam suspected there were times that also disappeared before the boat reached dock in Punta Gorda.

He checked the morning's catch in the live-well, and after he transferred some jars of stock to the boat in his trusty canvas, he poled back down the creek.

The blue smudge marking where the Gulf broke against Gasparilla Island slowly grew in size and clarity. The captain noted mooring lines were coiled neatly, awaiting dockage. He relieved Jim, taking over the wheel. They rounded an island and the Bull Bay fish-house, its lighter moored nearby, came in sight.

Two skiffs were tied behind it. One, of course, was Jake's. The other, it seemed obvious as the ice boat closed the gap, had to belong to one of the gentlemen fishermen who frequented the harbor in the winter. The skiff, if that word could be used to describe the craft, was large. The paint gleamed and the wood was waxed to nearly as high a shine as the metal trim. Attached to the rear was the largest outboard the two men had ever seen fastened on a small boat.

Jim looked back at the skipper as he rang the bells announcing their imminent arrival.

"Man could go blind, a sunny day like this, running that boat through the water."

Murdock nodded agreement.

"Not a practical fishing boat." He paused. "It might not do to judge too fast, Jim. But some of those over-important types wouldn't set foot in an old tub like Jake's there if it meant their salvation on the high sea. Not all of them are like that, mind. And a lot of them can fish rings around stop-netters with some little artificial bait. But that boat's got a look about it. I don't imagine any slimy old fish would ever be allowed to be pulled in over that fancy transom. Wonder what he would want with Jake?"

They had nearly reached the mooring, and Jake came out to tie off the boat as Jim tossed the lines. No one else appeared.

"Didn't think it was possible. You look more sour than usual, Jake."

"Got good reason." Jake clamped his jaw over a wad of chaw and started working it.

He was a short man. *A diamond in the rough*, thought the captain. Jake had a small head and shoulders, and the tiniest feet he'd ever seen on a man. One time, looking for boots to fit, Jake had finally bought some made for women—and size five at that!

But in between, his body sloped out in a grand manner. When the belt was reached, it sloped just as grandly toward those tiny feet. Jake always wore suspenders and belt. The captain figured the belt marked Jake's outer limits, a strictly ceremonial ornament. But the suspenders were clearly necessary. The only thing to stop the fall of those trousers should they lose hold on Jake's waist would be the floor.

Murdock climbed to the dock.

"Got some company, I see."

"Ain't got no company." Jake spat, perilously close to the shiny runabout.

"Buy you a boat, did you?"

He looked down into the beauty. The seats were lined with plump soft-looking cushions, brightened by wide red and white awning stripes. It looked never-used, like one of those pictures in high-society magazines.

"I can't imagine you chasing down tarpon in this, though that engine could run rings around the school," Captain Murdock probed. Jake wasn't often very communicative.

"This here's a pleasure craft."

"I can see it ain't no tugboat, Jake."

"Take a good look at that engine, Captain."

Then he saw it. The netting had been cut away close, but the prop and engine were wrapped in twine. It looked like fifty feet of net had somehow been jammed around that big motor.

"What the hell happened? Run over a gill net?"

"This sorry *captain* steamed right through it, even though Tom Craig yelled and waved him off. The jerk heard him. He had to have seen the net. But too much trouble to go around. He just figured his damn big engine'd cut him a path where he wanted to go. Too damn much net though. Choked that engine. Probably cooked it too. Sure's hell hope so. Knocked the blubber gut on his fancy cushions, too."

"You go rescue him?"

"Hell no." One more splat in the water.

"Ole Tom chewed on him for about half an hour. Threatened to leave him to the tide and mosquitoes. Ended up scaring him pretty bad too. That damn wind woulda saved him—woulda blown him upriver. Not that Mr. Moneybags was smart enough to realize that. Tom finally brought the boat here for security and took hizzoner back to Gasparilla Island. Ole Tom's getting a new net for his sorry old one, and some cash besides to make up for all his lost time and aggravation. Didn't know Tom could be a teacher, but he sure taught that fat old boy something."

Captain Murdock shook his head and turned back to help unload the ice." Think that old boy'll plan on doing any more boating around here?"

"Hardly think so. Think he had all the salt water he'll ever need. He was a sorry-looking thing sitting in Tom's skiff, I'll tell you. Don't think his pleasure cruise was giving him a whole lot of pleasure no more."

Jake deposited one more wad next to the shiny boat before turning to the task of unloading ice.

Mullet Jim had laid Jake's supplies on the dock, along with the Sears package. When Jake lowered the tong hoist, Jim fastened it around the ice, and guided as Jake cranked it up to the dock. Then unhooking it, he dropped the hoist back to Jim while he and Murdock slid the ice into the fish-house cold room. Years ago, someone had nailed a piece of tin to the dock—a slide into the cold storage. It didn't look like much but it sure made it easier to move the ice. The sun warmed the metal, and soon as the ice touched the tin there would be a puddle of meltwater. The ice slipped easily over it and into the storage hold. It wasn't long before they had the ice un-loaded and had cast off, leaving Jake and his fancy boat until the next day's pickup.

"We'll angle across the harbor to get to La Costa, Jim. I'd rather not try to cross the pass broadside to that chop."

"Soun's good to me. Steering this ice across that big mouth when it's talking loud ain't nothing I wanna do, Cap'n."

Captain Murdock kept the wheel. Soon swells again buffeted the boat. The rhythmic crashing hadn't changed in the past hour, and didn't seem likely to.

"I doubt Jake'll have much to load tomorrow. Nobody'd be outside in this. Probably not much to catch in the whole area today."

"Not many self-respectin' fish gonna be running off-shore today. They be hanging in their hidey-holes." Jim was in agreement.

They quartered the swell, working toward the south side of Boca Grande Pass. "Might be easier to go in south of Punta Blanca instead of working back to the regular channel. I think we'll have enough water."

"Not too much tide's gonna escape while that wind's blowing in that mouth. Think there'd be 'nuf water without the wind, even."

"True enough. And we don't want to get any nearer to the pass than needs be. We'll just slide right around that old island."

The wind, water, and motor all worked with the boat. In a short time they raised a hand to some watchers at the boatyard at the south end of Punta Blanca. They swept around into the bay and its fish-house, and soon were unloading again.

South lay more passes, more islands, more fish-houses. The morning was spent zigging and zagging across the sound, working toward the end of the line below Marco. When the tide started running out, the wind continued, creating a confused sea in the open areas.

Finally, about noon, past Redfish Pass as they headed for Wulfert, the wind dropped noticeably. By the time they reached Punta Rassa, the trees were nearly still.

"Now that we going open water, there's no wind to keep us cool, and the sun wants to fry my brains. Cain't believe it."

"Sure you can, Jim. It's always the way. Besides, ain't nobody ever told you the hardest place in the world to work up a sweat is on an ice-boat? Anyway, you got no brains to fry!"

"Ice-boat or no, I knows when I'm hot." Jim opened the hold long enough to grab a rag lying in the melted icewater. He wrung it over his head, yelping a few times at the cold, but persisting. Then he opened the rag and draped it over his head, and shoulders, anchoring it with his hat.

"Phee–ew, but that feels good!"

"Don't be using all that ice on yourself now. This sun's getting around to where we're gonna have to be stopping regular for extra ice. We're going to be just squeezing by this trip."

"Seems like we're running slower, too."

"Not the running. It's the stopping. We're slowed down unloading. Be the same tomorrow, coming back. Running shorthanded shows up. Be easier next time, with Bill back on board."

The off-shore water carried the imprint of the wind, even though it failed to reach this far. The water was rough, but the sun was bright and sky untouched by clouds. The ice was two-thirds gone. The boat rode high and easy as it sped along the empty shoreline. They could see the double white line where the waves broke on the bar and then again ashore, foaming up the beach. The beach was wide and unbroken, except for a few downed palms that had apparently washed ashore from some other area. The vegetation was low, mainly grasses. The few palm clumps visible were well inland, unlikely to be eroded anytime soon.

The changes along the way fascinated the captain every run. Each island was different—had its own personality. Ground cover, shape, some being eaten away, others growing. One infested with coons while the next had not a one. One filled with cabbage palms, another grass, or mangrove. At abandoned homesites or mounds, guavas or flowering trees flourished, sometimes sweet potatoes still tried to exist, or bananas. He never had time to do much exploring, but people living near-by would know what could be found and when.

Carlos Pass loomed. Captain Murdock again took over the wheel, while Jim went to keep an eye on the bars at the entrance. A dropping tide, and a shallow pass. But not difficult today.

3

Evan Pratt scooped blue crabs with that single-minded intensity an eleven-year-old brings to a favorite undertaking. He was absorbed with enticing a fat old blue with a mullet-head. He had tied the fishhead bait through its eye sockets with string—the eyes had long since disappeared. In truth, very little remained of the head, apart from the skull and some strings of skin fluttering loosely from it, that had not already been used nearly to invisibility. But that didn't seem to diminish the crab's interest. He stalked and scuttled toward the head as Evan, playing the puppet master, skillfully tumbled and rolled the bait to where he could snare Mr. Crab with a quick swoop.

He was not a boy catching a crab dinner. He was a coiled rattlesnake at the side of a trail waiting for a marsh rabbit. He was a man-o-war bird soaring elegantly in wait for his sea-gull servants to catch a breakfast he would commandeer. He was a barracuda striking a hapless silver shimmer that ventured too close.

When he dumped the crab into the bucket, he realized he had heard, faintly, the run boat's bells. The breeze blew hard enough to rattle the sea grape leaves. The surf sound was clearer than any bay noises. Even though a part of him had been waiting to hear the boat, he had very nearly missed it.

Evan gathered his two pails of crabs and the net, and spurted over the dune ridge to the beach. Wind urged waves up the beach enthusiastically. Even though tide was close to its high, a considerable swatch of wet sand gave firm footing as he loped northward toward home.

He hoped his mother hadn't been to the beach this morning—she would look at those seas and never allow him to row to the fish-house for the supplies. Even if it were only a half mile of calm water. Mothers were unreasonable. And Evan had noticed that his mother developed a more confining viewpoint for her children as her pregnancy progressed. It wouldn't be long before he'd not be allowed to leave the bare earth yard, defined by the pig pen on one side and the small garden plot on the other.

He crossed the ridge again on the path to the house. He didn't see any sign of his mother's footprints—a good omen. But then, even his own had been brushed away by the breeze sneaking through the twisting sand passageway.

When he rounded the side of the house, he saw his sister, Katie, hanging up a load of clothes. They joined many others. His mother, taking advantage of the sun and breeze, had turned out a big wash which filled the clotheslines his father and he had strung. They had also pressed several of the smaller bushes into service, to the disapproval of the chickens. Sheets draped over green bushes, bleaching in the morning sun.

"It's about time you showed up!" Katie's nose seemed out of joint. "Mom's gonna get after you, not being around to help with the washwater!"

"I didn't know she was washing. 'Sides, you and Nelly can carry water." Evan watched Katie's temper mount.

"That's your job and you know it!" she yelled. "It's not fair!"

"Don't get all upset. I'll empty it all for you." He changed the subject. "Look what I got!"

Katie loved crabs. Evan knew they would soften any complaining his little sister made. He started dipping out the washwater and threw it in the pigpen.

"Why don't you get the cooking pot? I'll restoke the fire and get some more water. We'll get these cooking and after I go to the fish-house we can all have crabs."

"O.K." Katie danced off toward the lean-to, calling to her mother in the house, "Evan's got crabs for dinner." Her sulky mood was forgotten.

Evan tossed out the last of the washwater and put more wood on the fire. The wood pile needed replenishing. He had been pointedly reminded of that last night.

"I'm counting on you, son, to pull your weight. Your mama cain't be choppin' wood and hauling heavy loads. You're the oldest and near a man. It's your place to be doing for her before skipping off somewheres. I don't plan to be reminding you."

And Evan's father wouldn't. Once, Evan had been shaken awake in what seemed like the middle of the night, to do some chore he had shirked. His father believed in making it clear that the easy way to do a job meant doing it right the first time.

By the time he was back with the water, Katie had brought the tub and was teasing the crabs. They rattled in their pails, snapping their pincer claws at the stick Katie waved at them.

While the water heated, Evan split some wood, carefully stacking it with a view toward impressing his mother with his industry. He looked at the horizon. It looked hazy, wavering with whitecaps moving in the open bay. He hoped his mother wouldn't notice that horizon and veto the fish-house trip. He chopped faster.

When the water boiled, he dumped in the first bucket of crabs, pushing back their energetic attempts to escape with the axe blade. In hardly any time, the crabs had started to redden and they moved only in response to the bubbles of the boiling water.

Finally the children's mother came out of the house. She led Ned by the hand, and as she waited for him to step down from the porch, she pressed her free hand to the small of her back.

Nelly grabbed the baby and more dragged than carried him to look in the steaming pot.

"I hear your luck was good," his mother smiled at Evan as she watched her two youngest children stare into the pot of crabs.

He returned the smile, relieved she wasn't upset. "Got a whole bunch. Mighta got more, but I heard the run boat and figured you needed me to get the supplies for you, too."

He took a breath and continued, "'Sides, Daddy'd like some fresh cooked crab for dinner for a change. Figured I'd take him a bunch too."

A slight frown crossed her face. She looked out past the dock and mangrove-fringed point defining their safe harbor.

Evan hurried on, attempting to draw her gaze from the water.

"Aren't you getting your yarn on today's boat too? I know you been looking forward to that." He regained her attention pulling crabs from the boiling water. The second pail started rattling as though its inhabitants knew their moment had come. Evan dumped them in the boiling water without ceremony. Katie laughed and the baby screeched as Mr. Crab, the big one, dove over the edge and into the fire. He scuttled out and ran without preamble, heading for the dock.

Everyone scrambled to stop him, forcing him up the shore. Evan got the tongs on him. Back in the boiling water he went, and Evan continued to hold him down with the tongs until his struggles tapered off.

"That's sure a nice mess of crabs, son." Mr. Crab's antics had diverted her. "If you were to bring home some extra ice, I believe the girls and I could fix a nice cold crabmeat supper along with some cob corn for your daddy. Meanwhile I know he'd like those hot crabs for dinner. Why don't you do that?"

Evan was elated."I'll chop the rest of the wood when I get back, I promise," he said, and ran for the ice tub. He put several crabs into a sack for his father and himself, and stowed them in the boat. As soon as he fished out the second batch of crabs, he carried the tub to the dock, untied the rowboat and was gone, afraid all along that his mother would change her mind.

He could tell from Katie's pouty look that she was feeling put upon again. He didn't want her to spoil his chance. If he stayed for dinner, chances are he wouldn't get to go at all.

He was right. As his mother and the girls went to the dock to shuck crabs, he could tell from her stance that she realized how windy the bay was and regretted allowing him to go. She even waved at him to return, but he waved back, deliberately misreading her signal. He put his back into the oars. He shot out of their harbor and, looking over his left shoulder, saw the fish-house.

It was an easy pull for him. Swells coming through the pass to the north swiftly carried the rowboat and he was close enough to the lee shore that the wind didn't bother him. He saw his father turn the corner of the fish-house and stand tensely as Evan rowed closer.

"Brought you lunch!" Evan shouted. He could see his father's shoulders relax. It was too close to his wife's time to be unconcerned by unexpected trips from shore.

He caught the rope and Evan passed up the tub with its sack, then scrambled up too.

"Got a fine mess of crabs in the bayou." He opened the sack for inspection. "Mama said if I bring back some ice she'll make cold crab and roast some ears of corn for supper."

"A real celebration, huh?" He carried the sack to the lee of the building where they sat, legs dangling over the water, to crack crabs and eat.

"Captain Murdock's going to bring your Aunt Emily up tomorrow." They talked as they cleaned their crabs. Silence fell whenever some morsels were ready to eat. Discarded shells floated on the swells, filled, and sank.

"Doubt it'll be much longer before Ned has to move over. He won't be a baby no more. Might be that baby'll come with no warning. I saw you pulling so hard on them oars I thought maybe it had started." His father reached for more crab. "Your Aunt Emily being here will ease your mama's mind well as my own. I'll know someone's there if I ain't. Emily'll be a comfort. You, you'll need to get the children out of the way, and do whatever your aunt says, of course, and come get me. When things start happening, there won't be no time for larking about." He paused to look severely at Evan from under his massive eyebrows.

Evan squirmed a bit. "I chopped some more wood, sir. Gonna finish when I get back. And Katie and Nelly are there."

"Your sisters have their chores, too. And they're what? Five and eight. Your responsibility stays on your shoulders. So hang around nearby. This is number seven baby for your mother. Such things happen fast." He got up and stretched, then rinsed his hands in a bucket of seawater.

"Grab you a Coca-Cola there, and I'll chop a piece of ice. Time you returned, and you'll find it's not so easy going back!"

In the shadow of the building Evan had nearly forgotten the wind. When he carried the supplies around to the boat he nearly lost his hat to a wind gust. He finished his Coke in four big swallows and sighed happily. As he replaced the bottle in the rack he heard a chunk of ice rattle into the galvanized tub. Grabbing the package of yarn, he scooted around and climbed into the boat.

His father watched approvingly as he stowed things. He placed the wool and rice where they would stay dry as possible.

"Pull over by the trees, now, outta the wind."

It was unneeded advice. They raised hands and Evan watched his father and the fish-house recede much more slowly than he could have imagined. Even in the lee of the island this was no day for small craft. The wind picked at the water, making a chop. He was glad to reach the trees, creaking as they were buffeted by the wind. Even though the tide should be running out the pass, he felt little sensation of being pulled along with it. The current was no help in regaining the dock and harbor. When he finally attained the sheltered harbor, his strokes across it seemed magnified, as the same amount of energy he had used to battle the swells shot him swiftly across its calm water.

He was tired. But he would chop a load of firewood this afternoon that his father would take pride in.

The girls took his line, and he passed up the packages. Katie, taking the prize yarn, ran for the house. Evan might have minded her grab for the prize before, but he knew she needed that special feeling too. He had brought the yarn ashore. Besides, to judge from the crab shells littering the bottom under the dock, both girls had been busy while he was gone.

Nelly danced alongside as he carried, with some difficulty, the tub of ice. She toted the lightest bag, a treat—bread baked in town.

"Mama said she shouldna let you go. The waves was too rough."

"I guess they were, but I did OK."

One of the roosters challenged him as he tried to place the tub on the porch.

"Get now," he chased him. Then he saw a hen nesting under the step.

"Look, Nelly. Did you know she was there? "The hen glared at him balefully.

"No." Nelly leaned down. Though she was in charge of egg gathering, hens often outwitted her, nesting in places where she couldn't get to—palmettos, cactus, sandspurs, and briars up on the ridge.

She diverted the hen and reached under, emerging with two eggs. "Awright!" Nelly was happy.

So was her mama. She delighted in the yarn—a particularly soft shade of yellow.

"It's like daffodils! And forsythia!" She swirled around. "Springtime flowers for the springtime baby." She patted Katie's head and gave Evan a quick peck on his cheek.

"Thank you, dear, and . . ." she raised her voice, . . . "Thank you Captain Murdock. Oh, he chose such a pretty color!"

She smiled. "Isn't this a nice day though! All the wash done. House clean. The crabs. Emmy coming. And this lovely lovely yarn!" She buried her nose in it as though she could smell the spring flowers she missed each year.

Her yard bloomed all year round—trees, shrubs, and vegetables. But in springtime she missed violets, lilies of the valley, the fragrant lilacs. If only they would grow here, she often said, she would be totally content. Too many shy flowers bloomed here—small and inconspicuous, often opening only at night. At that point her husband would, attempting gallantry, tell her that she bloomed better than any flowers. She would silently answer by turning red as a cactus fruit.

"I put the ice on the porch, Mama. Do you want it somewheres else?"

His mother looked awkward, he realized. He hadn't noticed how much she was changing, almost daily. But she still bubbled, seeming to float and bounce rather than move. Her hair, penny-bright, she piled high for coolness and her sea-green eyes roved like waves, constantly moving. Evan thought she was as pretty as the goddesses in the books she taught them to read. Prettier.

"I'm gonna finish the wood, less you want me to do something else?"

She set down the wool, eyes smiling.

"How do I know your father just 'talked' to you, Evan?" She moved toward him. "Yes, dear, go do the wood. Katie and I have everything well in hand."

Katie came in with another package.

"Evan can carry up the rice. That's too heavy." She set down her load with exaggerated relief. Evan went for the rice. The rooster strutted after him.

***

Before poling into the bay, Sam looked carefully through the tree wall hiding him. Seeing no one, and birds moving undisturbed on the mangrove roots, Sam pushed out of the creek and over the little submerged sand bar rimming the trees.

The tide was near full, and still. The sun was high. There was no breeze. The sky—milky blue and cloudless—looked faded from lack of rain. That intense blue of a fresh-washed sky lay hidden by dusty days of spring.

Sam doubted fish would be moving yet, but started the engine and cruised across the silky skin of water. His wake widened behind him in a smooth curve, eventually reaching under the trees to chatter in low voices at its welcomed shade. His was the only movement under that watching sun.

He reached the spot he had in mind, and shut off the engine. He could see he was early. He lay back for a little cat-nap. A tiny warbler chirped intensely in the mangroves, and a second, farther away, answered. They were marking their territory, preparing to raise their families. No birds were in sight, all remained tucked under their midday mangrove umbrella.

Sam set his hat over his face and dozed, his strong hands clasped comfortably over his midsection.

A short time later, something lifted his hat gently off his face and dropped it aside. Startled, Sam opened his eyes and managed to catch the hat just before it hit the water. The branch responsible reached out farther than most of the others, an advance guard for the forest of mangrove. He ducked under it and managed to push out enough to avoid tangling any further in trees, then poled back toward the flat he'd drifted from.

Still no breeze, though it often came on the tide change. The seagrasses pointed Gulfward, the water obviously hurrying to leave the flats.

Sam poled up to the main channel, just below where it branched into three smaller channels. As the tide dropped, fish retreated seaward via these underwater canyons, taking advantage of somewhat deeper and faster water movement to prey on smaller creatures swept along. On a rising tide, they followed these same roadways onto the flats until the mud was sufficiently covered to allow fish access to creatures and grasses birds had left behind. The underwater system opened the flats to larger fish as surely as a river tributary system opened prairies and unknown lands to explorers.

Sam fancied himself an Indian, waiting in ambush along the trail. Time would tell if he'd picked the right trail today. He anchored off to the side and prepared to throw the net. His eyes focused uptide of his position.

It wasn't long before the first scattered pod of mullet retreated and then recovered as his net arced gracefully, coming out of the sun without warning. He shook the fish free on the boat bottom to flop and squirm futilely as he quickly regrouped, throwing and emptying the net. Clouded water, where the net had dragged, drifted downtide in a puff as he emptied each net-full, leaving no warning sign for the next school of fish. They felt just a sudden flash of panic as the cotton line caressed their scales.

Time after time Sam converted the mullets' water-supported graceful movement into a frenzied thrumming against the boat bottom. Spraying scales and slime until exhausted, they panted, mouths agape. The next net-full of mullet revived their frantic attempts to avoid suffocating in alien oxygen-rich air. The rhythmic splash and drip of life-giving water, as the net deposited more mullet, would temporarily rejuvenate them. But that splash of water was a cruel tease, like a rope placed just beyond the reach of a drowning man. Their destiny was the fish-house scale. They would never again swim with the tide.

Even though he was the immediate cause of their demise, Sam could appreciate the panicked reaction of the mullet. Occasionally a lucky fish would flip over the side, and Sam mentally saluted its good fortune, rather than get upset. Big fish preyed on smaller ones, and Sam was a big fish. Nonetheless, bigger fish swam out there and preyed on the Sam's of this world. He'd experienced the other end of the net and didn't like it much. For him to live the fish had to die. But he sensed that if all the little fishes were gone, bigger fish would then be on the bottom. Sam didn't care to be at the low end ever again.

The skiff was heaped with mullet. Sam laid the wet net over the glistening pile and raised anchor. The tide urged his boat seaward as Sam picked his way to the stern to start the little engine. It was time to get to the fish-house.

4

Murdock rang the ship bell as the *Jeanette* glided toward the fish-house. Sam, in his loaded skiff, emerged from behind a point and motored to the back of the fish-house as though in response to it.

Friendly greetings were made all around. The ice would not wait. The men swiftly cranked it up and out of the lowering sun. Sam watched the operation, occasionally helping to guide a block, but basically staying out of the way. Unexpected help often became more of a hindrance, something Sam appreciated.

In short order the ice was unloaded, then Sam's fish. The trout were weighed and iced, then the mullet.

"Want this on your account or cash, Sam?"

"Put her on my account this time, George."

He turned to the captain as George disappeared inside to mark the credit.

"Brought you twelve jars, that right?"

"Sounds good. I believe I'll need another dozen next time—the good stuff, now."

"It's all prime, double-run."

"What I need. I got a dozen or two empty jars on board you can use, I know." Murdock turned toward the run boat and saw that Jim was already disappearing into the cabin.

He came out with a rattling burlap sack and passed it over, trading for the heavier canvas square. Again he went in the cabin, and returned with Sam's cloth. Meanwhile cash money had traveled from the captain's pocket to Sam's.

George emerged as the captain went back aboard, saying, "Probably still be running a bit late in the morning, George."

He nodded. "See you when I see you."

George tossed the line to Jim and the boat headed to open water without a wasted motion.

"He's got more distance than day left. Good thing the days are growing."

Sam replied, "Bill will be aboard next time—that'll get her back on track."

"Um." George moved around to the shaded north side of the fishhouse and sat on a wooden chair that had been sun and salt-bleached for at least a dozen of its many years. Sam, following, chose a sturdy crate.

"Considering it's just the two of them, they're moving along right smart."

"Better had," Sam rejoined. "That tide's a'moving right smart too. I wouldn't want to be caught in those flats off Cape Romano on no full moon tide with that lady." He leaned back against the wall.

"Just starting off the flats, that tide was rolling good. They'll be bucking it for real further south." George nodded. "That lady has the power though. Their only problem'l be the water. They won't have a lot covering the mud flats anywhere, especially tomorrow morning. Least the boat'll be empty down there."

"Good thing. But power or not there won't be an early start—they'd only be trapped in skinny water in the dark."

George reached behind Sam and pulled a ball of twine from the crate. Then he hooked another chair with his foot and dragged it to him. Its seat was gone. George started tying a new one. Sam watched a pelican land. The bird was ruffed with chestnut, and balefully glared at Sam with a phlegmy blue-eyed stare.

"What makes you so grumpy, bird?"

"Today's Monday," George said.

"So?"

"Yesterday was Sunday."

"That's an answer?"

"Sure." George shifted.

"The run boat passes through here every other day going south, and loads fish going north in the in-between."

"Yeah?" Sam prompted.

"Well, Saturday it went north. Loading fish means there's always some goodies the pelicans and gulls get to grab. Far as the pelican's concerned, going fish-filled one day means no fish the next. That would be Sunday. But today there shoulda been fish."

"You telling me that bird comes around only on fish days? I don't be-lieve it!"

"Believe what you want. Sunday confounds the pelicans. They adjust fine to ever' other day, but they get the rhythm down and Sunday comes. Hungry-belly Monday. What you see is the scout. Other ones sent him over to see if there wasn't some mistake. They know that boat's purely headin' the wrong way." George laughed softly. "What this is, is one plain mad bird. Looking for goodies, but he didn't get none. Happens ever' Monday, like clockwork."

Sam chuckled and settled back, watching the bird. It did look irritated, he had to admit. It didn't settle down, sit relaxed on the piling. Instead it shifted from one side to the other, craning its beak and watching George's movements with the twine. It kept flexing its wings slightly, and clattered its bill soundlessly. Sam scratched. The bird immediately had its eye on him, shifting its body in his direction, and lifting his wings like he was prepared to pounce. Sam smiled at the bird.

Suddenly it turned, its back to them. It glanced over its shoulder, re-volving that head and bill, and looked down its beak like a rifleman sighting down his gun barrel. He forcefully squirted a wad of guano, then flapped off. He didn't look back. The two men erupted into laughter. The white limey stain spread eccentrically on the water surface, rather like an oil spot, while the solids quickly disappeared below the dock on the tide.

"Now, tell me they don't think, Sam."

George wiped at his eyes, still laughing.

"I gotta believe you." Sam stood and shook his head. "And I believe we'd better have a pint on that. Nobody'd believe we were sober anyway."

He went to the skiff and brought up a pair of jars. Looking at the skiff, he picked up a pail from the deck and poured a couple of buckets of salt water over where the mullet had been lying.

"Got some cleaning to do tonight," he said as he handed a jar to George. "Least I do if I don't drink this tide out. Don't fancy bucking it, getting home."

"Let it slacken up, Sam. We'll slacken up too."

George smiled, and raised his jar. The men settled back and watched the mangroves deepen and become gold-tipped in the late afternoon light.

***

By mid-afternoon the woodpile had grown immensely, and the clothes had been taken in. Katie and Evan had worked through the stages of fighting, playing with, and ignoring each other. Their boredom wore on them. They wanted to roam the beach, yet knew they needed to stay near, at least until their aunt took over.

Evan walked to the end of the dock.

"Katie, watch," he shouted, and fell overboard like an uprooted tree. An instant later he was joined by Lightning, their short-haired mixed-breed dog. Lightning loved any excuse to jump into the water. Anyone trying to swim constituted an open invitation. He even tried to swim with the cormorants and pelicans—which those birds didn't appreciate at all.

The two of them splashed and churned the water. Katie ran for the house.

"Mama, can I . . .?"

"C'mon."

Katie was in her swim dress in moments, and poised to jump off the dock. The dog barked encouragement, and Evan splashed mightily as she hesitated. Finally she jumped, nose firmly held and pigtails flying straight up.

Mrs. Pratt settled slowly into the rocking chair with her wool. The children and dog chased each other under the dock, cooling off. The two younger ones still napped. She doubted Nelly would sleep long. If she heard the swimmers she would be up and ready to go immediately.

It would be so good to have her sister Emmy here. Amy Pratt's thoughts roamed. Her children would do anything needed of them, but they were children, after all. Sometimes Charles seemed to forget that, his expectations geared for an adult's capacity. And as much as the children knew of birth and death, watching their animals and wildlife, she didn't desire to share childbirth with them. Ned had arrived so quickly two years ago that Charles scarcely made it home from the fish-house. It was entirely possible again.

Still, Amy felt slightly guilty. Charles felt the baby would come any day. She didn't, but the prospect of having Emmy here for several extra days delighted her, so she let him continue to think it.

Seeing Emmy, sharing hours of talk and idle time—it was important to them both. It seemed that the births of Amy's babies were almost the only time they had to spend together. Otherwise visits were brief.

Evan and Kate floated on their backs now, talking, while Lightning swam circles around them. She suspected she was the topic of conversation. There were occasional glances toward the porch.

The children were curious, and, at their age, easily embarrassed. Yet they were practical, matter of fact. It was a joy to watch their growth, to teach them and see how they used what they learned.

Evan today. So transparent. He wanted to make the trip to the fish-house and he was so afraid she would refuse. And she nearly did, even knowing he would be watched by herself and by Charles each foot of the way. The wind had been in her ears all morning. She didn't want him to go. But she felt instinctively that she had to let him. The only way for a tree to grow tall is to stand back and give it room.

After he left she walked to the ridge. It was frightening to recognize that only this small strip of island protected him from the sea that she looked out over. How insubstantial the land appeared from that ridge, looking to sea. Its fragility could almost be forgotten here at bayside, but not there, where the shrubs struggled against the wind, and the board markers on the two small graves were sanded and bleached.

One marker ten years old. Another six. Evan's twin, always ill, had succumbed his first winter. And the infant—he barely lived two days before he joined his brother on the ridge.

Amy had come more than a thousand miles to reach this island, and probably not travelled more than fifty miles in any one direction since. Her children, she knew, would stretch the other way. She had to let Evan, and Katie, push against their limits here. Or they would never know how to reach out.

Already the soft yellow stuff in her lap was forming, preparing for the baby who would be soon using it. Likewise the children were being shaped—perhaps with more difficulty—they weren't simply strands of yarn after all. But Amy was responsible for knitting them into a finished product. It was a job she was happy doing. And good at.

Only a few moments had gone by when Nelly, puffy-faced from sleep and her warm bed, appeared in the doorway looking wistful.

"Go get your outfit on. I think a swim's just what we need." Halfway through her sentence, Amy talked to an empty doorway.

"Don't wake the baby," she called. Soon Nelly was back, presenting herself for help with buttons and ties. They went to the water hand in hand, Nelly pulling her mother as though she were a hungry dog sighting food.

They were much alike, the mother and daughter—quick, slim, auburn-haired and golden-skinned. The older two children were dark-haired and eyed, like their father. Amy's mother, on her only visit, had likened Evan and Katie to gypsy children living a gypsy life. The house had been included in that indictment. But then, the house had been hardly more substantial than the palm-thatched shack that had been her honeymoon home, except that it did have a tin roof. But her mother did not understand Amy's fascination with her adopted home any more than she had understood her own husband's compulsion to return to these same waters each year, lured by the tarpon in the sun. Although she didn't fear it, Amy's mother seldom went out on the water. She had a distaste for the undignified, jostled, sweat- and salt-stained condition water ventures invariably left her in. The scope of the sea was too broad, and deep. She preferred her adventures within a smaller scale.

Amy had been sixteen when without warning her father had died. There still was a hollow in her heart when she thought of him. It hadn't occurred to her then how very young he had been—not yet forty. He had given his family so much—social stature, travel, the polish of the finishing school she and Emmy attended, all his wife's and children's wants and wishes. Amy was so glad that he'd made himself happy as well.

She had had a privileged childhood—what her mother did not see was that her adulthood was as privileged. Her own hand shaped her existence here, without those social pressures that artificially shaped a less solitary life. She had no neighbors to gossip about whether she washed on Mondays or played on the beach with her children. Or to care how Amy raised her flock.

Her husband Charles was older than Amy by a decade, and had first met the family while fishing with her father. They had spent winters here, and the girls had adopted Charles Pratt. He was a man alone, who blossomed under their enthusiasm and interests. He, and they, found as much joy in watching horse-shoe crabs push across the sand as in hooking a monster tarpon. Between trips, he would write about his discoveries, and her father relived old adventures and anticipated new ones. When the sudden, tragic death came, Charles comforted them. He had become a part of their family. Charles still guided occasionally, but preferred being closer to home. His world, like Amy's, was focused narrowly.

But if Amy's mother could not understand, at least Emmy did. Amy thought Emily was more like their father—straddling both worlds—content in either. If Amy had become a disappointment to her mother in the way she chose to live her life, Emmy was a satisfaction. At least most of the time. She taught music and literature at the Smithson School. Winters she taught at the boarding school on the lovely barrier island to the south. Summers, the setting was the bucolic woodlands of Michigan. Emmy moved with the seasons, educating the boys. She also linked Amy and her family with their mother, who never ventured south any more, as well as with the wider world, which she brought with her.

Nelly waded to her knees. Lightning bounded to her, splashing. They tangled in a noisy, wet bundle at the edge of the water. Lightning delighted in seeing a new participant—the other two swimmers had tired out long before the dog had. Here in Nelly he had a new player. He was eager for her to swim and splash, nosing her into the water, doggy-paddling out and returning to beg her to come. Nelly grabbed his tail. He pulled her, her legs scissoring for balance, toward the other children.

Amy sat on the apron of the dock, feet dangling, and watched her flock. Occasionally she saw a boat heading toward the fish-house. Not that Charles would be overwhelmed today. Perhaps this evening they could walk the beach a little, watch the rising moon. Mosquitoes weren't too fierce, yet. And certainly the breeze should keep them away.

The children swam through the dock, poking at the barnacles and oysters. Evan came up with a strand of algae held across his nose—a gigantic handlebar moustache. Katie wouldn't be outdone. Her creation was a green curtain of hair, covering even her face. Then she sank under it, leaving the puddle of algae to drift in the tide.

"Be careful, now, that you don't find some stingers," Amy said. Jellyfish were possible this time of year. She didn't want those invisible tentacles across their faces and eyes.

Lightning was being ignored again. A coconut husk lay on the dock beside Amy. She whistled, then threw the dry shell as far as she could, still sitting. The dog immediately sprang after it, and once he had it in his mouth, brought it ashore for another throw. Dripping, he pranced onto the dock and dropped it beside Amy. Then he shook himself with pride and enthusiasm.

Amy was soaked. She sat at eye level to his shoulders, without a chance to escape. She tried to ward off the shower by throwing up her hands, and squeaked, "No, Lightning!" Solicitous, the dog started to wash her splattered face. The children could barely float for laughing. In self-defense, she hurled, side-arm, the coconut shell beside her. Thankfully, Lightning bolted after it again. She decided to get up before the dog repeated his trick.

But Evan called the dog, continuing the game. Amy wondered who would wear whom out. The giggles and splashes rose in volume.

Chickens pecked around in the seaweed that marked the high tide line. It was time to remind Evan about that, to have him pile it up on the heap near her garden. The chickens found plentiful nutrients in the weed. So did her tomatoes and beans, after thorough rinsing by thunderstorms. Charles was fond of saying if a thing hasn't been used more than once around here, it hasn't been used. It was true on the island. Old nails, tin cans, nets too rotted for fishing, everything could be re-used—in completely unexpected ways, too.

That was another thing that had appalled her mother. Amy couldn't explain it to her, though she tried. It wasn't that a tin can held kitchen silver because they could not afford a rosewood box to put it in. But a box was unnecessary, and took up extra room. It had to be shipped in special. It couldn't be used, in an emergency, as a receptacle for anything from wildflowers to bacon drippings. It just wasn't versatile. Perhaps a box would impress visitors. If they were inclined that way. But Amy's visitors were few, and they probably all had opted for the tin can too. Why inconvenience herself? To impress herself?

To her mother though, the life reeked of stoney-hard poverty. When Amy refused her mother's attempts to provide those unnecessary things, she blamed Amy's stubbornness and pride. Poor Emmy, she had the task of blunting their mother's urges to ship china dogs and ruffled dresses when dress goods and books were what they really wanted. Mother would vacillate between barrels of flour (certain they were on the edge of starvation) and the frilled and feathered hats and wraps that appeared each Easter in the city parades. That the family was comfortable and happy, that they had chosen this life over others, she simply could not imagine.

Amy's hunger for beautiful things was constantly satisfied by sunsets, and her flowers, and the mobile sculptures of birds wading in the bay, or chattering in the sea-grapes. Her beauties were constant and ever-changing. Unlike a static, manufactured, object.

The children, tired of swimming, now constructed moats and castles at water's edge. Soon, too, Charles would tie up his boat, and look for his supper. It was time to prepare it.

5

From her cottage porch near the school Emily could see the movement of the Gulf water. The surf at the beach edge was hidden by the ridge. The sun had just gone down. Some thin clouds, enough to catch the pink, purple, orange and lilacs, contrasted with the changing haze of color that the sky offered.

Most people turned away from the sunset spectacle once the sun touched the horizon. But its departure left subtler and more pleasing elements. Against that sky spectacle of color, and its vague, moving reflection in the shiny sea, the strong silhouettes of the palms, yuccas, and sea grapes grew black as she watched.

Emily walked to the porch rail, to look eastward behind the cottage. One cloud, a pink puff, hung there. The deep sapphire sky behind the adjoining key gradually lifted toward the zenith, overtaking the sunset's gaudiness with its serene, dignified color. The pink of the cloud faded to lavender, to grey, to invisibility.

She had almost forgotten the hairbrush dangling in her hand. Returning to the house, she began again to brush her hair. Nearly all of her belongings were organized, ready for tomorrow's trip to the dock. She pinned her hair securely, gave herself a quick glance in the mirror, and blew out the lamp. Pulling the door closed, she started up the path toward the little cafe a quarter mile away.

The pathway was dark with undergrowth, and mosquitoes loved to lie in wait for a passing victim there. It was no spot to linger as dark fell. The restaurant's lights were cheerful by contrast. She could hear voices through the open, screened windows as she approached.

"Miss Stanhope! Your friends are waiting for you. Come this way. We planned a special moonrise tonight just for your last evening here." The flourish with which Calvin Chadwick, the cafe owner, seated her could have been taken intact from the best New York City or Chicago restaurant. It didn't matter that this small, brightly-lit cafe was frequented by fishermen—commercial and sport—rather than stockbrokers, or that Calvin's uniform was twill instead of a tuxedo.

Their table abutted the eastern wall. Open casement windows began at table height, and extended to the ceiling. Strong wire screening, starred on its outer side by a myriad of insects, lined the opening. Beyond was the bay, some keys, and finally a paling of the sky which promised a clear rising moon. Her dinner companions, fellow teachers, had been idly gazing at the water, waiting for her.

"I apologize, I'm late I know. I watched the sunset when I should have been coming down the path."

"Not at all. We were, too. We simply were closer." Mr. Scholefield, the school's principal, inclined his head as he re-seated himself.

From the left, Alexander also bowed formally as he sat.

"Are you all organized now, Emily?" he asked.

"I think so. Calvin is sending some help in the morning to ship things north. And I've packed my travelling valise separately for my visit with Amy. What are your plans?" "We're both leaving on Thursday, via Fort Myers." Mr. Scholefield smiled. "Excited to see your new nephew—or niece? Do you have a preference?"

"No, and I don't think Charles or Amy do, either." She turned her silver, spreading her napkin on her lap. "Healthy is the main thing."

"Yes, your sister has lost one, hasn't she."

"Two, actually. One in childbirth."

"It must be a worry to her husband, alone on an island." The principal was newly married, and Emily had the impression he felt Charles was almost negligent to allow Amy to give birth in such surroundings.

Mrs. Chadwick arrived to take their order.

"Miss Emily, I've baked a tin of cookies and fudge for those children of your sister's. Don't forget it now, by the door."

She raised both hands in anticipation of Emily's protest and thanks.

"It's been so long since I've seen them. Tell them I said to come this way sometime!"

Mrs. Chadwick took their order and left as the moon entered the sky. It demanded the three diners' attention as it rose, partly blocked by the nearby key. Its spectacle dimmed conversation, and they ate in near silence as they watched it at the end of its rippled water path.

***

Northward, Amy and Charles left the house as Evan began reading *Alice in Wonderland* to the younger children.

The moon spotlighted their harbor, and the sugar sand path to the ridge shone invitingly. Charles put his arm across her shoulders, and they strolled over the ridge to the flat, wet, tide line. Slowly they walked south, sometimes talking but mostly watching ghost crabs skitter nervously, and listening to the creamy-topped little waves rush across the sand and shell. Night herons flapped away from the water's edge as the walkers interrupted their dinner. The birds circled back behind them to continue feeding.

The rising moon threw black shadows across the sand. It was easy to stumble over a half-buried palm mistaken for a shadow. They walked cautiously.

Charles' hand tightened on Amy's shoulder, stopping her. They stood silent. Their merged shadow, like that of some tall tree, reached the water's edge. One, two, three waves broke over their unmoving silhouette.

Now she saw it. Where the moon-whitened surf had run unbroken, there now was a confused, bowed area. A low mound, like a cluster of rocks, diverted the clean line. As she watched, it moved, ponderously intent. In a few moments, free of the water and moon-gilded, the turtle rocked toward the dry sand of the ridge. They dared not move for scaring her.

"I believe she's actually gonna nest," he whispered.

"Awfully early."

"I know, but this is beginning to happen all along the coast."

As they watched, the loggerhead climbed above the tide line nearly to the vegetation, and began rhythmically digging with her hind flippers, loosening and withdrawing the damp sand.

Once she was well involved in digging, they went to her, and kneeling, examined her progress.

Amy was interested in her soulful, sad eyes.

"I always wonder if they're in pain. In labor. If it's as difficult for them to move in the air as it seems. They are so much more graceful and agile in the water."

"I doubt they feel much pain."

"But she cries. Look, she's crying now." Amy petted the barnacled head softly. The turtle ignored them.

"That just keeps the sand outta their eyes."

"Perhaps." Amy gazed at the turtle a moment.

"Nonetheless, Charles, they are tears. She'll never see her babies. I prefer to believe she knows she'll never see them emerge, never see them grow. So it's romantic. So what!" She forestalled the teasing she knew he was ready to give her.

He smiled and shook his head.

"It's the mother in you. You think every critter is as soft-hearted as you are."

The turtle stopped digging.

"C'mere. She's ready to lay."

Amy knelt beside her husband, leaning on him. The moon had cleared the trees behind them, and the shaped hole was visible in the moonlight.

The glistening eggs dropped—two, sometimes three in a cluster.

"I don't suppose you're gonna allow this turtle on the table, are you."

It wasn't a question. He felt her head shake against his chest, and kissed her hair.

"Didn't expect so." His hand caressed her shoulder.

"Not the first one. Not yet."

"Softy."

"We don't need the meat right now."

"I know. I will take some eggs though. Be good for you, too."

"Mmmm."

The turtle's egg-laying rate was slowing. Charles got out his handkerchief and spread it in Amy's shortened lap. He gathered about a dozen soft, sandy eggs from the hole, a couple at a time while the last few dropped.

"This turtle's been in a battle or two—see the gouge in the shell?" He traced out a double crescent with his finger.

"She's lucky she didn't lose a flipper. Didn't miss by much." He tied up the eggs and they leaned away a little as the turtle started filling and covering her nest.

"I wonder how she'd manage without her flipper? She couldn't dig."

"They still try. I've seen them work and work at it, just the little stump moving, not doing any good. Running on instinct. Really sad."

Charles stood and helped Amy up. The damp sand and pregnancy made her more awkward than usual.

Sand flew now—the turtle wasted no time getting the nest closed and hidden. She started back toward the breakers.

Charles feinted toward the departing turtle.

"Sure, now? There goes supper!"

"Stop it!" She laughed at him, and they walked with the turtle to the water. Close to the trees, mosquitoes and sandflies were active. More air seemed to move at the surf line.

When the turtle felt the first wave rush and ebb under her, she paused. Then she followed the ebbing wave out eagerly, raising her head as the next wave wrapped around her. She was gone, as though she had never existed.

"She's done her duty."

"Mmm, time to rest awhile."

They turned back toward the house, but then Charles stopped. He turned her so the moonlight shown on her face, and slowly, gently traced her features with his fingers.

"Do you have any notion how dear you are?" His words were so low that the rattle of the shells in the breakers nearly covered them.

She lifted her arms, her hands moving around his neck and fingers tangling in his coarse, wavy hair. She drew him close. It was hard to imagine the years they'd been married. Her feeling for him remained fresh and luminous. It was some time before they separated, slightly, to continue homeward.

***

Many miles to the south, Captain Murdock listened to the soft buzzing snore Mullet Jim made. With Bill away, and the moon tide bugs fierce, the captain told the deckhand to hang his hammock with his. It made no sense for Jim to be fighting sandflies all night on the deck.

The captain could see the moon from his hammock, through the open hatchway, and was tempted to walk the deck, to exercise his demons. He knew he couldn't oust them. He'd given up that attempt. But if he tired them out, sometimes they let him sleep for a while.

No breeze stirred. Even through the mosquito netting, through his clothes, enough sandflies got to him to keep him uncomfortable. He would regret a foray outside.

He closed his eyes, and imagined his walk. The silver and grey flats, black oyster bars protruding from the mud. The channel the boat sat in, ruffled with fish movement as they crowded into the hole, awaiting the tide's advance to the black mangrove clouds in the distance. The sky would be pale—most of the stars washed away in the insistent moonlight. The fish-house a short distance away would be a spindly-legged silhouette, its pilings thickened below by the oysters the tide exposed.

There was no point to getting up. He shifted, trying to ease his body's need to do something physical. He moved again.

It wouldn't work. He knew that from the start. He would only wake Jim. Not for the first time. He might as well get up and be done with it.

As he went out quietly, Jim turned and muttered. *He'll be harassing me for night-walking again in the morning*, Murdock thought.

He went to the stern. Everything was as he'd imagined. Perhaps the sandflies were worse.

He lit his pipe, puffing a cloud around his head to discourage them. The tide had started to flow, and promised to come in strong. He could see a small oyster clump lying black in the mud nearby. The incoming water touched the cluster and wasted no time in isolating it. It would disappear quickly below the water.

A movement some distance away caught his attention. Another oyster bar extended from the mangroves out over the mud. A family of raccoons loped along it, returning to the trees. They'd been foraging out on the flats, and sensed the incoming water. It was time for them to return home, to settle in for the night.

He tried to convince himself he was sleepy. He needed to sleep. Sleep though was hours away, and he felt suddenly that the tide needed bringing in. The pint jar was in the engine room, near at hand. Lydie, though, Lydie was far away. Impossibly, unalterably, far, far away. He could control the tide, but never that sober reality.

The moon was overhead when Mullet Jim came out of the cabin to check on the captain. He found him asleep, half-sitting by the engine house, an empty jar carefully upright beside him. Little wavelets slapped the stern. He could hear tarpon roll in the channel. The tide was nearly full, pushing the boat away from the fish-house.

Jim put the captain's pipe in his own pocket and rubbed his eyes. The boss would wake and come to bed in a little while. Jim went back to bed.

***

Emmy had long been asleep, too, after her dinner and the stroll back to the cottage. Her colleagues had escorted her, and said their good-byes, as the chuck-will's-widows called. Despite the anticipation of tomorrow, sleep came easily.

When Charles and Amy returned from their beachwalk, they stood outside in the yard, watching their sleepy children in the lamplight, before going into the house. The window framed them like a photograph.

"A Christmas card," was Amy's reaction.

She went in, her hair flashing in the light, to bed and tuck in her brood. Charles, turning to check the boats, had to watch a moment more. He would keep and treasure that mental picture for the rest of his life. Even as he watched, another part of his mind knew that.

"A Christmas card indeed." A fitting symbol, he supposed, for a Madonna and children.

In a few moments more their light was blown out, as well.

6

The moon was nearly touching the western horizon, and eastward the sky had begun to pale. Mullet Jim looked across at the captain's hammock. He didn't know if its empty condition indicated he had overslept or that Captain Murdock had never returned to the wheelhouse during the night. Either way it was time to rise. He stuffed his blanket and mosquito bar into his hammock and went out.

Grayness dominated everything he saw. The sky balanced the soon-to-rise sun with the soon-to-set moon. It looked as though they would be on opposite horizons at the same time. The sea had shrunken to wrinkled lines, overwhelmed by mud and oyster banks which stood tall, allowing only tracings of the waterways to sneak guiltily through their soft maze. The mangroves seemed to float high over the flats like prissy mistresses drawing up their long skirts for fear of dirtying their hemline on the muddy sea floor. The fish-house seemed absurdly elevated, teetering tiptoe. Its grey boards had hardly changed shade from night to day.

The captain stood at the rail, in a position which suggested he had been standing there for some time. He was as grey, as bare-bones gaunt, as the landscape. Jim knew better than to harass him this morning.

Jim's nod was barely acknowledged. The captain's head did not move, but his eyelids flickered. Mullet Jim, stepping back, turned as the first ray of sun caught the air. The tide, as though unleashed by that light, began to re- conquer the flats. Several egrets spiraled down to the mud on the first hint of morning breeze. Jim looked for the moon. Already it was half swallowed by the sea. Its earlier powerful light was reduced to the feeble shine of a jingle shell on a wet beach.

Jim stuck his hand in his pocket and encountered the captain's pipe.

"I'll be starting the engine, sir," he said as he handed the pipe over to the captain. The captain's nod was a bit crisper.

Jim went to the engine room. This was Bill's home ground. When Jim had charge of the big assembly of metal, he felt somewhat awed and definitely nervous. He had refueled last night but starting that cold cantankerous engine was no job for an amateur. However it fired instantly. When it idled smoothly, he went out, checked the prop and rudder for debris, and signaled the skipper the all clear. As the boat slowly inched along the channel, Jim dashed forward to keep a lookout. Easing to the dock on a full moon low tide, when the water'd been stretched nearly invisible between that moon and sun, was a job for an expert. Which is what the captain was.

At the last stop before nightfall, they had unloaded the next-to-last of their ice and started filling the hold with fish. Then they'd made anchorage here after dark. They'd seen and exchanged waves with Elliot, the fish-houseman, as they anchored, but made no other effort to communicate overnight. When the boat engine announced the morning, Elliot had rolled out of his cot. By the time the boat pulled alongside, coffee was on the boil.

Jim swung the chute from the fish-house over the boat hold, and went in the storage room, cold and dark except for the square of light marking the chute opening. He shoveled and scraped the load of fish and ice to the boat hold.

Meanwhile Captain Murdock, his big enamel cup full of strong morning coffee, went over paperwork and orders with Elliot. Murdock could feel himself coming to grips with the day. Work was a shield protecting him from the night demons. When activity subsided for the day he sometimes, like last night, ran into difficulty. By the time Jim had finished emptying the fish-room and received his cup of steaming coffee, the captain had completed his work as well.

They reboarded, leaving Elliot to fasten the hatch door between the chute and fish storage while they battened the boat's hatch. In the wheelhouse, the captain slipped the boat into gear as the lines dropped onto the deck.

The flats were filling fast. The exit was complicated. Maneuvering through the bays was tough on a boat unfamiliar with the area. The rushing murky water often obscured the channels. It was easier to go astray at this point of the tide than when the water was dead low.

Stakes marked the trickier channels, if they hadn't been knocked down or moved by fishermen or storms. When too many strangers appeared in an area, the markers might mysteriously disappear overnight. The danger of running aground in a strange bay, especially on a dropping tide when sandflies and mosquitoes were hungry, was a certain discouragement even to the hardiest fishermen.

His head contained the only map a captain could rely on, and even that had to be revised with every storm and stage of the tide.

The fish in the hold would be joined by many more before the day ended. The two men worked their way north. It was the beginning of a long day.

It was a long morning for Emily as well. Too well organized, she ended up repacking her valise simply to occupy herself. The majority of her things had already been taken to the mail dock, to be sent to her mother's address in Michigan. She had dusted and re-dusted, straightened and re-straightened, every item in her cottage. Even her book wouldn't hold her attention. At last she gave up. She put her valise on the porch and made a final round, checking locks and windows. She would spend an hour on the dock by the post office. At least she would have someone to chat with.

"I knew it!" The voice startled her. Emily spun around to see her fellow teacher.

"Alexander!" she exclaimed. "You surprised me! But why are you here? Did I forget something?"

"No." He smiled at her confusion. "I just knew you'd be pacing the floor for half the morning here, and then be rushing up to catch the boat an hour before it even passed Punta Rassa! I thought you might like a hand, or some conversation."

"That is sweet of you, Alex. I think I can cart it all, but it's nice of you." Emily had a net bag, in which she planned to carry Mrs. Chadwick's box of treats and some books, whatever didn't fit in the valise.

"After I've come all this way, you can't refuse my strong arms." His cottage was less than a hundred yards south of hers. "Besides, I'm going up to the store."

He took the valise and waited for her to gather up her other things. When Emily first taught at Smithson eight years ago, Alexander had been one of her students. Five years later he had returned as a mathematics teacher, and had now finished his second year of teaching.

"Alex, give me your opinion. My sister's older boy is eleven. The last time I visited Amy we discussed the possibility of having Evan enroll in our school. He's a bright boy, and Amy's done well in her schooling of all the children. But the time is coming when he'll need more. He's never been out of this area. He should expand his horizons." They started down the path. Emily continued, "I know your situation was somewhat similar. I guess I'm asking your opinion of the advisability of Smithson for someone in Evan's position."

"He's eleven, you said."

"Yes, soon to be twelve."

"How mature is he?"

"Oh, I think he's typical. Teases his sisters, tries hard not to see his chores. But a responsible boy."

"He's the oldest?"

"Yes."

"That tends to teach responsibility automatically."

"I suppose it does."

"Well, when I went to school here I lived at home. Evan wouldn't be able to do that."

"We realize it would mean boarding. But I'd be here. He could even live in the cottage with me."

"Teaching him independence is one of the reasons he'd be going to the school," Alex pointed out." Living with his aunt, especially if she's a teacher, probably would be a handicap."

"I see your point. I'd be nearby if he needed me, but don't get too close."

"Exactly."

"You boarded in Michigan?" Emily inquired.

"Yes, but that's only half the school year. Your Evan would be taken from a very restricted world and dumped into a much larger one. Even if you're near it could be difficult."

"His grandmother is in Michigan too. Perhaps if he boarded here, and lived with me and his grandmother there. Michigan could be frightening for a boy unfamiliar with it."

"How well does he know his grandmother?"

Hmmm, Emily thought, and then spoke. "That's probably a real point. Not well. And my mother isn't very pleased about Amy's 'wasting' her life on a Florida island. I don't know how she'd react to Evan." She stopped to look at Alex.

"Well, yes I do. I don't mean to imply she dislikes her grandchildren or any such thing. She'd come to life if she had the opportunity to mother— or grandmother—Evan. But she has a very formal view of life. I'm concerned she might say something that could hurt without realizing. I just don't know." They continued toward the dock.

"My mother feels somehow that Florida is a thief. That this coast seduced our father, befriended Amy, and even influenced me to some degree. It's not a full-blown neurosis, mind you, but looking at the process from her viewpoint, it's understandable. She lives nearly alone. When she visited Amy and Charles she couldn't see past the sandspurs and roaches. I think because she was afraid to. Florida has become her enemy, the other woman. It stole her husband and children. She simply can't admit to any good feeling about it.

"For Evan, leaving Florida would be a big move by itself. To suddenly hear remarks about his family's indigent life-style or feed-sack shirts would be bound to affect him. He'd end up anti-grandmother or his upbringing."

"That's scary, Emily. Sounds like an awfully big jungle for an eleven-year-old to have to find his way through. It could be a real problem. He'd spend the rest of his life feeling guilty, whichever choice he made. But if your sister just kept him on-island, that would be worse for him."

They reached the dock and sat in the shade of a red-skinned gumbo-limbo.

"I don't know how qualified I am to give advice about children. I'm surely no parent, or even an uncle. But, maybe, if your sister started his schooling here, where Evan would be separated by only a small distance, and could go home sometimes, it would be easier. Could you talk to your mother this summer before he leaves? Maybe make her realize what unthinking remarks could do to the boy? You seem to feel she isn't likely to be deliberate about it." He paused. "Maybe if she realized she was gaining a grandson by not badmouthing his upbringing, he would gain by all of it—grandmother, school, and home.

"A boy learns so much more than math or English from school. You know that, certainly, and I'm sure your relatives do too, or they wouldn't be wrestling with this can of worms.

"I can speak for myself. If I hadn't gone to the school, if I'd stayed here and at the Virginia house, I would have done just fine. But meeting other children and teachers was the best part of my school years. I learned about life-styles and places I couldn't have even imagined. Some I'd not want to have to experience, too. Certainly a boy like Evan would be stretched tremendously."

"He's so isolated now," Emily said. "It would fill his biggest lack—the variety of people he has no idea he's missing right now."

"Yes. His family means everything to him now. It'll be hard though. He'll have some trouble adjusting. But, Emily," he turned toward her, "don't forget, and don't let your sister and brother-in-law forget, that if they delay because they're afraid he'll be homesick, it will only be harder on him later. This is the right time—he's got all his values down, his roots. They wouldn't do him favors by waiting."

"You're right. Thanks Alex. You're confirming what Amy and I had thought. Your viewpoint is important—you've been there."

"Well, it's never the same, but I hope I've helped. I'll see you next month, Emily. Meanwhile, enjoy the new baby!" Alex waved and headed for the store.

It wouldn't be much longer before the run boat arrived. Several people passed by, stopping a moment to chat or wave as they passed. Most were locals, the winter crowd already gone. Emily missed this place's openness and friendliness each summer. It wasn't that way in Michigan even though she had known the people there longer. Acquaintances she'd grown up or gone to school with became distanced by the protocol of their day-to-day life in the north. A spectrum of friends was difficult there, compared to the islands.

The captain had not spoken an unnecessary word all morning. Jim managed to be everywhere he might be needed before it became essential.

The boat seemed crisp and efficient in all its moves. Docking, loading fish, casting away, all occurred with speed and silence at each stop.

Now, as they docked, Mullet Jim saw Miss Emily jump up and gather her things. When they were moored, the captain left the wheelhouse and went to her, taking her bag as he gave her his arm. By the time the captain had escorted Emily aboard and seated her, Jim had the hatch open, chute set up, and had started to direct the flow of fish.

In a couple of hours Miss Emily would be at her brother-in-law's fishhouse. Jim suspected the captain would be having a long two hours. Maybe Miss Emily would put him in a better mood, though Jim hadn't seen the woman yet who had managed that trick.

The captain returned with his sheaf of paperwork, and soon they were off again.

Jim, coiling the bow lines, passed near Emily.

"Hello, Jim, you're looking well!"

"Thankee, Ma'am." He nodded. "And you are doing well? You're happy about that baby, now?"

"Indeed. It's such a fine excuse to stay longer, you know. Jim, how's your mother? I haven't seen her for years."

Jim flashed a smile. "Oh, she be doing fine. She's allus asking after you and Miss Amy, whether I'd seen you, how the chillen is doing. You know, Miss Emily, Mama allus felt you girls were her special charges, she just loved you two to death!"

"No more than we loved her, Jim. I never have time in town. But I've got to say hello to her one time. How's her health holding up? All right, I hope?"

"She's real healthy, 'cept some rheumatiz once a while. She see you, she be happy a month, Miss Emily. I'll tell her you was asking."

Jim looked at the wheelhouse. The captain didn't seem inclined to turn over the wheel. He stared ahead as though this straight stretch was a major test of seamanship. Emily intercepted Jim's look.

"The captain seems pre-occupied."

"Yes, Ma'am."

"Well, I won't disturb him. I'm going to sit there in the shade and read, if it's not in the way."

"Oh, that's just fine, Miss Emily. Anything I could get you, let me know, please?"

"I'm all set, Jim, thank you." Emily settled down near the wheelhouse, and smiled at the captain. He didn't seem to notice. She opened her book and started to read.

Some minutes later she realized she hadn't absorbed a thing she'd read. The boat's motion and the passing islands were seductive, drawing her attention. Putting the book down, she went to the rail and watched the hissing green water part around the bow. She could see an infrequent brown or gold leaf turning in the water, obeying the complicated demand of the current, or an occasional fragment of seaweed, or deeper glint that may have been a passing fish. Mostly though, it was a near-monotone clouded-jade-green rushing past her eyes.

She was nearly hypnotized when the dolphin broke the surface to her left. For an instant they locked eyes, and it re-entered the water, leaped once more, and turned away.

Emily spun toward the wheelhouse, but the captain had seen it too. His arm extended commandingly toward the flats. When she saw the splash of water, she thought tarpon. But then the dolphins' bodies and heads appeared, and she realized they had cornered a school of jacks. The stunned fish slapped the water, being tossed and batted by the pod of gray predators. The feeding frenzy continued as the boat moved north.

Captain Murdock came out of the wheelhouse and gestured to Mullet Jim, turning over the wheel. Then, lighting his pipe, he walked toward Emily.

"I never tire of them," Emily said, straining to see the last of the feeding ground.

"They are well-designed machines, top in their field."

"Oh, but Captain, more than machines. To compare them to a cold machine when they are so lovely . . . that isn't giving them enough credit."

He shook his head.

"I disagree. Machinery, properly designed machinery, can be beautiful in the extreme. Consider efficiency, economy of motion, achieving the intended result without waste. An object can be lovely, in and of itself, certainly. But doesn't it become enhanced when utility is added to the beauty? Comparing the bottlenose dolphin to a machine credits it with an added dimension."

"I don't know. Your argument's confusing to me. I have to agree useful things can be beautiful. And beautiful things useful—sometimes. But often not, Captain. If beauty were judged only by its usefulness, what would happen to flowers, music, literature, painting . . .?"

"I don't judge only by usefulness, now, Miss Stanhope. But usefulness increases beauty in my eyes. Your examples of beauty though—I'd argue that they're also useful.

"Certainly flowers. Without a flower the seed wouldn't set. The entire reason for the flower is to attract a bee, or bat, or whatever. Even if it's not beautiful by our standards, it must appeal to the pollinator, or the plant won't reproduce. A flower is using beauty to continue its essential reproduction.

"The other things you mention—the arts. Maybe the usefulness of music isn't entirely obvious. Or Shakespeare. But it communicates, it can tell me something I wouldn't otherwise experience. A painting can show me a country I'll never visit."

"Yes. Perhaps we are saying the same thing. I don't think of a machine—like your boat engine—as beautiful. Only useful. But it is both, isn't it? I suppose I never realized it before." She turned to face him, studying this rather surprising man.

"You've provided me with a different perspective, Captain Murdock."

"Oh, I believe you see it similarly to the way I do, but perhaps weren't thinking of the whole. It could be taken even further—if we cannot see the beauty, or usefulness, of an object, perhaps it means we haven't found the secret of looking at it in the right light, not that the secret does not exist. It would be an interesting exercise to determine what a dolphin, or a pine tree, finds useful. Or beautiful."

"Everything has a reason?"

He nodded. "It's likely. We—meaning mankind—tend to consider ourselves too significant. As though we're the key to making the sun go round."

"The tide to rise?"

"Perhaps that's the reason for our disasters—the hurricanes and vicissitudes of life remind us of our puny unimportance. We have such hubris. We pretend to make a difference in the world. We inflate ourselves." His animation was gone. In its place had appeared a pain that Emily found difficult even to look at.

"Utility is the only reason to continue on when beauty dies. In the end, Miss Stanhope, we do not matter in the least."

He did not look her way. He roughly replaced his pipe in his pocket, and left.

Emily found herself speechless. Her hands were painfully squeezing the boat rail. It was an effort to release them.

She returned to her seat and picked up the book. She was blind to its pages, and blind to the passing sea as well. Her thoughts were on a philosophical, anguished man.

Except at the fish-houses, the captain remained at the wheel. He didn't speak with her again.

7

It had been a difficult day for the captain. Last night Lydie, his wife of too few years, had dominated his dreams as she did so often. The after-effects of the nightmares dulled and darkened his responses all morning. One part of him moved, robotic, in his normal daily rhythms. Another sector of his mind was sardonically amused as it calculated the effects of his sullen mood on the long-suffering deckhand, Jim. Murdock's self-loathing wore him out. It seemed to him other people moved through their lives unencumbered, while his burden had fastened to him like a stone carapace. If he were to set it down, he would die like a turtle stripped of its shell. He guessed that was a part of his punishment.

But the mood had eased. Escorting Miss Stanhope aboard brought him farther away from that darkness. It had been a pleasure, discussing a civilized topic with an interested woman. Perhaps it was incongruous—a drawing room discussion on the dock of a boat laden with dead fish. But intelligent conversations didn't always happen in likely places—in fact, he had found such reputed places often barren, only populated by people who felt the "right" tie or alma mater could substitute for real thought. They brought parrots and mynah birds to his mind, creatures which could be taught to talk, but not to think.

Then, without warning, he had seen Lydie's expression in Miss Stanhope's eyes, quizzical, thoughtful, enjoying the conversation. His bright, beautiful, trusting wife who, as much as she loved him, he cherished and loved her more. Lydie knew that he would never allow hurt or pain to come to her. He wondered, not for the first time, what the depth of her disillusionment had been. When had confidence turned to doubt, doubt to fear,

fear to despair, and, ultimately, life to a lingering anticlimatic death?

For Murdock, Lydie had been forests of pine and salt water cascading over jagged rock, evenings by a snapping fire with friends, saws whining and the smell of fresh-cut timber. He managed mills and superintended logging operations on thousands of Maine acres. Some of those acres belonged to Lydie's family. It was inevitable that they would meet.

Life had been so good. He hadn't fully realized it then. But, looking back . . .

They were young, well-off, bright. They were in love. Their marriage had been the season's social event. And they did enjoy society. They enjoyed their time alone even more. They explored their surroundings as well as each other, expanding their physical and mental horizons. They wandered pine woods, tidal pools, mountains, little off-shore islands . . .

It was, indeed, the best of times. Perhaps it was inevitable that the worst of times must follow, that such beauty and happiness must be replaced by horror. Great heights imply great falls. Perhaps the sensible course is on flatlands, where a fall is scarcely noticed. Melodramatic, that. And worse, untrue. But the symmetry of it was compelling for him.

Later he had fled to opposite environment. No rocks, just mud. Where the only mountains were changing clouds. The water was salt, but warm, and largely placid. Mangroves replaced pineland. Even the sun was different, setting in the water instead of rising from it. He had abandoned his lifestyle, his living, his friends. He learned the sea and its moods, determined it would never again surprise him with anything he should have knowledge of.

His life had changed, but it was inadequate. Despite abandoning everything, despite his resolve, Lydie was not left in Maine—she came with him. In honesty, he would not have wanted to be without her.

He did not want to forget Lydie—only that last leaving of her—those morbid imaginings of her last hours—days—alone and abandoned. That would haunt him, always . . .

Autumn. The leaves were at their loveliest, and Lydie was eager to visit an island off the coast, isolated but not impossibly far, which had a quantity of hardwoods in its center. Even from the mainland, at the town docks, it was possible to see that trace of color there. She planned a lovely autumn frolic beneath those trees.

So they packed a basket and set out. It was late in the fall, but island trees hold their color longer than the mainland because of the tempering effect of the water.

The day was beautiful, with a glittery jumpy blue sea, a south breeze, and mare's tails' clouds gauzy above. It did not take long to row to the island, and as they approached it became clear that the autumn leaves would put on a special show this day. Lydie had been right to pressure for the excursion despite the late season.

They spent hours walking, the breeze rattling the yellow and red canopy, occasionally releasing handfuls of leaves, which came spiraling down like confetti. She found a stream—a rivulet falling from rock and running through leaf mold and rock to lose itself in the earth. They drank from it and imagined other creatures doing the same. In spring violets would become a purple carpet here; in winter the icicles of the frozen spring would turn into a fantastic gargoyle of its summer self. So much to see—birds, small creatures, rock formations—it was Eden.

They were tired when they found a sunny valley with springy tall grass. Lydie declared this would be their lunch spot, and dropped into the sweet-smelling meadow exhausted. They ate. Afterwards they kissed and dozed in the warm sun.

He woke in the shade. Lydie was asleep, slightly flushed, still in some sun. Her image was even now engraved behind his eyes. He could still taste her skin, as he kissed her awake.

"It's late, Miss Alice-in-Wonderland," he whispered.

"It is, isn't it. A wonderland, I mean." She sat up. "The Roman gods couldn't ask for more than this idyllic place." She smiled, touching his face, "An idyll, with my idol, my love."

He laughed at her silliness, and stood, pulling her up.

"The sun seems to be telling us the idyll is over. It's a long way back."

"I don't want to leave—why don't we stay here, forever?"

"It's a tempting thought. Or it would be, given food and lodging."

"Always practical," she sighed.

They started back to the boat.

As soon as they left the shelter of the island's interior, the breeze they had enjoyed suddenly became a wind. Clouds moved quickly. They realized that they had waited too long on their picnic.

Lydie looked up. "I think we're in for a storm."

"I believe you're right." He looked at the sea below them, seeing the waves white-capping. "We'd better take some shelter. We won't be crossing in that." He heard some thunder rumbling.

"I'll get the oars and sail canvas from the boat." He pointed to a spot behind the ridge. "Maybe we can set up a lean-to over there, wait out the weather.

"You look for a good spot, I'll be right back."

He started down the slope and paused. "Did you wish this on us?" he shouted to her.

Lydie just laughed and disappeared in the other direction.

When he returned, hauling the contents of the boat, she had cleared a spot of leaf litter and branches, and was busy breaking spruce branches for their seat. In a short time they had a shelter.

The sky darkened steadily. They moved rocks onto the sail edge to anchor their lean-to. The wind strengthened, and before long sheets of rain began to blow.

They huddled close, and ate some of their remaining lunch. Hours went by, the storm easing and then increasing in strength. By this point they realized they had been trapped by the first "norther" of the season— knew they could be isolated here for days.

"It's all right," Lydie reassured. "We have jackets, some food, matches. We'll be a little hungry, and uncomfortable, that's all."

Just before sunset, the rain quit. The clouds started to thin to the north, showing color in the few torn patches of clear sky. Lydie got up and went to the ridge. Her form against the wildly moving setting sky-color seemed a silhouette painted on glass.

"It's awesome—these waves! Unbelievable!" she called. She turned toward the lean-to, and took a step. He saw her fall, in slow motion, slipping on moss or a rock, but couldn't move toward her in time to stop it. It was no more than five or six feet that Lydie slid. She was laughing, embarrassed at her clumsiness, as he reached her.

She put out a hand, and he raised her, but before she was fully up, her expression changed. She screamed as the pain took control.

Scooping her, he took her to the lean-to. As soon as he saw her ankle he knew it was broken.

They looked gravely at each other. Lydie shivered, and he grabbed the coat to put around her. The temperature was dropping rapidly with the sun's disappearance.

"I have to straighten it, and tie it up, love."

"No." She was trembling. "It really doesn't hurt right now. Please."

He kissed her. "Let me get a fire going." He let her rest, hoping she'd sleep, and gathered wood.

Pain was marking her face. They knew he would have to bind the ankle.

Finally he straightened and bound the leg, and Lydie slept, or perhaps fainted. Either was a blessing. It was full dark. They were cold, without food, and no one knew their whereabouts. The sea was impossibly rough for the rowboat to attempt a crossing.

Through the night Lydie moaned and tossed. She began to run a fever. By morning it was obvious he would have to chance the water alone, leaving her, to return with a larger boat and medical help.

He cut poles to support the sail lean-to, so that he could take the oars. He placed everything in her reach—the fire, more wood, the jackets, the remains of yesterday's lunch. He filled the jug with water.

"It's all right, really. It won't be long. It's daylight. You'll be back in a couple of hours." She couldn't hide the pain though. "Go on. I'll be fine."

He held her, hesitating.

"If you don't go now, darling, you'll never get back." She smiled.

He kissed her, said nothing.

"I love you, but GO!" She waved her hand. "*GO!*"

"I'll be right back. Lydie, I love you."

"I know, please . . . take care!" Her hand pushed at the air urging him away.

Finally he left her and carrying the oars, climbed to the ridge to look at a still violent sea.

"Good-by, darling, I love you!" Lydie's voice from under the lean-to propelled him to the boat, and in moments he was soaked by sea-spray as he strained at the oars.

Rough as the water was, he made good progress. The island receded steadily. Then, out of its lee, the wind and waves grew fiercer. He continued without a pause, driven by the knowledge of the suffering Lydie was enduring. He had slipped sideways from his starting point, was being compelled to the south. Waves thrust against the side of the rowboat, forcing his angle more southerly to avoid swamping. The boat was ankle-deep in water. He shivered uncontrollably—he'd left his coat for Lydie—but as much from fear for her and the strain of trying to get to the mainland quickly as from the cold. He could not rest—the wind pushed him three yards south for each yard he gained toward shore. He didn't want to land on a deserted part of the coast if he could avoid it. Time was too important.

He risked a glance behind him, and was appalled at the distance to go. Even more, the swift movement of the houses slipping to his north frightened him. He realized how completely his craft was at the mercy of the wind and sea.

He continued on, mechanically. The waves and wind would have been more bearable with ominous, stormy skies. But it was a clear-washed, deceptively lovely sky. People on shore would be commenting on the beautiful day—"if a bit brisk." They would have no inkling of the fight he was making—the struggle to save Lydie's life.

The trip had taken an hour yesterday—today he had already strained three times as long. The shoreline wouldn't approach his boat. The reason finally occurred to him. The tide had started running out. Caught by tide and wind, he was being taken to sea, helpless. No sign of life appeared around him. Still, he pulled for shore, calling Lydie's name to himself.

When night fell, he was miles off-shore. He could see some faint lights. He dozed, he rowed, he shook with the cold and wet. All he could envision was Lydie, lying under the sail canvas as the fever and pain mounted from her ankle.

By morning he seemed closer to shore. The sea was calmer, the wind blowing less hard. The tide should be favoring him. But his body was weakening rapidly. He'd had no food for nearly two days, no water for one. His strokes were jerky, uncoordinated. He struggled on.

Shortly before the third night fell the fishing trawler, returning to port for the night, noticed the little boat.

The man in it was unconscious, his skin blistered and cracked by the sun and salt.

Murdock didn't regain consciousness when they brought him aboard. He did moan once or twice as they dragged him over the railing.

"He's been out here days."

"No sign of a water jug, nothing."

"One step from death, he is."

"He was."

"It's not over yet, mate. He has a battle still to fight."

"That he does."

He was quickly in a doctor's hands, and at mid-morning, Murdock regained consciousness.

"How do you feel, sir?" the nurse bathing his face said.

"How . . .?"

"Some fishermen found you drifting at sea. They brought you in."

"Lydie!" he shouted hoarsely.

"Easy now!" she soothed. "Your wife, that is? Tell us her address, we'll get her a message, don't worry."

"No!"

The nurse was startled. The doctor came in, having heard the commotion.

"Lydie . . . needs help."

The doctor winced, looking at his nurse.

"Was . . . Lydie . . . in the boat?" he asked.

"Yes . . . o." his mind would not function properly. "No, she's hurt, on the island. Must get help."

"What island—where, sir?"

"Take you, needs a doctor."

"Yes, we'll go right away, but where?"

"Broken ankle."

To the nurse, Dr. Howe said "Get my bag ready. And nurse, this must have happened days ago. Exposure, infection, fever,—pack morphine and have plenty of manpower. Have a boat—a large one—ready. Let's hope we are in time."

Murdock, assisted on both sides, was put in a car and they quickly arrived at the docks where the boat waited.

Five days ago, he and Lydie had set out to that island from this same dock. He pointed across the dead-calm sea at the island. No color showed. The leaves were brown now, dead and blown off the trees, after the first touch of the nor'easter's winter weather.

"All right, Murdock, we'll find her. Nurse will take you back to rest."

"No, I'm going."

"I don't want to argue, sir. You are in no condition to travel. Conserve your strength for your wife."

"I must go. I will go." It was futile and time-wasting to argue with him.

The doctor sighed and nodded.

The powerboat reached the island in fifteen minutes. Murdock pointed to the landing, silent. He attempted to get out with the others.

"No, you don't have the strength for that hill," the doctor said. "Just tell us where."

"Over the ridge. Lean-to."

The men ran up the ridge, pausing at the top. They went more slowly down the other side. Murdock, alone in the boat, succeeded in climbing out. It seemed to take hours to climb the hill. He could hear nothing from the other side. Under his breath he kept saying "Lydie, Lydie." his talisman, a chant.

The doctor saw him first.

"Get him out of here," he ordered.

"No," Murdock cried, "Let me be." He struggled with the men who tried to turn him back to the boat.

"Let me be with Lydie."

The doctor tried to reason with him. "Murdock, it's too late. Your wife . . . she's been dead for two days at least. You don't want to see that."

Murdock stared at him uncomprehendingly. Then he growled, unearthly. The three men, startled, were left behind as he plunged down the slope.

The lean-to, half-collapsed over Lydie, looked abandoned. The wind had piled leaves against and on it. The firewood had not been burned. The fire he'd started before leaving was half-burnt, had been allowed to smolder out. Even the water jug seemed untouched. The coats were folded as he'd left them. The leaves were brown and curled, half- covering everything, a blanket partly drawn over the scene. But Lydie . . .

It was grotesque, some cosmic joke. All Lydie's beauty had been sucked into the ground, and a fetid, mushrooming gargoyle had grown to replace it. It had Lydie's clothes, her hair. It was a mockery of her. A corruption.

Murdock screamed, and could not stop. The men caught him, turning him away. He stood rigid. The doctor snapped,

"Cover her," nodding toward the sail. Murdock collapsed. He knew nothing more for many days.

By the time he recovered from his pneumonia, all semblance of fall had disappeared into a snowy winter. He was taken to a cemetery, where they told him Lydie's body lay. He erected a stone. In his heart, though, he knew she lay on spruce branches under a tarp, being slowly buried by weightless ribbed curls of dead leaves. They sailed, falling effortlessly, covering.

He tried to continue his life. But the house, the mills, the country, the pines, the mountains, everything he encountered summoned Lydie's memory. He knew he wouldn't be able to continue, not if he were to remain sane. When autumn came, and leaves started to color, he fled. He went south, as far as he could reach, away from the fall that haunted him.

8

The sun was high. Emily had been sitting in the ever-shortening shade of the wheelhouse for an hour, letting the wind of the boat's passage blow her mind clear. From her position at the bow of the boat, the hiss of the water along the hull was more distinct than the sound of the engine. She amused herself with a game—by turning her head slightly, she could vary the pitch of the sounds around her. She could increase both the engine noise and the sibilance of the water, or balance the breeze's roar in her ears with a sudden sweet call from an osprey overhead. She felt rather than heard the engine's bass in her private symphony. Pressing her head back against the structure of the wheelhouse increased that effect. The captain unknowingly contributed variations on her theme with each change in boat speed or direction.

It was a pleasant pastime, as she idly watched the islands approach and pass the boat. The waterway was empty of any human presence. She seemed to be rushing through a dreamscape. She closed her eyes.

When she opened them, alerted by the change in pitch of the boat engine, the sun shone full in her face. The boat had turned, threading into the short channel leading to her brother-in-law's fish-house. She could see Charles standing on its deck, shading his eyes with one arm.

She stood and waved, a gesture he returned exuberantly. Then she saw him turn abruptly, and walk to the back of the fish-house. She looked north to see the wake of the little powerboat leaving the Pratt's harbor. That would be Evan, coming to the fish-house to ferry her home.

Her anticipation mounted as the run boat worked, ever so slowly it seemed, into its position by the fish-house. Charles wore a grin that would not quit as he paced. He caught the mooring lines, slipped them over the pilings, and jumped on board before the boat was completely stopped at mooring. He hugged and lifted Emily in one motion.

"It's so grand to finally see you here, girl," he said. "Amy 'bout talked me to death the last few days, what with all she's got planned for you."

"She hasn't forgotten a certain baby's arrival, now has she?"

He laughed, "You'd almost think so. Not that any of the children have slowed her down overmuch." He hoisted her valise to the dock.

The captain left the wheelhouse. "Miss Stanhope, have a nice stay, and give my regards to your sister." He smiled, as though he too were infected with the excitement of the meeting. The moment temporarily erased whatever dark place he had been in.

The men gave an arm to Emily, though it was an easy transition to the sturdy structure of the fish-house. Jim, already at work, shifted fish to the boat. The three walked toward the office. The sound of the little boat seemed near.

"Here comes Evan, all excited!" said Charles.

They all stared in surprise when the boat rounded the corner of the fish-house. Amy Pratt had come to pick up her sister. Tossing a line toward her husband, she maneuvered the boat with aplomb. His reaction, slowed by surprise, was clumsy as he fumbled with the line.

Emily laughed. The captain's head shook as he smiled. Charles seemed torn between his total surprise and a desire to scold his wife.

"I might have known," Emily said.

"Why isn't Evan in that boat?"

"Because I wanted to meet Emily, Charles. It's been months since I've been on the water. And it's such a lovely day."

"You shouldn't be doing that in your condition."

Amy rolled her eyes, sending a sly grin toward her sister and Captain Murdock. "Charles, darling Charles, I do appreciate your fussing. But I'm a healthy, competent, person. I'm very capable of steering this boat a half mile. Honest!"

Charles looked exasperated. "But the baby . . ." he started.

". . . undoubtedly enjoyed the ride as much as I did," finished Amy.

"You may as well admit defeat, Pratt." The captain grinned. "An obstinate woman will never be defeated by us mere men."

Charles smiled weakly, "I believe you're right."

Amy laughed. "Spoken like a man who knows, Captain."

Captain Murdock, with a faint smile, inclined his head noncommittally. He stepped toward the office.

Amy delayed his retreat a moment.

"Captain. I was so delighted with the yarn. The color is lovely, and it's got the softest hand—the baby will enjoy it as much as I."

"As soon as I saw it, I knew it would be perfect for your child. I'm glad it struck you the same way, Mrs. Pratt." He nodded at both women, and went into the office.

"Well, I'll save my tongue lashing for later, Miz Pratt!" Charles swung Emily's valise into the boat, and helped her into the bow seat. "But don't think I'll forgive you this trick," he warned, wagging a finger at his wife.

Amy's response was to blow him a kiss as she swept the skiff away on an arc heading back to the home harbor. Charles watched until they disappeared.

He entered his office, where the captain was involved in papers. "Coffee? Or a Coke?"

"Thanks. Yes, coffee, that'll be fine."

Charles poured from the always-steaming pot, his mind still on Amy's escapade.

"I'm willing to bet that woman planned on coming out here all along. She persuaded me to leave the powerboat so Emily wouldn't be inconvenienced going to the house. She left me believing Evan would be coming out here, but now I think about it, she never said that."

"She's a strong-willed woman, Pratt. But if she wasn't, she'd never make it out here. You'd be in town, going to parties and dances, and running for mayor or some other foolishness."

"You're right there. But she sure makes me worry sometimes. What if something happened?"

"On that little boat ride, what would happen? Babies don't come that fast. She needs to get off that island sometimes too. Bet she left your boy hopping on the dock."

Charles laughed. "I'll bet she did at that. He'll be afraid I'm gonna chew him out for letting her come, and if I can't always rein her in, no eleven-year-old will!"

"She's a sensible woman, they both seem to have good heads on their shoulders. Just relax."

"Easier to say."

"Yes, I know." In a lower tone he said, as if to himself, "All too well." Murdock paused meditatively.

"You're a lucky man, Charlie—appreciate what you have. It might be easier reining her in, but you'll spoil what's there if you do."

Mullet Jim appeared in the door.

"Time to go, Jim?"

"Yassah, Cap'n."

The two men looked at each other. The captain laid his hand on Charles' shoulder before he turned to leave. Murdoch's mysterious past had almost surfaced. Charles knew that that moment had passed, for now.

"Thanks for taking care of Emily, Captain. It is appreciated."

"It was a pleasure for me, Charlie. In truth."

A few minutes later the run boat left. Charles seated himself in the breezeway which divided the fish storage from his office. He propped his feet against the wall opposite, precariously tilting his chair. He looked completely relaxed, almost asleep. Internally though, a feeling that had been coming on for some days churned.

On the face of it, it seemed absurd. In fact, he wondered if his age made him worry too much.

A new baby arriving—was that so big a change? Babies had certainly come before. Amy had no major problems with childbirth.

Then they had discussed the possibility of Evan's attending Smithson School. Losing his older son to a larger life would be a change, for all of them. Evan was bright—he would do well. He wasn't cut out for a sleepy existence like his father. It would be tough to let him go. Difficult for Evan to go. But overall, once they got used to the idea, best for him. Charles didn't feel that was the cause of the feeling nagging him.

Nonetheless, he was perturbed. Suddenly he felt distanced from his life, as though he were watching a film—a strange sensation, an emotion he had never experienced before—he was generally a practical person. Last night, watching Amy and the children through the window, and again today as her boat pulled away, his senses seemed to wrap the moment in cotton wool, in the same way Amy so lovingly packed her grandmother's Christmas ornaments each New Year's Day. Precious, fragile, irreplaceable. There seemed to be no reason for the feeling. Maybe he was coming down with a cold.

Charles set his chair down with a crash and got his hammer. Several planks on the south side of the fish-house needed renailing. It struck him that some hard physical labor was just what he needed. An hour or so of pounding nails before the fishermen started bringing in their afternoon catch should cure his nerves.

***

Aboard the boat, Mullet Jim anticipated reaching town. He wanted to get to the card game tonight. Saturday had been payday, but he wouldn't get any money until tonight. Because banks didn't open until he was well out on his run Mondays, his mama did his accounts for him. He still lived at home and shared his paycheck freely. But he always kept some money aside so that he could dress and go on the town. He liked to play the role of an experienced seaman on leave for the garden and stable boys from the big hotel uptown. He was a kingpin on shore, and played it to the hilt—greased hair, wide snowy collar and gold stickpin, hand-rolled cigar and a glass of bootleg rum. He enjoyed the card playing, too, and often won.

Punta Gorda was a different world from the boat. One evening he had actually passed Captain Murdock on the sidewalk without the skipper recognizing him. If the captain thought at all about it, he had probably assumed that that nattily-dressed dude was an off-duty chauffeur for one of the several millionaires who drifted in or out of town on their mysterious business. At least Jim liked to think that. His mama kept his clothes immaculate—probably better than the captain's own, although Jim guessed if the man didn't go anywhere he had no reason to dress.

And the captain didn't.

Each night ashore he would turn in his account-books and orders, and do whatever small shopping favors he personally took care of. Then he went to his empty house, ate the meal his housekeeper had left, and did not emerge again until he left for the morning run. The townspeople speculated fruitlessly on how he occupied his time.

He had declined dinner invitations until they were no longer extended. His housekeeper shed no light on his activities. She saw him each Sunday. He was polite, presented his requirements for the week along with her pay and housekeeping money, and that was that. She was not curious. Apart from an occasional unreplaced book, or rinsed dishes, and the unmade bed, the house would be as she left it. She spent four afternoons there—Tuesday, Thursday, Saturday, and Sunday. The captain paid well and punctually. Nothing else concerned her.

Before Mullet Jim could play cards, he had more fish to load. They were getting close to the last stop—Bull Bay.

"Cap'n, d'ya think that fancy boat's still at Jake's?"

"Probably not." He emptied the dead pipe. "In fact, the owner of that craft is likely in Tampa or beyond at this point."

This afternoon the mouth of the pass was table-top smooth. Yesterday's wind evidenced itself only in the milkier-than-usual color of the bay water. Sediments that floated downriver to become bay bottom hadn't completely settled yet. "The hold's still got plenty of room for fish, Jim?"

"Yassuh. Not a record haul today."

"Hardly surprising. The mackerel have played out now. Hot water fishing coming up."

"An'de rain."

"Fish don't mind."

"I do w'thout da lightning, Cap'n."

Captain Murdock smiled. Jim had a genuine fear of lightning—in fact the first time Murdock had seen Jim's reaction in the middle of a big storm, he had thought the deckhand was playing an elaborate joke. But the summer storms terrified Jim. It was only when the boat was in the midst of an intense storm that Jim's fear overcame him. Then he would hide in the engine room, and actually cover his head—with a blanket, oily sacks, whatever he could find. The captain and engineer let him alone during these spells. Before the captain realized that was the best course, he had confronted Jim—first with cajoling, then threats and curses. Once or twice he attempted to physically move him. But Jim's vibrating body had become rigid. The captain got nothing out of him except a monotonous moan, which started when the storm surrounded the boat and ended only when the storm had receded. Luckily for all of them, the boat was powerful and speedy. They did not remain long in those situations. All during the rainy season, Jim kept a special eye on the barometer mounted on the boat. He ran a cloth over it several times each day, watching with intense interest any movements of the needle.

His fear had been born in the 1921 storm, when he had been caught in the Ten Thousand Islands, unable to make any headway or reach shore. Five people had been on board. Two were lost at sea during the hurricane, and the other three, Jim included, had given themselves up for lost after four days adrift. After the captain heard about Jim's experience, he gave the deckhand a lot of credit for continuing on a job at sea. He overlooked the man's small idiosyncrasy.

"You're right—rainy season's nearly here." They rounded one more island. "But now here's Bull Bay."

"Doan see the boat, Cap'n."

Only Jake's skiff was tied to the fish-house today. Jake caught their mooring lines and then retreated to his office without a word. When Jim started to empty the stored fish he could see that Murdock's prediction yesterday of a poor showing of fish at Bull Bay had been right. The captain's job, to complete his paperwork, would take longer than Jim's.

"Well, Jake." Captain Murdock had followed him to the office desk. "Things get all straightened out between your fancy boater and Tom?"

"Weren't my boater. No need to wish him on me."

The captain began adding a row of figures, letting the silence stretch on a little. Finally Jake said,

"It's straightened. Tom had to threaten the law oncet they got to shore. That sorry guy thought he was gonna walk away, oncet his feet got on land. Turned out he'd borried the boat so he dint care bout it. Tom had to chase him to the Inn and raise a ruckus in the lobby. Tole the clerk to call the law and blocked the way to the stairs. Just kept on carrying on high until the guy give in."

"Isn't that desk clerk some relative of Tom's?"

"Windbag never knew that. Yeah, a cousin or somethin'. Played right along. He got his net money and then made the guy hire somebody to come back with Tom for the boat. Made him pay in advance, too. Figured he'd never see him again, once he got near the train station. Hell, Tom even tole the desk clerk he'd probably oughta check to see this guy was paid up—he liked to walk away from his debts."

Jake and the captain shared a laugh.

"Bet he liked that!"

"Tom said the guy never said a word."

"Hope he doesn't plan on stopping upriver on his way somewhere else."

"You'd probably not run up against him, Captain."

"True enough. The hotel there can have him. They like appealing to the fancy crowd—but they find plenty of phonies in the bunch."

"Like those binder boys a few years ago, in Miami. Selling the same waterlogged lot ten times over. Least until that hurricane taught them something about Florida."

"Jake, don't count on anything teaching that type. There's no storm gonna teach them. That wind blew them away. But they'll return, soon as they smell the money again. It doesn't matter what they sell, long as it turns a profit to line their pockets. They build a front and get to the right pigeons, and then they're on target for their kill. I've seen them spend their last dime to polish their shoes, so they can go up and dance in the hotel ballroom all night. Their belly'd be empty but they figure shoe polish is the way to some rich debutante's heart. The better investment. Wonder how so many people can be so stupid."

"They figure we're the stupid ones. Not grabbing at the goodies. Who knows? Maybe they're right."

"Hell, Captain, if you believed that, you'd be cutting the fool up on that fifth floor ballroom too."

"I've been there, Jake. But you're right. I hope I never carried their attitude with me."

"No chance a that."

"Thanks." The captain swept his receipts together. "Anything you need this trip?"

"Nah. Probably not till the weekend. 'Cept I could use some business."

"The wind's down now. Fishing will pick up."

They left the office, and walked toward the run boat. Its engine rumbled. The boat seemed impatient to be headed to the home stretch. Jim was more than ready. He had one mooring line off and stood on deck holding onto the boat. Jim turned loose and moved to the other mooring. As the captain took the wheel, Jim completed casting off. Jake and Bull Bay were quickly left behind. Jim spent the rest of the trip tidying the deck and getting set for a quick departure once they reached the town dock, with its lines of fish sheds and railway cars.

In the wheelhouse the captain was enjoying the upriver run. Running east, up the wide river mouth in late afternoon, it seemed as though every leaf was detailed by the sunlight. Wet mangrove roots shone red, exposed by the retreating tide. Most of the birds were treed, waiting with a snake's patience for their evening meal. One sunny indentation held a couple dozen pink spoonbills which reminded him of outsized, fantastical dogwood blooms out of a New England spring. Other trees blossomed with egrets, or pelicans with beak and body tucked into a solid grey mass. The captain could feel the cold blue eyes of each pelican he passed. From each perch, their eyes fastened on the moving boat and mentally escorted it upriver.

Then town appeared, dominated by the block-long hotel. The old docks extended into the river beyond it. A bridge would soon be replacing them. At the new docks, closer to the boat, locomotives shuffled boxcars around—he could see their movements. Undoubtedly they were waiting for the fish in his hold before pulling out.

The run boat was on time, despite not having the engineer on board. The captain had done well as usual. They tied up, and turned the boat over to the on-shore crew. Jim left and the captain entered the office shed. Another run was over.

9

The moon had gone from full to new. The run boat coasted south and north, a metronome to the passing days. For the children, the excitement of their aunt's coming to visit faded with the routine of the days. The adults had their own concerns and plans. Even if it affected the children, they were unlikely to be interested in details the adults mulled over.

Their mother and aunt talked about baby names, about family never seen in Florida, about their childhood. Soon the children slipped away to swim or play. The concept that their mother had a wider world to draw on, once accepted, became less extraordinary for them.

One day Katie noticed a little green heron in some buttonwood overhanging the bayou that was their harbor. She had been watching it idly when she saw that it had a nest nearby. From that point on the children checked the nest every day from a discreet distance. The flimsy gray stick nest, with three blue eggs, became in time a moving mass of fluffy gray furballs.

Too young to be captivated by the babies, Ned didn't fuss about them. The other three bickered and fought until Evan suggested they each name and "adopt" one baby. Thereafter the only arguments were about which chick they were looking at.

Their father told Evan it was a mistake to get attached.

"You'll never get close to them. And if you did, it would be bad for the bird. Evan, most bird families lose one or two of the babies before they grow up. Sooner or later, the nest will be empty." He paused, and commented, "You can't tell them apart anyway. They're all alike—like triplets."

Evan knew his father had a point.

"Just the same, Dad. Mom and Aunt Emily are twins. But they're different too. Even if they look alike."

Charles sighed. He didn't try to dissuade the boy any more.

Evan couldn't decide if he loved or hated the idea of going away to school. He had done considerable thinking about it while sitting in trees watching clouds build, or walking the beach tossing shells at the gulls.

One warm afternoon, his mother and the younger children had lain down for a nap. Aunt Emily looked at Evan, sitting alone on the porch.

"Why don't we take a nice swim in the surf, Evan?"

"I guess so. Not much breeze here. I'm getting hot."

They walked over the dune ridge to the eye-dazzling beach. The sand was too hot to stand on. They ran for the wet sand. The sea was very calm, hardly lapping on the shore. It felt delicious, as cool and crisp as its minty color implied.

Emily waded out waist deep and settled into the water, letting herself float with only her head out of water.

Evan splashed out beside her, and then sank, leaving his empty hat to float on the surface while he tadpoled in a circle around her. When he reached the hat again he spurted up into it, popping high in the air with water streaming from him. The hat hung in defiance of gravity from the back of his head.

Emily splashed him, in return for the tidal wave of water he'd just sent her way.

"You look funny, Aunt Emily. Like a coconut with a hat on, floating out to sea!"

"Cheeky boy." She sent another stream of water his way, with a backhand of the surface. He just laughed and swam farther out.

"C'mon out here, Aunt Emily. You can sit on the sand bar." He stood up to show her that the water was only knee deep. Emily dog-paddled slowly, watching the bottom. It was nearly exclusively sand, with an infrequent shell or fragment, or a trail marking the wandering of some tiny creature. Occasionally a movement betrayed a small, nearly translucent horseshoe crab, or a hermit crab scuttling along with his stolen house. Mysterious holes of varying sizes were scattered across the sand. Some had piles of ropy- looking sand alongside. By the time she reached Evan, she had become totally absorbed in the seemingly barren ocean bottom.

Evan had been exploring too. He handed her a large, fragile, sanddollar as she neared his head. Balancing on one hand with his legs streaming out behind, he flipped at the edge of another with one finger, partly exposing it. Then he pointed out several others.

The two floated along like tailing redfish, concentrating on the bottom and letting the current wash their bodies in a gentle rocking motion.

After a half-hour or so, Emily rolled over. The water felt suddenly icy on her sun-warmed back. The change in position was refreshing. She sat on the sandbar, leaning back on her arms. She tilted her hat forward over her eyes and faced the island, watching the birds pick at coquinas and seaweed along the shore.

Evan sat too. His toes floated to the surface, and he pulled down his left leg, then right, alternating as the other gently rose. Still intently watching his toes, Evan said,

"What is Michigan like?"

"It's a beautiful place. But very, *VERY*, different from here."

"I guess it would be. Is it cold?"

"Not in the summer. Actually winter here is something like summer there. It can get pretty cool sometimes. The lake water is cold and deep. You can't see across it, just like the Gulf right here. But the beaches are brown sand, or pebbles. And the sand dunes can be huge—taller than the Indian mounds here."

"I don't guess there's any mangroves."

Emily smiled. "No, there aren't. Pine forests, farms, maple trees, and birches. Nothing prettier than a clump of white birches on a lake shore, with deer peering around them."

"Deer?"

"The hunter awakes! Yes, lots of animals. Some you know, others you've only heard of. I've seen raccoons and otter. Porcupines. They will intrigue you, I think. There's supposed to be bears, and wolves. Some of the birds you see here too, others will be new.

"It's rocky, hilly country, because there used to be glaciers and ice covering it."

"The ice age."

"Yes. A long time ago. But there is quite a lot of snow and ice in the winter now. I don't know how your grandmother stands it. I try to persuade her south for the winter. But she can be a stubborn lady."

"Tell me about her. Is she nice?"

"Oh, Evan, yes. She's as grumpy and stern as she can be, just to cover up how soft-hearted she really is. Do you remember her at all?"

"Not really. I know she was here, but I don't remember it—just Mom and Dad telling me about it."

"Well I can describe her, if it helps. Her hair is white, and she dresses it very elegantly, piled high. I always think like a Spanish princess, though she's not at all Spanish in temperament. Very cool. Kind, as long as she approves of you. She's my height, blue-eyed, slim. Her hair used to be blonde, before Daddy died. She is very graceful—you can't imagine her ever getting her hands dirty. Then you walk out the back door, and there she is on her hands and knees, working at the soil around her roses or something."

Emily smiled and continued, "I've accused her of never sweating. She'd only smile sweetly and say, 'Emily, a lady doesn't sweat, she glows.' And that's what she is, a complete lady."

Evan seemed to puff protectively.

"My mother is a lady, too."

"Indeed." Emily smiled. "Only your grandmother feels some things are extremely important which Amy or I do not. I doubt your mother bothers with white gloves. Your grandmother still finds that shocking. Gloves are as essential to her as shoes." She paused. "Come to think of it, your mother is a bit lax in the shoe department with you children."

"But what's the point'a wearing shoes in sand . . ." Evan's voice trailed away as he realized his aunt was laughing gently.

"You understand, Evan. Etiquette has to yield to practicality sometimes. Your grandmother doesn't care to yield. And in her world she doesn't have to." She lay back, floating free of the bar. "People don't always want to acknowledge that circumstances differ, that their solution won't necessarily work for the other guy. It threatens them somehow, to take account of differences."

"You love her."

"Of course. She's my mother. But not just because of that, Evan. She's a loving and good person, and she has not had an easy life, even if she's been well-off. It's a little like climbing through the orange tree's thorns, loving her. The oranges are worth a few scratches. Especially when you take into account that the tree is not deliberately reaching out to scratch you."

"Ev–an." Katie was calling. Naptime was evidently over. "C'm–'ere."

Katie was at the water's edge as they waded to shore.

"Evan, there's only two babies in the nest! C'mon."

Evan and Katie ran over the dune, leaving Emily to wade out alone. She took a sweeping look along the Gulf before returning to the house. Some fluffy thunderheads were forming to the south, and little clouds nearer to hand seemed to have heavier, grayish bottoms. Rainy season started to look real. Those clouds were about the color of those green heron chicks, she thought. The image of a helpless, drowning chick being swept out by the current flashed in her mind. She grimaced. Charles had tried to warn them.

Amy and the children were on the dock. The women's eyes met. Amy gave a slight shake. No doubt about a missing chick. The girls were crying, and Ned joined in, though he wasn't sure why. Evan looked ill. All eyes were on the nest, and the two fuzzy chicks. Mama heron was nowhere in sight.

Nelly looked hard. "That one is Chick," she declared. "I know it," she continued defiantly, obviously expecting a battle.

Katie looked again. "That other one is Dusty. I named him 'cause he looks like a dustball, under the bed." She cut her eyes toward her mother, half-expecting a reprimand for not cleaning under her bed. She sniffed, thoroughly.

Everyone looked at Evan. He didn't look back but continued to stare at the baby birds. They returned his stare—all eyes, beak, and fuzz.

Finally he said, "Yes. That's Chick, and Dusty. I reccanize them both. Guess my baby found a different nest to move to." He left the dock and went toward the beach, closely followed by the dog.

The women exchanged glances again, and Nelly shouted, "Look, here comes the mommy-bird to feed them."

She was right.

***

That night Evan asked Emily if she wanted to walk the beach.

"You haven't seen a turtle yet this year, have you, Aunt Em?"

"No, and I'd really enjoy that!"

They left the house once it was fully dark, and walked north toward the pass. Emily was certain Evan wanted to talk, but he said nothing all the way to the pass. Gradually she let her thoughts drift, listening to the night sounds—the crunch of their footsteps, cry of the night birds, tinkle of shells and water. The beach at night seemed more sound-filled than the same place by day. It was not the types of sounds, but their volume. At night she seemed aware of each nuance of wave, each shell turning end over end. A ghost crab ran, and it was almost possible to hear each of its appendages in the sand. In daylight that would seem incredible. It was as though the weight of sunlight dampened the whispers of noise. But at night those sighs and whispers rose, and mixed with the indefinable scents of night blossoms and the salt breeze. It was a magical blend.

"Evan, it was a nice thing you did for your sisters today."

"What?"

"The baby birds."

"Oh." He scuffed the sand as he walked. "They were their birds. I know mine's probably dead. But they don't have to hear that."

She put her arm around his shoulders briefly. "It does get painful sometimes, growing up. But you were thinking of your sisters as well as yourself. That was sweet, and considerate, because you fell in love with those babies too."

Evan squirmed. Emily smiled to herself when he changed the subject.

"I been thinking. Maybe I'd like to go to Michigan this summer with you and see how I'd like it. And if I do, that's fine. And if I don't I'd still have been there. Would that be all right?"

"Fine with me, Evan—as long as it's something your parents will agree to. You'd rather jump into school in a totally strange place, then?"

"It's gonna be strange—might as well get it all done at once."

They began walking, retracing their steps, when they encountered a large trail crossing theirs, going up the beach.

"There's a crawl! And only up—it's probably still there Aunt Em!" Evan's whisper was excited.

When they went up the beach they found the diligent turtle nearly finished laying her eggs. They stood by as she ceremoniously closed the nest, spraying them with damp sand as they got on their hands and knees next to her. Once the nest had been buried they followed her on her laborious crawl back to the sea.

"Daddy says they come up the same beach all the time."

"It's amazing to think how they find their way back."

"You see that one's shell. It'll be easy to spot her again with that double bite out of the shell."

As soon as Evan mentioned the turtle's damaged shell after they returned to the house, Charles and Amy claimed prior knowledge of her.

"She's a lucky turtle. The first one we saw on the beach this year."Charles chimed in. "That's your mother's turtle—she saved its life a couple of weeks ago. So you can't lay any claims, Evan."

"Now I have a pet turtle!" Amy declared. "Next time she comes around I'll have another pet—one I'll fuss over more than a turtle, I imagine!"

Charles turned to Amy in mild alarm.

"Are you feeling all right? Is it time?"

"Of course it's time, or almost, love!" Amy laughed.

"I doubt it'll be tonight though. By the time that turtle returns—what, two weeks or so?—I imagine the baby'll be here. That's all I meant. Don't panic."

"I'm betting on two or three more days, Amy. I've been watching. It won't be much longer," Emily concluded.

"Evan, if things start when I'm at the fish-house I expect you to come get me right away. In fact, I think I'll take the rowboat, and you can come in the powerboat for me. That'll save time."

"OK Dad. But does that mean I hafta stay out there while Mom's having the baby?"

"I'm afraid so. Someone needs to be there, son. Besides what would you be doing, here?"

"Missing all the excitement," Emily interjected with a laugh.

Evan pouted, just a little.

"Evan and I have been talking," Emily became more serious. "I think you should go over it with your parents, as long as we're all together."

"Well, I think I'd like to go to Michigan with Aunt Emily when she goes. Go to school up there and see grandmother, and all."

"So soon?" Amy looked worried. "I'm not sure I'm prepared to lose you that fast, Evan." She looked at Emily. "Or whether mother would be prepared."

"I'll write to her tonight. I don't see any big problem, Amy. It'll be good for her."

Charles objected. "Amy will need the boy around to help her this summer with the baby here."

Evan had not thought about the baby, past its arrival. He slumped visibly.

Amy had watched him. "Charles, other than cutting wood, the girls and I can do fine without Evan having to be here. You can help us there."

He nodded. "It's up to you, Amy. And how well you get through this delivery, too. I'll let you decide. But no final decision until the baby's born."

"Fair enough. I say let him go then. Emily, write mother and we'll plan on losing our first-born this summer."

"Thank you, Mom," Evan popped out of his chair to give her a big hug.

"Now," Amy responded, "it's time you got to bed."

"And me too—daylight comes early," Charles rose and yawned.

Emily got out her writing paper and adjusted the lamp as the room emptied.

Once the letter was written, sealed, and addressed, she tucked it under the lamp so Charles wouldn't forget it in the morning. Then she blew out the lamp and went to bed as well.

10

When Emily got up the next morning, Charles had left with the mail. It was raining—showers which had built up over the Gulf washed the islands in a gentle, soothing way. At dawn when she had opened her eyes for a moment, the sky outside seemed to glow orange. The rising sun had stained the misty rain, and it seemed like the interior of a sunset cloud. Now, an hour later, the sky had turned gray and darker than the dawn.

She found her sister at the table with a cup of coffee. Amy had apparently been reading, but had pushed the book away as the light level fell.

"Should I light the lamp?"

"Don't bother. It's pleasant. The children are sleeping late, too."

Emily poured her coffee and sat at the table. Looking at Amy had always been like looking in a mirror—at least when one of Amy's pregnancies didn't distort the image. She teased her sister.

"I think you have more laugh lines than I do, Amy."

"Let me see." Amy looked at Emily closely. "Probably just as well the light is dim, Sister! But I'm sure I do—I spend more time in the sun."

"I expect the sun only emphasizes the lines. You seem to be thriving on this life—you are always smiling."

"I admit it has been all I've wanted, so far. Maybe you ought to try it, Em."

"Now." Emily shook her finger.

"You're beginning to sound like Mother with her 'settle down' theme. She's afraid I'll be an old maid schoolmarm."

Both women shared a smile.

"Well, don't fuss about settling down. Things 'settle' to the bottom—cream 'rises' to the top. I seem to remember our mother saying that—do you?"

Emily nodded, amused.

"What you 'settle for' is always less than what you strive for."

"And 'settling will leave a bad taste—there'll always be the nagging thought that things could have been better, if you'd tried a little harder,'" Amy finished in a sing-song voice.

"It's a dirty trick to turn her own words into weapons, Amy. It is." They had fallen into a familiar conversation of the past weeks. "I don't believe she'll ever completely recover from Daddy dying so unexpectedly. It put a crease in her bonnet that won't ever smooth out," Amy sighed. "She imagines it happening to herself, and is afraid we wouldn't be cared for or something. She certainly taught us—and we're adults—why we shouldn't be able to care for ourselves when we've had such a grand pair of teachers for parents escapes her. But Emily, she's never gotten to know Charles. She's never gotten over the feeling that fishing is a game or sport, not a living. So Charles can't be supporting us." Amy sighed again. "And you—you don't even have a POOR husband!"

"How will we ever manage?"

"Exactly."

"I don't think she can be reassured. I think she's not entirely rational on the subject."

"It's understandable. Everything she had once has drifted away—husband, children, all her values. The world keeps changing the rules on her. She needs to expand her life, but she's too busy trying to shore up what she already has."

"Evan could be a help for her, Amy. Force her to concentrate on someone else."

"Let's hope."

Amy picked up her knitting. "I want to finish this today. Since it's going to act rainy all day, this afternoon we'll corral Evan and get his measurements—order him some proper things from Sears. We can't have him looking like a poor relation."

"That sounds good. I'm going to bake some cookies. Chase away the damp and treat the little ones."

"Don't forget us big ones, Sister!"

Emily started assembling ingredients in the kitchen and Amy went into the front room. She sat in the quiet room and her fingers picked up the flow of the knitting in the same rhythm as the tick of the mantel clock. Once that rhythm was established, as was often the case, her mind picked up the thoughts that were nagging at her.

Their mother had been one of the twin's prime conversational subjects the last two weeks. The lady was simply too vital to be closing herself off as determinedly as she was doing. Each summer as Emily went north, her impression was that her mother had become more shut off, more fortified, yes—more petrified—than the year before. It worried Amy. She even considered a trip north herself, although it would not be easy. Even though Charles, bless him, had suggested her mother live with them a portion of the year, Amy realized that would be unworkable. She would not even come south with Emily in the winter, and Amy was certain she would enjoy the seasonal visitors near the school if she did. The lady was stubborn. She had become soured on Florida, and that was that.

Whether adding Evan to her mother's life would be a help or hindrance Amy could not guess. Perhaps it had come to the point where any movement might be better than stagnation.

Thunder rumbled and lightning flashes were more frequent and disconcerting. The wind and rain picked up, demanding attention, and pulled her mind away from her mother, and even the knitting. Nelly came sleepily into the room.

"Why's it so dark, Mommy? The thunder woke me up. Is it still night-time?"

The day had begun.

At the fish-house Charles lit his lamp. The rain promised to continue all day. He had some netting to mend, but that was an outside job. Accounts were all in order waiting for the run boat, and it wasn't likely he'd have many fish to weigh in today. This kind of rain would keep a man bailing more than fishing if he were to venture out.

He had wedged the door nearly closed, to keep the rain from blowing in. Through its crack it was hard to tell the difference between the sky and sea. All landmarks were gone, and the clouds were as torn and dark as the water. The tin roof drummed with the deluge. Sporadically, a wind gust twanged it in a way that seemed to threaten to rip a panel of the roof free. Charles knew the roof was secure, but he involuntarily started and glanced upward when that happened.

He paced to the little window, but the view was the same. When he left the house, Amy was fine—no sign of labor. But storms often brought babies—and he wasn't happy about Evan coming out here—even in the powerboat—if the birthing should start. In this deluge it was too easy to become disoriented in a small boat.

He picked up some thin strips of buttonwood he had put aside weeks ago. He had lost his favorite net-mending shuttle overboard last week, so today seemed like a good day to concentrate on carving another. Carefully he began forming what looked like a spear head, about six inches long and two inches wide. He tapered the point and edges, but not its base. When he roughed out the shape he wanted, he placed it on the table near the lamp, and holding it steady, he scored an arching line a half inch or so from the thinned edges. Then, inside that line, he scored a second.

Slowly working from both sides, he hollowed the space between the double line until he removed that section of wood. The shape roughly re-sembled that of a candle nearly filling a cathedral window. When its sym-metry and shape finally pleased him, Charles laid it aside and began another, larger shuttle needle. By mid-morning he had roughed out a few of varying sizes. The weather had changed little. The rain poured off the roof in sheets from all sides. Thunder was muted—distant, or drowned out by the noise of the rain.

Taking a break, he went to the door with a cup of coffee. The sea quiv-ered, but was relatively smooth. The force of the rain dampened down the wave action.

If the storm was as widespread as Charles suspected, he didn't envy Murdock's job of threading through channels and passes this day.

He finished his coffee, sighed, and put on his oilskins. Keeping well under the roof line, he circled the building, checking on everything. He wanted no rainwater in gas drums, or items lost overboard. When he reached the spot where the boat was, he knelt down to try to peer between the planks of the deck. That was futile. Resignedly, he stretched out on his stomach, and hung his head over the edge to peer under the fish-house. A second's glance was sufficient, and he scrambled backwards under the eaves. The boat floated high and dry, protected by the bulk of the fish-house, so that it didn't fill with the rain. He had gotten more water-logged checking on the boat's lines than the boat had gotten all morning in the weather. It was no more than he expected.

The system he had rigged up to keep his boat dry worked admirably. What little inconvenience he encountered working it under the fish-house each day during rainy season was more than compensated by the fact that he had nearly eliminated bailing the boat during or after rainstorms. He devised his set-up shortly after he had raised his swamped boat from the bay bottom one stormy day.

He tied a second set of painters fore and aft, besides the normal ones he used to moor the craft at the house dock. These were longer ropes, particularly the bow line. When rain threatened, he eased the boat under the fish-house when he arrived. His procedure was to pass the long bow line through an eye bolt he'd mounted on a convenient piling well under the house. Then he backed the boat out to the edge again, letting the painter loosely run through the bolt. Getting up on the deck, he would then pull the boat back under the fish-house by pulling the bow line taut while letting out the aft painter—basically making a pulley. When the boat was positioned where he wanted it, he merely left enough slack for the tide, and tied off the boat. The whole operation took little time, and was much easier than attempting to manhandle the skiff onto the deck, or bailing in the rain each hour. Even during wind-driven storms when the waves slapped the bottom of the fish-house, there would be little water on the boat bottom. In fact, checking on the boat was probably a foolish exercise in the rain, but it was a habit that no man dependent on a boat would willingly break.

He went into the fish room. The ice he had chopped and spread this morning had not even started to melt. Charles doubted another block of ice would be necessary today at all, unless more fish were brought in. That seemed unlikely in the storm. He closed the door, barred it, and hurried back to the office to shed his wet clothes.

***

Evan was restless, full of nervous energy and not able to work it off. He went to the porch to watch the rain. Nothing moved outside except an occasional tree branch. The chickens were doubtless huddled under the house. The day seemed to stretch out endlessly. All the women were busy with things—even his sisters were engineering some complicated play for their doll's benefit. Ned was sleeping.

He went to the kitchen, and stole some warm cookies from his aunt. "Evan!" His Aunt Emily sounded exasperated. She slapped toward his hand as he reached for more cookies. "You need something to do. Go upstairs and pack this little box." She handed him an old cigar box. "That's for treasures only. Nothing practical—nothing you can purchase at a store. Just things to bring your mind home if you get lonely in Michigan. You'll have to think over what is important to you, and sort out some of your odds and ends. Maybe that will keep you out of the cookies until we're ready to get your clothes ordered. Go on!"

She shoved him out of the kitchen.

His mother smiled at him as he walked past, a little puzzled looking, examining the box as though it might hold an explanation.

"It's an excellent idea for you, Evan."

"But what would I be taking in here?"

"You won't figure it out all at once. Em and I packed a box like that when we came here our first winter." She smiled at his puzzlement. "Your grandfather's idea. It works. Just put some things in there. You'll think of others, and be taking some things out and others in for several days. It'll come to you."

Evan went up to the loft and sat, looking around. Obviously, he would take the picture of the family standing in front of the house. Aunt Emily had taken it last year, and even a couple of chickens and Lightning the dog had managed to slip in. It was rather stiff—no one seemed to be smiling, although they had been excited enough while the camera was being prepared. Nell stood in front of her parents, who held Baby Ned between them. Katie and Evan stood next to, and a little in front of, each adult—Katie next to their father, and Evan by their mother. It was very symmetrical and formal-appearing, and everyone was dressed in their finery because they had been going to Boca Grande that day.

That had been a marvelous day. Aunt Emily had left by train the next day for Michigan. But before that, the family had an elegant overnight stay at the Inn, complete with a proper formal dinner in the dining room. The children had been awed—eating the same food as the men who ran the world—or so it seemed. Crystal chandeliers winked. Soft heavy tablecloths and napkins with a glistening design, white on white, covered dark tables surrounded by brocaded chairs. A number of times gentlemen had approached his father to greet him and talk a few minutes. Evan's heart had swelled, and his palms became damp. He had not realized that his father was so well-known—so respected—by millionaires! And his mother, too. They asked about her mother, admired the children. It was a revelation to him.

After dinner the family strolled to the beach and back, standing for a few moments by the nearly vanished remains of the once lovely Inn bathhouse. A hurricane had toppled it when Evan was a baby, and another storm had completed its destruction. His parents tried to recreate it for the children—telling them tales of their courtship there, and pointing out landmarks that remained from a time past understanding for the children.

As elegant as the dinner and the Inn were—and evening dancing had capped that night—the children were captivated more by the movie matinee.

They had sat on folding chairs in a big tin barn, watching the film and drinking soda Mr. Pratt had bought across the street. Ned spent his film time lining up shells on the sand floor, oblivious to the wonders the rest of the family were experiencing. Halfway through the picture, a thunderstorm drove rain on the roof with a fierce thrumming sound. It made the whole adventure more memorable.

The next afternoon, shortly before putting Aunt Emily on the train, they had gone to a band concert at the Inn. Several people had pressured Emily and Amy to sing. It had been a long time since the Stanhope girls had visited, but they were remembered. Finally, to everyone's delight and enthusiasm, and the children's amazement, they did sing.

It had probably been Evan's first concrete realization of a world beyond his own. It glittered impressively. He had decided, going home, to be a railroad man—a millionaire railroad man. His mother smiled at his enthusiasm and replied cryptically,

"Be whatever you like, so long as what you are and who you are don't get confused."

And his father, not usually prone to confusing remarks, added, "Riches are more than money, Evan."

As the months passed, that world receded somewhat. But he had looked through that door. And the picture somehow stood for both of those worlds in his mind. It went into his box along with a roseate spoonbill feather and a lucky bean. On his windowsill was an albino lightning whelk, about three inches long, that he'd found one cold blowing winter day. It went in the box too, after Evan had relived that cold morning—and how marvelous it felt to return to the shelter of the house and have the warmth of a big mug of sugared coffee, as well as everyone's admiration of the prize shell. He began to understand he was packing memories, in a physical way. He found himself absorbed, and was surprised at the hour when he was called down for his fitting.

After dinner that night the family played charades. It was a ploy to tire the children since they hadn't been outdoors at all, and a treat, letting them stay up a little longer.

Charles entertained them by describing in mimicry the bedraggled condition of Mullet Jim and his skipper by the time they'd reached his stop. He hadn't glimpsed Bill, the engineer, and the captain told Charles that he hadn't seen him all day either.

"He went into the engine room this morning, and the engine started. It hasn't stopped so I guess he's still there, but he's not coming out to see if the rain slacked off any." Charles had a talent for reproducing the accents and body movements of people he described, and the captain seemed to be wryly draining rainwater out of his pipe as he talked to Charles, right in their lamp-lit room.

"Which reminds me," Charles continued, lapsing into his own persona, "Captain Murdock left a bottle yesterday, and I'd forgotten to bring it home." He produced a quart bottle of fine Cuban rum. "This is in anticipation of the baby's arrival, for a celebratory drink and so forth, he said." Charles grinned. "He said I'd better not drink it all because he would check to make sure I had brought it home!"

"Where on earth did he get that!" Emily exclaimed.

"You're not serious, Em! No doubt traded some of Sam's potent shine for it, at any of a dozen fishing smacks up and down the coast."

"He just struck me as very upright, I guess."

"That's fair. I think he is. But this alcohol thing—most people can't see any reason for it, and the captain's one of them. You'd never catch him running people or guns along the coast like some do, though he certainly would have the opportunity. But some likker—who's hurt? Besides," Charles deliberated, turning the bottle meditatively, "it is always good to have something in the house—for medicinal purposes, you know." There was some general laughter as they returned to charades.

***

The rain seemed just as heavy the next morning. After eating his breakfast with Amy, Charles commented, "It's probably a good thing this weather isn't a month or two down the road. It'd likely turn into a real hurricane on us. As it is, it makes me a little nervous. Particularly with you ready to complicate my life." He patted her protruding belly fondly, and then held her in a rocking embrace as they stood by the door watching the dreary sky.

"Seems like I'm in no hurry to leave," Charles said into her fresh-smelling hair.

"I don't envy you that trip, love," she replied.

His hands moved slowly across her back and shoulders.

"I don't envy you what you've got ahead, either. But I do most assuredly love you, Mrs. Pratt." The kiss was prolonged. Neither wanted to break away.

"I don't plan a baby today—I want some sunshine for our child—so don't fuss." She stretched up to give him a quick kiss. "Stay dry, Mr. Pratt. I love you."

He sighed. "Guess I gotta go, like it or not." He hitched his hood around his face and opened the screen, loping across the yard. He turned toward the house and threw Amy a wave as he reached the overturned boat on the beach. In moments she was watching an empty shoreline. She closed the screen door softly.

11

For Amy a rainy day constituted a break from the ordinary. It was a physical relief for her to rest her eyes from the tropical sun. But the hours stretched interminably the second morning, and before long she wondered if the sun would be gone forever. She was more than ready to walk the beach or pull garden weeds. The combination of a house full of children and another rainy day didn't appeal to her. She had become restless.

Everyone slept still in the early morning darkness, so she attempted to go back to bed. Even though the rain was a soothing noise, she could tell after a few moments of lying quietly that sleep would not return. She had been too wide awake already. She couldn't get comfortable—the bed seemed to reject her. Besides, when the baby arrived she'd have to stay in that bed for some time. No sense in wasting her time there now.

She sat on the side of the bed and looked at the room. A pair of windows faced east, bringing mornings inside. She could see portions of the bay through the trees on clear days. An opossum family had raised their young outside in one of the trees this spring. No one knew they were there until Amy had awakened to a crashing and rustling in the bushes. Charles had shined a light on them, the mother frozen in stillness with a multitude of babies clinging to her back. Amy could feel the fright emanating from the mother and coerced Charles into dousing the light. She refused to let him catch it despite his objections. Something always seemed on display— whether sea grapes, cardinals, warblers or moonflowers.

Inside, the room was spare, but it had a certain elegance. The iron bed was creaky, but rust free, painted white. A delicate cross-stitched quilt was folded over the footboard. It covered the bed in winter. Two oak dressers with crocheted doilies under the celluloid hair brushes and mirror were aligned along the unbroken side of the room. The beaded wallboards, laid horizontally and painted white, rose to the ceiling from a dark wood floor. The walls, adorned with several small paintings and photographs, also held the door to the kitchen as well as the pair of windows. An oil lamp with a blue glass shade relieved the white and wood tones, complementing the blue quilt with its handsewn white design. The only other piece of furniture was a sewing rocker, a low, armless oak rocker with a cane seat.

She pulled it around to face the windows and sat. This room remained brighter than the others even in the rain. In the front rooms the porch roof obscured what little light could get through the clouds. Amy rocked, and watched the rain outside the silent house.

In her mind she checked off her list of needs—anything she would possibly require in the next few weeks—and decided, once again, that she had probably tied up all the loose ends. Everything seemed in order, waiting for the baby's grand entrance. Captain Murdock's pass south this morning would bring some additional supplies, and tomorrow Evan's clothing order would be in the mail.

Amy smiled to herself. Maybe her nervous flutterings weren't caused by the rain. Maybe it was simply being all prepared, without the play proceeding. Time for the baby to make its appearance, center stage.

The moonflower vines covering the trees outside the window vibrated with the force of the pelting rain. She could barely distinguish color—only sullen shapes and silver rain. Thunder rumbled low in the distance, and though it hardly seemed possible, the sky seemed to be growing darker. The rain tapped on the windows like mad fingers beckoning for attention. Getting up to light the oil-lamp seemed to be too much effort, so Amy watched the room dim as she rocked silently.

The lamp was lit at Sam's little house. Yesterday he had talked with Bill on the run boat. Sam had decided he was due to give himself a few days on the town. His brother Bill was also a bachelor, so Sam usually stayed with him when the town mood came on. Sometimes Bill was a bit too precise and persnickety for Sam's taste, but that was probably what came of being an engineer. Bill had always tended to be a bit more rigid than Sam. He had a hefty dose of the fire and brimstone their daddy'd preached up and down the coast years ago. Although Bill knew about Sam's sideline, it was a subject that remained closed. Bill managed to disappear whenever Sam had business dealings with the captain. The two brothers circled warily around many subjects the same way, and it didn't interfere with the indisputable fact that they were the only kin the other had. Although Bill was the elder, Sam was by far the better-known brother, whether because of his innate friendliness or his product, no one seemed sure.

Sam was tempted to catch the down-coast run this afternoon just for the ride. Nothing to do in the rain. But then, the boat would seem mighty crowded in this downpour, and he didn't want to be on the wrong foot with Bill even before he started his visit. Better to wait until tomorrow. Maybe George out at the fish-house would be ready to play some cards this evening.

Sam settled back in the old armchair. It had been sun- bleached and worn until its fabric was nearly without color or design. It was a little ragged and dirty in places, but the chair was sturdy and comfortable, molded over years to the precise lines of Sam's body. Much of the time Sam spent in his house he could be found in that chair. In fact, many nights he didn't bother to go to bed, but slept in it as well. He had a direct view of his boat and the bay from there, so no one could enter or leave Fishhawk Bay without Sam's being aware of it.

Sam and Bill had been born and raised among these islands. Sam thought they probably had more time afloat then on land, truth be told. Their daddy had been a part-time circuit preacher, a part-time shopkeeper, a part-time husband and father, and, it turned out, a part-time scoundrel.

The scandal had surfaced when Sam was about eight. He could remember distinctly the screaming and crying that went on. Mostly because his usually staid mother wasn't prone to such outbreaks. They had all gone on one of Daddy's preaching and selling circuits. When they reached a little settlement in the Ten Thousand Islands, their daddy suggested they set up camp on a small island some distance from the settlement. Their mother, sure of a reception and room at one of the parishioners' houses, wanted to go to the dock. She insisted over his objections, and the boat headed reluctantly (as Sam now remembered it) to the dock. Looking back as an adult Sam wondered if his mother had had a premonition, or had even been told somehow, of what awaited them. He couldn't decide if he were imagining a strained trip or whether the ensuing scene had come as a surprise to his mother.

At any rate, the boys scrambled ashore and the adults came more slowly. As they reached the end of the dock, a large woman, very blonde and clearly with child, hurried toward them. A younger girl-woman of perhaps twelve followed, obviously a daughter.

"I'm so glad to see you're finally back, Mr. Preacher–sir. I been looking every day for you. Come, come." The woman flapped and stuttered, and plucked at their father's shirt sleeve. It was apparent even to the boys that this blonde mountain was dim-witted beyond all normal bounds.

"Come," she chattered, while the daughter stood back silently. The woman didn't seem to see the boys or their mother. Their father acted embarrassed and reluctant.

"Aren't you going to introduce us, Wilbur?"

Sam's mother was angry. Sam could feel it radiate. Belatedly their father muttered everyone's Christian name, as the mountain tugged him toward a shabby house. At the step, Sam's mother took a stand.

"Helena, is that your name? I didn't understand. What is your last name?'

Helena was now on her porch. Their father as well. The boys and their mother had to look up at them.

"Who is your husband?"

The fatal words had been spoken. Helena beamed. Their father was ashen.

"In this house," Helena said proudly, "I'm Mrs. Preacher–sir. Not in the church. Not in the street. Just here. Come, come," she pulled at their father again, into the house.

Their mother was transfixed for an instant. Sam could visualize her expression even now. Then without a word to them she went inside and shut the door. She did not knock, an action Sam had never before seen her make. When the voices started to rise Bill and Sam walked down to the water.

Sam had no idea of what was happening. Bill was no help either, saying only "I don't know" to every question. It took years before it all fell into place for Sam. Helena had given the circuit preacher a room. The warm weak-minded woman had been an easy conquest for the traveling preacher—who had allayed her fears with a very limited marriage. He shared her bed and bounty, and she never said a thing beyond her house. Perhaps someone added one and one when he saw the preacher and the pregnancy in a woman living alone. Perhaps he had never even been suspected. Perhaps the wrong question had finally been asked at the right time.

Sam never remembered how they returned home, or when he realized his father was no longer a member of the family.

The boys and their mother moved to town. Their father, the former part-time preacher, former part-time husband, wandered the coast selling some meager wares and drinking heavily. With every binge he tried to justify himself to embarrassed people in dozens of settlements. He was never mentioned at home. Several months later their mother died of pneumonia. As an adult Sam decided the primary cause of death was embarrassment. After her death, the boys sometimes saw their father for short periods but it seemed almost a relief when he disappeared in a storm when Sam was twelve.

Sam never saw Helena again. Or the baby that would be, he supposed, his half-brother or sister. But once he had seen the daughter.

He had been in Fort Myers with several other men, picking up supplies for a fishing boat he was working aboard. He was fourteen at the time, and after dinner one of the men decided it was time to introduce Sam to a "new form of entertainment."

Sam didn't grasp their line of thought at first, but soon realized what he was being introduced to. He had grown up relatively unsupervised since his mother's death, and although Bill would be sure to straighten out any of his tendencies to go too far astray, Bill wasn't here.

So as the evening wore along Sam had some whiskey surreptitiously pressed upon him, and eventually the group came to the decision that Sam should be taken to the rooms over the barber shop. Sam knew what was planned, and was heady enough with whiskey and talk that it didn't matter.

He should have lost his virginity that night. Perhaps he did. He wasn't sure. When he finally was shoved through that upstairs door into the dim, musty-smelling room with the rumpled bed, he was ready to "become a man."

The girl, half-dressed, sat in front of the windows. She rose and turned toward him as he came in, and before Sam had caught a full breath she smothered him in her warm breasts and wrapped her arms around him.

"So, my sailor-boy," she crooned, and without any preamble moved one of his hands onto the cotton of her camisole. When he seemed frozen momentarily, she kneaded his hand under her own a few times, and he felt the tissues of her breast, felt her nipple shrinking and hardening under his hand. Without conscious thought he leaned forward and his hand searched for bare skin. His whole body shivered as he found it, and he hardly realized that she was undressing him until her warm hands grasped and pulled at him suddenly.

He let out a cry, but she was leaning against him in such a way that he could only collapse backward on the bed. She burrowed into his side and constantly moved her hands on him, bringing waves of warmth over him. He still had not gained a full breath. Each intake of air brought powdered warm scents and spices to his nose. Her legs were bare now, and his hands were touching her as eagerly as she was caressing him. She held him tightly and rolled back—he was now over her—when she opened and wrapped her legs over his. The heat of her seemed to burn him. She forced him close and with her movements and hands, centered him. Then she guided him, hands grasping his hips. As he penetrated her, she gurgled a sigh and he squeaked in surprise.

He popped his eyes open and for the first time saw this woman who held him captive in a basket of her arms and legs. She did something, without moving, to the part of him buried in her that made him squeal again. Her blonde hair was long and scattered, her body stretched out from their joining to a face that was slack, open-mouthed. Her eyes opened and she moved again, almost an impatient motion.

"C'mon sailor-boy, it's easy. You like it fine, doncha." She pulled him toward her. It struck him abruptly as she spoke that he somehow knew this woman. The slack face reminded him . . .

"C'mon, sailor boy, come." She pulled impatiently at him and bucked her body against him, but in that instant he shrank out of her as he recalled the blonde woman pulling at his father, and urging, "come."

He scrambled to the door, hoisting his trousers with one hand and opening the door with the other, and fell down in the hall. As the door clicked shut he saw her surprised face above jiggling breasts as she lifted herself from the bed, and then could hear her laughing through the door.

The men were around him immediately, and they laughed too.

"Can't cut it yet, sonny, eh," one jeered. He unclicked the door and spoke inside. "Doan bother gettin dressed, baby, I'll finish what the pup started." He went in and closed the door while the others lifted Sam and buckled him into his pants.

"Doan worry kid, you'll get the hang of it."

"He got further along than you ever did, Shorty."

Their words bounced around as they dragged him back downstairs, but Sam wasn't focused on them.

"Boy sure musta been impressed w'Sally, he's in a stupor."

They sat him down, and tiring of baiting him when he didn't respond, turned to their bottle again. When the leader sauntered down the stairs, carefully placing his battered hat on his head, he announced, "That tart tried to charge me double for the trick—claims the boy got going fine, then just quit. Told her I only pay for my sugar a sack at a time. Them couple a ounces she spilt filling the sack don't count." He favored the group with a satisfied leer as they chuckled. He slapped Sam, saying, "She says you got what it takes, once you git used to it, son."

As talk went on to other things, the son of the preacher wondered about Sally, upstairs. The daughter of the preacher's woman. It was the only time he ever saw her.

Sighing with the memory, Sam got out of his chair to refill his coffee cup. He disturbed his cat, who glared at him before it turned and settled into the warm hollow Sam had just vacated.

"I'm coming back there, girl, better not get comfortable." Sam warned as he went to the stove.

But the cat ignored him.

12

When Amy heard her sister stirring, she went to the woodstove and pulled the coffeepot over to bubble. She stuck a wood splinter in the stove, and when it ignited she touched it to the oil wick. She had the lamp in one hand, splinter in the other, and turned to set it down on the table as Emily came into the kitchen. The cat spotted the flaming splinter. It leaped from its chair and streaked to the back of the house. Startled, Amy turned. Her foot tangled in the small throw rug she stood on. Her balance gone, Amy found herself falling. She tried to set the lamp and splinter down as she went.

As she fell to the floor, Amy watched the lamp shatter on the corner of the table as it left her hand. Oil and glass showered her as she collided with the floor. The rush of breath knocked out of her seemed echoed by the 'oomph' of the igniting oil and Emily's scream.

The flame's brightness hurt Amy's eyes. She scrabbled and crawled away, pushing at the fire frantically.

Emily called to her. Amy couldn't understand the words. Her head was filled with a rushing sound, blocking out everything except her need to escape the light and flame. She gained her feet, and stumbled toward the door. Emily—Emily was hitting her with the rug!—she was holding her—pulling her to the floor! With a savage pull, Amy freed herself and ran outside—into the blessed rain—straight into the grey bayou.

Only with the cold shock of that salty water extinguishing her burning clothes did Amy start to feel her burns. She gasped in shock, and swallowed a quantity of seawater. Choking, she reached toward Emily, who was running, carrying the smoldering rug. She fell into her sister's arms, and they collapsed on the beach.

"Amy! Oh, Amy—let me see—is it bad? . . ."

"The babies, Emily, the babies . . ."

Emily whirled around. There was some scattered flame along the path to the water—remnants of Amy's dress. Emily dunked the rug in the water and ran back to the house. Amy could hear a cry start that sounded like Nell, then other voices.

Evan, moving fast, had reached the kitchen to see his aunt chasing his mother—in flames!—to the beach. He was transfixed for an instant before it dawned that the table dripped oil flames to the floor. He grabbed the broom and slapped at the flames as his aunt rushed back in with the dripping rug. They beat out the fire with all the fear and fury of parent birds mobbing a black snake inexorably approaching nestlings.

Emily didn't waste a motion.

"Get a blanket. Watch the glass . . ."

She was gone.

When she came to Amy again, her sister was trying to stand, shaking with the chill rain and reaction. Emily reached toward her, but flinched back at Amy's scream of pain. Blisters bubbled along her arm and body. Sand glued itself onto her skin through the burned fabric. Amy's hair was scorched, burnt half-away.

"Amy, can you walk?"

Amy's face was contorted. She nodded, determined. Emily supported her on the right, unburned, side, and they struggled up the stairs to the porch.

Amy was crying silently. Evan, holding a flannel blanket open in front of him, stood in the doorway white-faced.

"Momma . . ." he whispered.

Amy held onto the porch post.

"We have to get the dress off, Amy, now."

Amy nodded tightly. Her knuckles were white as Evan's face.

"Evan, close your eyes and hold that blanket. I'll take it when I need it."

He nodded. His eyes were scrunched. The tears escaped anyway. It was an eternity of darkness, with the smell of the scorched kitchen, the rain plunking compellingly, and worst, hearing the sharp, stifled intake of breath and the smothered cries of the women as Emily carefully but frantically tore the clothing from Amy's burns.

Finally he felt the blanket being taken from his shaking fingers.

"Go open her bed, Evan. And we'll need warm water, some torn sheets for bandages, ointment—whatever you can find. Send the girls for sheets—try to calm them, now. Hurry."

He turned and over Emily's shoulder, for a second, met his mother's eyes.

Her eyes were hot with pain, but he could see in their depths that she continued to extend comfort to him. His shaking eased and he ran for what his aunt needed while Emily moved her sister slowly into the kitchen.

Amy took hold of a chair.

"Please, Em, the blanket."

Though Emily had held it away from the wounds, the blanket still touched.

"Can't stand it, Em." Amy was shaking. "But I'm so cold. It hurts so."

It was all Emily could manage not to hug her sister.

"It's the shock, and the rain. We've got to make a tent around the stove, trap the heat, and get you washed—that sand and salt water only makes it worse. Can you stand alone a minute?"

Amy nodded.

Emily went to the stove and manhandled the table close to it. With the broom she shoved glass aside. The coffeepot still boiled. Evan had water on to heat. The girls cut a sheet into strips.

"OK now, tack the edge of that blanket on the wall, Evan. Anchor it with these chairs. Your mother's chilled and I must clean up the burns, so we'll rig a tent around the table here, trap the heat. Just pile up chairs and we'll drape blankets.

"Nelly. Bring me that bottle of rum your Daddy brought home. We'll get some of that in her with coffee.

"Katie. Every blanket and pillow you can find. Put them in her room while we're doing this.

"We can't let anything touch her burns. It's too painful. But we have to figure some way to keep her warm in there."

The children scattered without a word. Evan tacked a blanket up and stretched it to the table, tacking it again and then tied the end to a chairback. Emily stirred the doctored coffee.

"Soon as that water's warm—we'll start cleaning the wounds."

He nodded. Emily carried the coffee to Amy.

"Drink it now, we've got to get some heat in you."

Emily could see that Amy's strength dwindled with each second. She drank some coffee, reluctantly.

"S'ready, Aunt Em."

"OK, we're coming."

"Lean on me, Amy, you know better where it doesn't hurt."

"No place," Amy tried to smile. But each motion made her flinch with pain.

At the stove Amy managed to perch sideways on a chair. It gave her support as she endured Emily's gentle laving and drying. But when Em tried to pour a trickle of water near a sandy blister, she screamed.

"Wait, Em." Amy looked close to passing out. "Please."

Emily realized she was shaking more than Amy. She sank to her knees a moment. The sisters looked silently at each other. Finally, Amy said.

"Do it."

At last the worst of the washing was over.

"Let's get you in bed before we try to bandage the burns."

"I don't think I could stand your spreading ointment on it, Em."

"Maybe if I put it on the sheet, Amy, and laid it on you slowly, it wouldn't hurt so bad?"

"I don't think it could get worse, but it does. Em, I'm so scared." Amy's voice was barely a whisper as she concluded the sentence.

"We have to manage. We will. Amy, you're being so brave. And so are the children."

"Yes. All right. I'm trying."

"Let's go."

When they got in the bedroom, Emily was surprised by a half dozen bamboo poles jammed along the far side-board of the bed. The tip of the pole closest to the foot-board was tied down around the near side-board with twine. The springy pole arced over the mattress.

She saw at once what Evan had in mind. The poles would support the bedclothes without their touching Amy, making a cave which would be warm and relatively comfortable.

Amy achieved a smile as they maneuvered to the bed.

"My own lean-to. It's great."

In a few minutes Amy lay on her right side while Emily put pillows behind her. Her eyes were closing.

"Em, I think I'm going to sleep. It feels so good."

Emily tied down the poles, and draped blankets across them.

"OK, Amy, relax a bit. I'll fix the bandages in a little while."

Amy was immediately asleep, almost snoring. The rum in the coffee was having its effect.

Emily sat on the rocker and for the first time, really scrutinized her sister's burns. The damage appalled her. Much of Amy's left side and arm were oozing blisters. Another nasty blister marred her cheek and scalp where considerable hair had burned away. More hair would need to be cut away—later though. Finally her eyes rested on Amy's swollen stomach.

Emily shivered.

She recognized how wet she was, and rose to change. When she opened the bedroom door, the three children stood waiting.

She raised her finger to her lips.

"She's asleep, thank the Lord."

She searched their frightened faces.

"I won't lie to you. She's in a lot of danger. And if the baby starts to come, it won't be easy. But we'll take each step as it comes.

"Katie, can you and Nell take care of Ned—feed him some breakfast—and yourselves too?"

Kate nodded. "But I want to see Momma."

"Yes, but she must rest first, you understand?"

"I know, but . . ."

Emily hugged her, hard. "Darling, we are all frightened, and have a right to be. What is important now is to help your Mom all we can." She kissed both girls as they went upstairs to Ned, whining in his crib.

She looked at Evan. "You couldn't have done more, you know. I'm really impressed with you."

"Is she gonna die?"

"Oh, Evan." She locked eyes with him. "I certainly hope not. We have to keep looking for the best."

She put her hand on his shoulder.

"Would you stay by her door, in case she wakes up? I want to put on something dry. Then would you please go for your father?"

"All right."

He put a chair by the door and slumped into it, leaning his head on the jamb. Emily touched him, and went to change.

The vision of his mother covered with flame as brilliant as her geiger tree blossoms wouldn't leave his eyes. How often both his parents warned about the woodstove or lamps. His mind couldn't accept that such a thing had happened to his mother. She was always so careful.

Katie slipped quietly into the kitchen. She took some bread and a jar of jelly, and started back. Taking food into the loft was not allowed, but both knew it was better than bringing Ned into the kitchen. When Evan looked at the food his stomach rolled, threatened rebellion. He looked at his sister instead.

She had been crying, he could see. But she was coping, attempting to do her part. Evan sat a little straighter as he watched his little sister leave the room.

He stood as Aunt Emily returned, and as she nodded at him, he went out the door to the dock.

Although the boat needed bailing, he ignored the water and worked to start the engine. When it caught he slipped the lines from the dock, and full throttle through the rain headed for the fish-house.

Only as he left the bayou did he wonder what he would say to his father.

Charles heard the motor long before it arrived and stood in his rain gear watching the boat approach.

No doubt about it, he thought, watching its jerky, too-fast approach. She's in labor. The boy's a bit excited, scared, from the look of it. He waved to Evan to calm down, to slow down. The boy ignored him, slewing around to approach the fish-house as though he expected Charles to leap in on the pass.

"Baby or not, son, you need to take more care here." Charles started lecturing as the boat bumped into a piling and stalled. Evan grabbed the deck and looked up at his father, and something in the look chilled Charles unexpectedly.

"Momma's burned bad. The oil lamp exploded." Evan's sooty, tear-streaked cheeks and soaked clothes conveyed more than his words. It seemed to Charles that the words didn't form any intelligible meaning. But he jumped in the boat and pulled at the engine while another part of his mind puzzled over what Evan had said.

The engine caught. They raced for the house, leaving the fish-house empty and open.

Evan huddled miserably in the bow, not attempting to say anything over the engine. He doubted his father would have known anyway.

They entered the bayou at full speed. Charles cut the engine just as it looked like he'd hit the dock. The boat settled into its wake. Charles hopped on the dock in the same motion.

"Tie it," he ordered as he ran toward the house. Evan had to scramble to grab the dock before he drifted too far away.

Until the instant Charles jumped onto the porch and breathed in the sooty burned smell coming out the kitchen door, he had managed to deny the reality of what his son had brought to him. His mind refused to accept it.

But the fresh-burned smell stopped his rush. He had the same feeling when he had unexpectedly grounded in mid-bay on an oyster bar. The physical stoppage nearly threw him on his face. And like his boat bottom on that bar, he knew damage was significant. He didn't want to look.

Emily had heard his approach. She hurried to the door, one hand drawing him in.

"Charles."

No smile, no easy banter. No "It's going to be OK," no "don't worry." Charles entered warily, as though the house had been mined. Emily, always so comforting, only looked at him, with a seriousness, a sadness she rarely betrayed.

"Shhh, she's sleeping," she said as Charles seemed to swell in fear.

Relief loosed by her words nearly made Charles collapse. His eyes left hers and took in the charred floorboards and disheveled room. Glass glinted against the wall. Blankets sagged on chairs, the askew table was piled with containers and cloths. The bedroom door was shut.

As he moved toward it, Emily hurried after him, restraining him with her hand.

"Charles, she's badly burned. I won't be surprised if she starts into labor any time."

He looked at her, feeling the steady tremor in her touch. Charles was surprised—a display of nerves wasn't Emmy's way, no more than Amy. He glared at her.

"I won't lose her," he growled. It was a declaration, almost a threat. He quietly opened the door and slipped through, leaving Emily with her head bowed, muttering a fervent prayer that he be right.

The tented bed gave Charles a nasty start. It had been moved, and the unfamiliar shape looming against the meager light of the rain-streaked windows had an eerie effect. Once he had been hunting through some swampy bog near the Everglades. That day he had turned to his side in time to see the rising bulk of a black bear appear fifteen feet away behind some bushes. He felt the same icy sweat at his bedroom door as he had that day. As then, disaster loomed black, and Charles froze. The bear, upwind of him, dropped down and ambled blindly away. It had never seen Charles.

But the bed did not move. It seemed to pulse, larger, with each of Charles' heartbeats. He released the tightly-held doorknob and moved toward Amy's uneven breathing.

She was curled on her side, nearly naked. He had never seen Amy drunk, but her posture suggested that to him now. The blanket covering the upper part of the bed-tent was rose-colored, filtering the small amount of light further. It made the sheet Amy lay on look pink, and cast a glow over her skin.

Her reassuring appearance strengthened him until, as he approached, he saw the gleam of blisters and ointments. As he knelt beside the bed the swollen parts of her body and arm, the burnt-back hair, became distinct. As he watched her, fascinated as a trapped rabbit watching a snake, her fingers trembled and twitched, and she moaned softly.

Charles was afraid to touch her. He couldn't see how far the burns extended. He talked to her, quietly.

"It's gonna be OK, sweetheart. No time at all, it'll be alright, Amy. Stay strong, darlin', I'm here now, and I won't leave you. We can do it, together, you and me. Just like always here, darling."

Her fingers relaxed, but she didn't open her eyes. As gently as he had ever touched anything, he touched his fingers to hers.

13

Evan came into the house as Emily sank into a kitchen chair. He looked at his parents' door, and then at his aunt. She held a hand out toward him, and when he reached her, they held onto each other without speaking. Holding him close, she leaned her head quietly against him, encircling him with her arms.

Evan realized with a shock that he was giving her comfort, instead of the reverse. He patted her hair, uncertain of what to say. She seemed exhausted, in need of gathering strength.

Finally Emily rose. She smiled at him.

"I need some coffee. And so does Charles, I'm sure. What about you?"

"Yeah, OK." He sat in her vacated chair, and watched as she poured the hot fluid. He felt as limp as the sea-lettuce floating under the dock.

"What are we gonna do?" Evan talked into his coffee cup.

Emily sat down.

"I don't know. I can't imagine taking her in the boat to Punta Gorda, in her condition in the rain. Getting a doctor here seems nearly as unlikely. But if the baby starts coming—and it will, soon—I don't know how she'll be able to stand the combination."

She gazed at Evan. He was so young.

"Did you notice, had the run boat been through?"

He shrugged, unsure.

"It's going south, anyway." She spoke to herself.

The bedroom door opened and Charles crept out, sitting down soundlessly. All three stared into their cups.

"At least she's sleeping," he finally said.

Emily picked up the rum bottle from the floor and put it on the table.

"She has little choice," she smiled wryly. The bottle was several inches low.

"Could we get her to town?" Charles ventured.

Emily shook her head.

"We could barely get her to the bedroom. No, we would hurt her more than they could help in town, I believe."

Upstairs, Ned could be heard whining. Emily looked around the kitchen.

"They need to come down. They've been shoved up there too long."

She started cleaning up the glass.

"She'll be waking up soon. Then who knows what will happen. The run boat's gone on down?"

"Yes. Maybe we could get her on it tomorrow," Charles sounded hopeful.

Evan looked into his coffee again. Emily broke the pause finally with a doubtful,

"Maybe."

George watched from his doorway as the boat eased to the dock. Mullet Jim stood patiently on the deck in the downpour, waiting to tie up. He didn't wear a slicker. His shirt was dark with large irregular patches where it clung to his body. He had an old felt hat on his head that directed a cataract down his back. He didn't seem to notice.

He tied up and started into the ice house, but George yelled at him.

"Forget it, Jim. Ain't even a pinfish in there today."

Jim flashed him a grin and sidled toward George, staying under the roof overhang as much as he could.

"Nobody fool enough to be fishin' today," he laughed.

"Yeah," George replied. "Dry run today."

Jim cackled. "Dry run. That's right." He laughed some more. "Dry run. Driest I seen it all spring."

The captain started out of the wheelhouse. Both men waved him back in the same instant. Murdock raised his arm in acknowledgment and shut his door again.

"How come the captain's got a slicker on in there and here you are runnin' around like that? Ain't you allowed one?" George cut his eyes slyly at the dripping Negro.

Jim's grin flashed again. He took off his hat and drained it.

"Doan like them oilskins. Not less the winter wind's cutting strong. They so hot inside I gets as wet as I'd be 'thout 'em, and I cain't move 'round way I need too. They 'bout useless, for me."

"Work up a sweat shovelin' out the fish I imagine, under that."

"Too true, yassir."

"Tell Murdock Sam'll be looking for him tomorrow. Doubt they'll be any fish though."

Jim raised his hand, heading for the mooring lines.

"Wait."

George went in the office and brought out a bottle. He handed it to Jim.

"I'll take it off Murdock's order tomorrow. 'Spect he'll like that tonight."

"Thankee sir. 'Spec' he will."

George continued to stand in the doorway as Jim reboarded and passed the bottle into the wheelhouse. George raised an arm in response to the captain's dimly-seen salute, as the motor drummed louder and the boat separated from the fish-house.

No pelicans hung around today. They knew a lost cause too. The boat had to make its round, fish or no fish. The pelicans didn't waste their energy. They were probably all tucked in the mangroves, sleeping. And, surveying the grey wet world outside his door, George decided they had the right idea, like always. A little nap sounded like a fine idea.

***

Sam wasn't aware he'd been dozing until the cat jumped off his lap. The punch of the cat's back paws springing off Sam's untensed belly made him start awake. He focused on the cat's hind-quarters and tail disappearing through the tear in the screened door as his eyes opened.

The rain drummed darkly. It was impossible to guess the time of day. It didn't matter anyhow. This sort of day the world hung suspended. Nothing happened but the slow breathing of the tide. And that was a shallow, sleepy movement, as though it knew that few birds would venture out on exposed flats teeming with rainwater.

He shifted in the chair, and let his eyes drift closed again.

***

Rosa, the housekeeper, brought the mail to Mrs. Stanhope at breakfast. When she picked up the envelope she immediately recognized her daughter Emily's handwriting. The letter was not a surprise. She'd had a restless night's sleep. She had dreamed of Florida through the night. Amy and the imminent birth were on her mind.

She opened the letter quickly but methodically, and was immediately assured of the even keel of life on the little island. Her instantaneous reaction to Emily's proposal, bringing Evan north with her, was annoyance, and she set down the letter to eat her meal. But before she was finished with breakfast, she realized that she was planning trips and treats for her grandson's stay. She had decided to welcome the boy here.

After dressing, she sat at her desk to write Emily. She found herself daydreaming—remembering her trips south with her husband and children. The majority of the morning slipped away in silence, as most days did. She realized she had written little.

"Rosa."

"Yes, Ma'am."

"This letter. It's from Emily. She wants to bring Amy's older boy here for the summer. For school—and to get to know his grandmother."

"What a marvelous idea, Mrs. Stanhope! How old is the boy now?"

"Eleven."

Rosa gasped. "He'll be grown up before you know it! It's hard to imagine when the girls—seems like just yesterday they were children, Ma'am."

Mrs. Stanhope agreed.

"Nearly grown. Not long and they'll all be grown."

She turned back to her desk, tapping her finger. She found herself looking at a copy of the same photo Evan had carefully packed into his memory box—Amy and Charles, and the children. Her fifth grandchild was soon due. And she knew none of them—had seen only Evan and Katie as babies.

She started the letter to Emily once more. Rosa's footsteps echoed in the hall as she went on with her morning rituals. Just as, on this side of the double doors, Mrs. Stanhope kept faithfully to her schedule. Her day was full, as was every day delineated on her calendar—every day full, and, the thought penetrated suddenly—so very empty. Her daughter was preparing to give birth on a primitive island for the sixth time. The sixth time! She was not needed. That was what she told herself each time. But today, suddenly, she realized she was wanted, and had always been. That she had closed herself off from her grandchildren—from Franklin's grandchildren.

Again she was lost in thought. But this time she felt a further stiffening of an already erect backbone. She had made a decision. Now she would carry it out.

"Rosa," she called.

By late afternoon Mrs. Stanhope had waved good-by to Rosa from the window of a train bound for Washington and south. She couldn't help being amused by the stunned expression on Rosa's face. She wondered if surprise wasn't reflected on her own. It had been a long time since she had acted on impulse—it didn't seem a fitting way for a widowed lady of her standing to act. Why did it feel so marvelous, then? She felt decades younger. She had nothing to do—other than watch the land pass outside her window. Rosa had a list of people to contact—engagements to break. And a telegraph to send to the Punta Gorda Hotel reserving her room on arrival, and instructing management to hire her a boat and captain for her stay.

She leaned back in her seat, not at all tired. The excitement of her decision had energized her. She looked within herself, remembering—without the bitterness of his absence—the walks, the dances, the lovely nights under south Florida skies with Franklin. Remembering how much he'd loved the water and the land there, she could not wait to see it again. The same land that had inflicted the pain of his absence seemed now to promise the balm of his presence. She was rushing to her children and grandchildren. But first, she was coming home to her husband's memory. She blanketed herself with those memories as the train pushed eastward toward the night.

***

Sam again woke slowly in his chair. The view of the bay hadn't changed at all—the rain drummed as insistently as it had his last awakening. The amount of light hadn't increased. But now it felt to be late in the afternoon. Perhaps it was only because his belly was empty. George would be expecting him soon. He quickly fed himself and got organized for his run to the fishhouse. George would feed the animals as needed while he was gone. The dog was asleep in the corner, where he'd been all day. The cat hadn't returned. It was probably under the house, along with the chickens. The hens seemed a little more restless and squawky than this morning—no doubt keeping a beady eye on the cat. Neither cared to leave the dry crawl space for a rainy dash to other shelter.

Sam didn't worry about his chickens. They were plenty tough—in life and in the eating. The cat had felt the sharp tap of hen's beaks before, and knew well there were easier pickings elsewhere. They had their own armistice underway.

What little light that got through the rain had started to fade. The deluge would be no fun to navigate through, but doing so in the dark didn't appeal at all. Sam wrapped his bundle of clothes in some oilcloth, blew out the lamp, and hurried to the boat. He bailed and got the engine started after several moments of fiddling.

He followed the mangrove shoreline. It was much faster cutting across the bays between his house and George's fish-house, but in this sort of weather the tide and wind could put him well off-target. Vision was limited, and Sam had always had enough water skills to know that the cautious sailor was the one who eventually lasted to become the old salt. Chances were, with his knowledge of the water, he'd be able to hit the fish-house dead-on. But chances weren't necessary. So he skirted the edges until he came to a long point. At its end, he struck out at an angle into the monochrome grey void. After a half mile or so of open water, Sam spotted a darker grey shape to his left. The fish-house looked hunched against the storm and deserted.

The tide flowed through the pilings more strongly than Sam had expected. He tied off the skiff and lifted his bundle up to the walkway. Then he scrambled up. He heard nothing from George.

He carried the bundle around to the other end of the building, where George's office and bunk were. He opened the door to the dark room and yelled,

"Wake up, you lazy old snake," and left, laughing, as the heaving confusion of blankets on George's bunk telegraphed that he had indeed snuck up on George's blind side.

Sam walked the skiff around near the door and allowed the tide to ease it under the fish-house before he tied off. Back under the scant overhang, he shook himself much as his dog would have done and slipped back into the office, shutting the door behind him.

In the few moments he'd been gone, George lit the lamp and put a pot of water and coffee grounds on the stove. There weren't any curtained windows or geraniums, but the room felt cozy and welcoming after Sam's little sea journey.

"You trying ta scare me into an early grave, you lowlife?"

"Can't be done old man. You already outlived your whole generation."

George cackled in amused agreement. The younger man unwrapped the dripping oilcloth and pulled out a dry shirt and pants. He stripped off his sodden ones and sighed in satisfaction as the dry ones went on.

George pointed mutely to a line strung close to the far wall. It already had other clothes draped on it. Sam added his oilcloth and clothes.

"Think the cisterns are all full?"

"Ha. Just maybe."

Sam finished settling in and drew up a chair to the table.

George, yawning, leaned back on the chair's two rear legs. The two men sat inactive, listening to the steady roar of the rain.

"Tide's running fast," Sam broke the silence.

"Gulf's likely filled up and overflowing this way," George grinned. "This storm don't act like it wants to go away."

"Think it might turn into something?"

"Nah. Water ain't warm enough. But it'll by God wash the dust off the roof."

Sam noticed George had been rubbing his bad hand with the other. He jerked his head in a nod toward George and asked, "Is that acting up with the rain?"

George looked a little surprised, not realizing he had been favoring it. "Yeah, it is a little. Ever time we get a serious rain. It just aches, like." Sam nodded in understanding.

The coffee was boiling now. Sam pulled it off the hottest part of the stove. On the shelf next to the sack of sugar was a bowl with several broken egg shells. He picked up a couple, and crushed them over the coffee, dumping the bits into the black fluid.

"Want a cup, George?"

"Think I will." George shifted position. "There's a pot a'purloo there a chicken walked through, if you're interested."

Sam poured two cups. "Not at the moment. Ate before I left. But I'll pile a plate-full up for you, long as I'm playing maid here anyway."

"Do that. My insides are rubbin' together, feels like."

The purloo steamed when Sam lifted the lid. Big globules of water rolled across the underside of the pot lid. Sam let the liquid drip back into the pot.

"Smells good, hafta try some later."

He heaped an old china plate high with the rice and meat mixture and replaced the lid. He set the plate by George. Then he brought the coffee cups to the table.

George got up and put the sack of sugar on the table. When he sat again he pulled a spoon from the tin can full of utensils sitting between them, and scooped a generous spoonful of sugar into his cup. He stirred it a couple of times, and then with the same spoon he began shoveling in his dinner, eating silently and methodically until the china's blue bottom was again exposed.

Sam, just as silently, gingerly sipped the cup of coffee he hunched over.

Outside, the dark day turned into night.

The rain beat on.

14

Evan and Katie sat at the top of the stairs looking down at the kitchen. Ned and Nell were asleep—their afternoon naps had overtaken them.

From time to time they could hear their mother's voice over the murmuring of the other two adults. It would rise, wavering, like a badly played flute, and be cut off suddenly. The sound of scrapings and footsteps would sporadically float up the staircase as well.

"What do you think's happening?" Kate whispered.

Evan concentrated, but couldn't hear anything clearly. He shrugged in bewilderment.

Suddenly the bedroom door clicked open below and Evan heard his father's voice continue, ". . . do something!" His heavy tread was quickly followed by Emily's more hurried steps.

"Charles, think a moment." Her voice rose. "What good can that do?"

"I can't stand around and watch her die!"

Katie gasped and grabbed at Evan. He held onto her arm just as tightly. Perhaps they were heard, or sensed, in the kitchen. The voices dropped lower, although they still heard snatches of the argument.

"Charles, the run boat will get help here as quickly as you could. Probably quicker . . . chance of your getting in trouble or losing your way in this storm . . . Charles, if you're lost and Amy dies . . . think of the children, Charles!"

"I'm not gonna get lost for Christ's sake. You think I don't know this water—storm or not?"

"There's always a chance in this kind of weather. It'll be night too. But even if you made it the run boat would get there soon as you. You know that."

"But it won't be back here until tomorrow. You expect me to just sit?"

"I know it's hard. But Amy needs you here. And the boat will be early with this weather. Evan can meet it. I know the captain will do everything. The doctor wouldn't ride in your skiff in the storm, even if you were fresh, let alone planning to come right back with him after you fought the waves all night and day to get there. Use your head, Charles."

Their father paced the kitchen. The silence lengthened. Emily spoke again.

"I might not be able to cope. If she goes into labor while you're gone, I will need you." Her voice sounded defeated.

Charles suddenly entered the hall and stood staring up the steps at his children. His face appeared furious. His eyes pinned Evan and Katie. They were immobile.

A frozen moment passed. Evan felt like a mouse, when a barn owl swoops past. He was afraid to move, afraid it would bring destruction upon him. Stillness was safety. Though he stared right at them, Evan felt his father was not seeing his children at all.

All at once the fury died from his face. His eyes dropped. He turned back to the kitchen, to Emily sitting at the table with her face in her hands. He touched her shoulder gently.

"You're right. Of course you're right. And above anything I must be here for her." He squeezed her shoulder, and went quietly back to his wife.

Evan silently crept down the stairs. He peeked into the kitchen. Aunt Emily's head was on the charred table, pillowed in her arms.

The room was quiet. It was only by a convulsive shuddering in her body that Evan knew she was crying.

Evan waited quietly in his father's office for Captain Murdock's boat. Although the rain continued, it had begun to ease. Evan was alone for the first time in twenty-four hours.

The office was dark, but he had no intention of lighting the lamp. Perhaps not ever. He had sat in the empty room for perhaps an hour, imagining many times over the same unimaginable sequence. Tears had come, but his face stayed wooden. Evan knew how precarious his mother's condition was. He heard the boat's bells from what seemed a great distance, went to the door, and watched the familiar ballet-like movements as the boat subsided alongside the dock. As he draped the lines Jim handed him over the post he asked, "OK if I come aboard?"

Jim waved him forward with his grin.

"No fish today, Jim. But I need to see the captain."

"He's up in the wheelhouse, son."

Evan headed for it, and the door opened as he approached.

"Your father taking the day off since things are so busy, Evan?"

Evan didn't return Captain Murdock's smile.

"No, sir." He stood firmly. "Captain Murdock, we have a bad problem. Dad's to home with Momma. She got burned yesterday—upset the oil lamp. Bad burned." Despite his resolve a tremor went through him as he spoke. It didn't help that the captain's eyes had grasped him fiercely. He had paused in the midst of lighting his pipe, and shook out the match without taking eyes off the boy.

"I . . . I think they're afraid she's gonna die." The last words came in a rush, with a squeak at the end. Evan was horrified to feel his lips wobbling, despite his attempt to stop the trembling. He turned away and stared out the window. The captain grasped—and nearly crushed—his collar bone.

"The baby?" he said.

"Hasn't started yet. Aunt Emily's real worried bout that."

"Yes. She needs a doctor, least a nurse or midwife. I'll bring someone. I better go to the house first. Your boat tied up?"

Evan nodded. Captain Murdock shrugged on the oilskins and left, stopping to say a word to the engineer. A moment later Evan saw the comma of white foam behind his boat as Murdock buzzed to the island.

The engineer came up to the wheelhouse, and another man appeared behind him. It took a moment to recognize Bill's brother Sam. Evan had not seen him in some time.

Bill looked directly into Evan's face.

"Real sorry about your Momma's trouble, boy."

Evan nodded thanks. The spasm of tears had subsided.

"Sam here was gonna go to town with me, but he thought he'd stay and run the fish-house for your Daddy a few days. We know his heart ain't here right now."

Sam stood forward. "I don't need nothing special from your place—got enough grub here till the boat comes back, and if I can borry your row-boat there, I'm happy. Captain'll be back right soon, so I'll put my things in the office, sounds all right to you?"

"My Daddy'll say you needn't give up your time, and . . ."

"I know that. I want to. And he doesn't need worrying over this place right now. Here—carry this over, boy." Sam shoved a bundle abruptly at Evan.

***

Captain Murdock knocked at the screen. No one was in the kitchen. He wrinkled his nose at the oily charred odor permeating the wet air and knocked again. He heard the movement of feet on the stairs, and a girl peered around a corner hesitantly.

"Hello, child. I'm Captain Murdock from the run boat. If your father or aunt can come to the door, I'd like to speak with one."

The girl didn't speak. Without taking eyes from him, she knocked softly on an inner door.

He heard a voice and saw the girl point toward him, then run into the hallway.

Emily opened the door farther and saw Murdock's large silhouette against the screen. After being momentarily startled she recognized the captain and hurried toward him.

"I don't mean to interrupt your nursing, Emily. I wanted to see what might be needed."

"It's alright. Charles is with her. She's not sleeping, really, but rests between outbreaks of pain. She's lost so much strength.

"But . . . I really don't know what can be done. The blistering is over most of her upper body and on her face and head. We've used everything we can think of on the burns. But it's very bad."

"I'll bring the doctor back if he's in town. And whatever he thinks, of course. What—Emily, what do you think?"

She raised her head, almost defiantly, it seemed.

"She's from a fighting family, Captain. And she has everything to live for. The burns alone could kill many people. With the other complication . . ." Emily's voice slowed and the captain could see a glint of repressed tears in her eyes.

"Are you all right? Charles?"

"I'm managing. And the kids . . . Charles though—he seems to be flying apart. He's scared, I know, but he's almost making it worse, I think . . . he wanted to go to Punta Gorda in the storm and dark last night, or even to try to take Amy. He's so afraid she won't live. I don't know if you realize how important she is to him—and him to her."

The captain stared at the bayou.

"I think I understand," he said.

He turned toward Emily.

"I won't hold you up any longer. Tell Charles I said staying with her is as important as anything he can do. We'll be back as soon as possible."

He raised his hand to Emily and strode to the skiff.

The run boat droned steadily up the river toward town. The wheelhouse was dark; the two men were quiet. The rain streamed on the river surface, producing a fog that hid the rain drops as they hit the surface. The banks were sensed, rather than seen, looming asymmetrically to the left or right as the boat moved with the channel.

Jim piloted the near-empty vessel, while the captain watched the fogged waterscape pass. His thoughts remained at the Pratt homestead, and they were somber as the weather. A mental image persisted—the powerboat approaching the fish-house—Amy's bright hair flying—and the expression on her husband's face, a complicated blend of surprise, dismay, and a certain baffled pride. However it came out, the Pratts' world had changed yesterday. For the rest of their lives events would be measured as happening before, or after, the day of the fire.

A thin dark line formed in the distance. They had reached the city docks. The captain laid down his pipe, and relieved Jim of the wheel.

Jim hurried home through the rain. The doctor would be aboard early tomorrow, and Captain Murdock warned his crew of an early departure. No partying tonight.

The streets were empty of any movement. The hotel was all but closed—the season nearly over—and no sensible person ventured into streets that seemed more like shallow over-flowing creeks.

Jim's mother was at home. He could see the light through the rain. Her work stopped in the rain. She needed bright sunlight for the drying, or her endless exertions over the line of wash and rinse tubs were useless. Jim went in the house to tell her about Amy Pratt.

Jim woke up to the smell of his mama's breakfast cooking. Last night when she heard of the accident she wouldn't even hear Jim's remonstrations as she informed him she was going down-run to help Amy Pratt. Years ago Ida Jewel Kresson had nurse-maided Amy and Emily. They needed her help now, and she would go. Before she went to bed, she had left word with a neighbor who would do her washing while she was gone and packed a bag.

Jim hoped the captain was in a good mood. He certainly wouldn't be expecting another extra passenger. If he took it in his head to refuse Jim's mother aboard, Jim didn't know what might happen.

Jim and his mother saw no sign of dawn as they walked to the boat dock. The rain had stopped, though clouds still seemed thick in the blackness. Lights burned on the fish dock in preparation for the early start. Jim saw the skipper in the wheelhouse, already preparing for departure.

"Wait here, Mama, while I talk to de captain." He left her standing under the ridged tin roof of a pole shed near one of the sets of railroad tracks that ran the length of the pier.

He stepped on board the boat and knocked at the wheelhouse door, uncharacteristically.

Murdock raised an eyebrow at the Negro's behavior.

"What's up, Jim?"

"Morning, Cap'n." Jim entered and seemed at a sudden loss for words. He scratched his cheek and looked around the place as though he had never seen it before. Finally he faced the captain and said, "Mama's decided she should go help Miz Pratt. She's waiting over at the shed with her things. She's planning to come aboard if it's alright with you."

Jim looked uncertainly at his captain, whose surprise turned into a bark of laughter.

"Sounds like she's got her mind made up."

Jim grinned in relief.

"Yassir, she do. Miz Amy and Miz Emily are her babies, you know?" She not gonna take a 'no' too good."

"More credit to her. I don't see how she'd do any harm. We'll take her over. Get her aboard so I can meet this lady, Jim, and get her settled in. Doc'll be here soon, and you got work to do."

Within the hour all the ice was loaded and the boat coasted down river in the dark. The water ran dark, roiled, and swift as the thousands of acres of flooded wetlands upriver began to shed their rain overflow. Occasionally a thump alongside would startle those aboard—a tree branch or other debris flushed from inland rode the river-rollercoaster to the sea. They hardly registered with the captain as he concentrated on keeping to the channel in the dark rush of water. When dawn finally began to grey in the east, he gave a big sigh and rolled and stretched his neck and shoulders, stiff from his concentration in the blackness. As dawn broke, the channel gave way to the wider expanse of the harbor. The boat's bow seemed to lift with the brightening day, and rush on hopefully.

15

Amy felt suspended. The burns were a constant pain she could sometimes relegate to the back of her mind. Like being out on the bay in mid-afternoon sun, unprotected, there was no escaping the burning. So she ignored it as much as possible, even though the intensity had increased a hundredfold.

Mostly she concentrated upon a narrow circle within her own body. She felt each drop of blood in her veins, was aware of its movement through her limbs. She could hear the breath in her lungs, almost see the air she expelled with each exhalation. She watched redness grow to blistering on her body, could feel the rush of her body's defenses to each pustulent eruption.

Whenever the bedroom door opened, a flurry of wind currents raced over her sensitive skin like a sandstorm. Even movements of people in the room stirred up windstorms. She was aware that people were there, but paid them little mind. Their voices were sea-whispers on a shore miles away. The smaller circle of her body kept her attention. Only rarely did her focus widen to include an area beyond her bed, and then briefly she would record a still image of Emily carrying something, or the sound of rain, or the darkness beyond. Then it would tumble into the kaleidoscope of other snatches, other images.

She glimpsed for an instant her father triumphantly pulling in a tarpon, a tree—dead, or unleaved by winter, a receding wave across the beach underfoot, a furious naked baby with waving arms, skin red and wrinkled. Each vision was as quickly gone, silent within the deafening ragged wind of her breath, the echo of her heartbeat. And lower, faster, the fainter sound of another heartbeat.

She could hear, too, the moaning her mouth made. Some inner part of her, irritated by the mewing, wished it would cease. But her mouth was a separate entity, and ultimately, ignorable. It was on the surface, that borderline between the distant strangeness her sister and husband traveled in and the only important world, deep within her pain and self.

That second heartbeat seemed to grow louder, more insistent. Amy could feel her senses swirl around that muffled pulsing, that portent. She seemed to be rushing toward it with each thump, sucked unconsciously to it and as suddenly distanced again. There was no pain in her rush toward the pulse, but no volition either. She was pulled and released rhythmically, a hooked tarpon inevitably pumped boatward by a skilled fisherman. Each advance closer, each retreat less far. It was a rising sea level, ever-rising, hesitating only to climb ever higher. Each hesitation, each contraction of the flood, was a benchmark for the next wave. The sound and feeling crescendoed and eased within her, each cycle building in intensity until the background disturbance of her burns ceased to exist for her.

Except for the younger children, the household did not seem to know the difference between night and day. Emily or Charles kept watch over a withdrawing Amy, an Amy who seemed to no longer know or acknowledge them.

The children huddled in corners like wounded animals, afraid to show themselves or draw an adult's attention, hence somehow, surely, adult wrath. Emily and Charles, though, were blind to them. They paced heavily, fruitlessly, from kitchen to porch to bedroom. Charles stoked the stove, picked up wood without looking at what remained, boiled coffee which he carried like a sacrament. One time Emily stirred up a pot of rice and offered it with a wave of her hand as she returned into the bedroom.

Katie had pressed against that door, insistent on getting to her mother. She finally succeeded in seeing her, unresponsive and mumbling, her body red and bubbled in such a way that Katie instantly conjured up a memory of the crab boil. Evan followed her headlong rush to the porch, and found her vomiting over the railing while the impersonal rain poured on.

The doctor would be here overnight. Evan moved his things into the girls' room. The animals grew hungry. He fed them. The wood basket emptied. He re-filled it. He cooked some eggs. He fried some meat. He bathed faces and covered sleeping bodies. He stared out windows at the constant curtain of rain. He tried not to think. Whenever, accidently, his eyes and Katie's met, both lowered them guiltily, as though eye contact might somehow steal life's spark from the bedroom beyond the kitchen.

Each time the bedroom door opened or shut, their eyes jumped to it, and as quickly away. Hours passed without a word spoken.

Kate went into the front room. It felt almost museum-like, deserted. Probably no one had been in there since the fire. The room felt cold, damp, and abandoned. She shivered. She sat on an upholstered chair and traced the pattern of the thin rug with her eyes. The clock ticked insistently. It sat opulently on the pine mantel-board, one of Grandmother Stanhope's gifts, as out of place with its decorations of carved marble rearing horses and a snarling tiger as if those creatures had suddenly come alive on the island.

Evan came to the door and looked at his sister. After a moment he sat in their mother's chair. A basket with the left-over yellow yarn lay beside the chair. Evan picked up the small yarn ball and rolled it across the floor, holding onto its end. It made a pale line across the rug and into a corner. He pulled the string slowly, allowing the ball to unwind further as it gradually came back. After he had dragged it back, he again tossed the yarnball across the floor, until he had a pool of spilled yarn around the chair.

Katie watched him without comment.

When all the yarn was unwound, Evan began to ball it again. The clock continued its ticking. At each quarter hour it chimed hollowly. Evan wound and unwound the yarn several times. Neither spoke. It seemed as if each clock tick pushed back into their throats any words that might be present. To say what they imagined might make it real.

Outside, rain dripped from the roofline. Only dripped, Evan suddenly realized. And it was brighter, as though the clouds were thinning. He dropped the yarnball into the basket and went to the window. It was not raining. The woods beyond the house looked strangely bright with sheets of water surrounding the mangrove and buttonwood roots. Some of the chickens ventured out from under the house, stepping daintily on the wet ground, looking around suspiciously.

The clock's hour chimes sounded eight times, startling Katie. Evan turned to her, saying, "I'm going to bail the boat and check the engine, so it'll be ready soon as Doc gets here."

She nodded as he left. Suddenly the room seemed awake. Even though the sun didn't yet shine, the rain had stopped. The room contained a brightness, a renewed hope that it had lacked a moment before.

Katie got up and started out of the room. She stopped to pick up a cushion and plump it as her mother had done so often before. She replaced it, eyed it critically, nodded like a pleased bird, and left the room with a smile.

When Evan finished bailing the boat he was drawn toward the path over the ridge. It surprised him to see a set of footprints firmly marking the rain-soaked sand. His father had walked this way this morning.

Evan followed his footprints. The vines and branches hung in the path where they'd been beaten by the rain. Most had scallops of water balanced along their lower edges, last drops reluctant to fall to the ground. Evan could clearly see where Charles had brushed some of the bushes, knocking the droplets off. He must have soaked himself, Evan thought. Evan weaved around most of the overhanging branches but still got uncomfortably wet. He anticipated wet leaves and avoided them. The sand was pocked like an orange-skin by the rain. It dawned on him that his father's footprints no longer marked it. In the same second that he stopped in puzzlement, he realized he had just passed the path to the graves. He retraced his last few steps. His father had turned there.

Evan felt chilled. Charles seldom visited the graves. Yet there he was now. Evan pivoted and quickly reached the beach. An urge to flee took hold of him and he ran down the shore, ran until he staggered and gasped for breath. Still he moved jerkily along until he had to collapse in a heap on the beach, panting from his race.

The surf had cut away a shelf at the tideline, scouring indentations around fallen trees decorated with shell fragments. The shelf was seat-high, layered with shells that seemed to have settled out largest toward the bottom, smaller above, until the smallest fragments made up the upper layer. Evan's feet hardly indented the hard-packed lower beach, but the upper one, where he sat, felt soft as a rotten log. He could see long cracks to either side of him that ran parallel to the shoreline several inches back from the eroded edge, cracks which would invite the next high wave to tumble another segment of the sand ridge. Evan leaned his hand on the sand landward of this gap, and that slight pressure caused a small area of the face of the slope to crumble.

He pushed the sand back up against the slope. Some stayed, most rolled down to dissolve in the foamy surf. Suddenly anxious, Evan twisted to his knees and began to push the sand back against the slope it was slowly separating from. He scuttled hastily along twenty or thirty feet, reuniting the parting sands in a frenzy of activity, when a rogue wave washed over his legs and against his repair work. The sand collapsed, rippling to either side of him like a falling house of cards, repaired section falling as quickly and impassively as the unrepaired parts. Evan knelt in the swirl of water and bowed his head in near-tears. It was only mid-tide. For hours yet the shore would be attacked by the water, would disappear helplessly into the sea.

He got up by leaning heavily on the sand, pushing himself erect like an old man. The spot where he had knelt was now indented and washing away—his simply being there had eroded that spot worse than the surrounding beach. It was as though he had been a fallen tree the sea had dug around. Evan started to walk back, seeing that each footstep he had earlier made was now a hollow, with a tail streaming seaward, leaking sand.

So fragile, it would not stay. His mood veered to the bitter and he stomped, deliberately making the sand fall. It would not stay. He reached a long, unmarked stretch, and in the soft sand, in large wavering letters, stomped M–A . . . M–A. He stepped back into the surf and looked at it. A little wave touched an M delicately. It trembled to Evan's eye, but remained. It would disappear, but Evan did not want to see it. He turned away and left his cry, unheard and unseen except by the foamy waves, to the sea's mercy.

When he got back to the house, Nellie had gathered a basket of eggs. Both girls stood on the porch. Evan's stomach jumped at their expression.

"What is it?"

Katie replied.

"Auntie Em said Momma's starting to have the baby. Pains are coming."

Evan started for the kitchen.

"She said to stay out the way."

"Maybe she needs me."

"She said *stay out.*"

"I hear you."

Evan shut the door between them. Emily came out of the bedroom, bee-lining for the stove. Without slowing at all she said to him, "You'll go for the Doc. I can't spare your Dad, and neither can she. I expect it'll be a little while yet, but she's hurting herself moving around. Probably be as well if you go over there now and be ready to bring him back right away. Go ahead, now."

She waved at him in a shooing motion and reentered the bedroom with the kettle.

"I'll take some eggs to Sam." he called after her. She didn't bother to reply.

He picked up a palm-leaf basket and Nellie put a half-dozen eggs in it. All three walked to the dock. Evan got in the skiff. Nellie passed down the basket after he had the motor burbling, and Kate untied the mooring lines. He would wait for the doctor—wait for a miracle. At the fish-house he would not have to watch the sand inexorably washing away.

Fishermen were moving on the bay this morning. Little matter that fishing would be slow after the storm—they needed to stir around after being closed up for days. Besides, they optimistically repeated to each other, ". . . fish'll be hungry after all that long, too . . ."

Evan barely had time to tie up the skiff and take Sam his eggs when he saw the run boat bearing down from the north. Moments later, he shuttled boxes into the skiff while the Doc, an arthritic-looking man with thin hair and a thick waist, supervised. An old black woman with hair like iron filings and arm muscles that Evan suspected would be the envy of many men, was being helped into the skiff by Mullet Jim. Evan didn't know who she was. He was flabbergasted when Jim said, "Take care of Miz Amy, now, Mama, and your own self." And to Evan, "Watch out for my momma, now, young'n."

Evan had never visualized Mullet Jim as anything but a fish handler. That he had a momma, and that she was right here, going to help his mama, was amazing to grasp. He looked at Sam and the captain, and Doc. That they too had mamas whom they cared about clicked into place almost audibly. It was a revelation to him. He had become aware of a kinship with these others that had not before been visible to him. The run boat was hours early. These people were here, because Evan's mother needed them. He got in the skiff blindly.

The little skiff reentered the bayou long before the run boat finished its ice stop at the fish-house. Before it returned to this spot tomorrow, the nightmare Amy Pratt fought would be known up and down the coast. She and her family would be prayed for and thought about by neighbors dozens of miles away. Even neighbors who never met her still knew the battle she waged as intimately as Amy's family did. They knew her ordeal could be their own.

16

As the boat moved steadily south on its rounds, the morning grew brighter. By early afternoon the sun, still hazy, was steaming the woods dry. Although Mullet Jim stayed on the shady side of the boat between stops, his face and body still ran with sweat.

At Carlos Pass, the captain went in the office to tell George about the drama up the bay. After George expressed his shock at the Pratt's trouble, Murdock said, "Sam's helping out at the fish-house for Charles. He doesn't know when he'll be back. He said if you want to stay in his house instead of here, do so. Might be easier for you. Or the chickens would manage if you'd rather cart the cat and dog here."

"I'll think on it. Not real keen on changing beds."

The captain nodded in understanding.

"The boy said the baby was about to arrive, huh?"

"Yes. Doc got there just in time I guess. And Jim's mother—she's delivered a few babies in her time I'm told."

"Sure has. Old Ida Jewel probably birthed half the little pickaninnies in town. Not to mention a quarter of the white folks. Fact, I believe Bill there, and Sam too, have been introduced to the world care of Ida Jewel."

The captain grinned. "That so? I'll have to talk to Bill about that."

George laughed. "You 'spect him to remember?"

Murdock drew on his pipe. "If any man on this entire coast remembers day one, I'd be betting on Bill," he rejoined.

Chuckling, George nodded agreement as Murdock picked up his receipts and went out. George followed.

"Phew, that sun. It gets impressive when it's come back after so long."

"True enough. But better on the water than in town while it's sucking all the rain back out of the puddles," Murdock replied. "Cast off, Jim."

The boat retraced its path through the pass. George watched it shrink. The sun rode hot and high. He returned to the office and arranged a chair in the cross-breeze between the door and window. No reason to be uncomfortable. He could watch the water and hungry birds, or sleep, as he chose.

The captain was in a cross-breeze too. He had propped open his front wheelhouse window and the door. As long as the boat churned steadily along he was in the teeth of the breeze. The shaded little room contrasted with the brightness beyond. As he coasted south, he noticed several trees down, and sand-spits reshaped or missing from former locations. Storm-related changes. His eyes always roved the water, but after heavy storm blows that trait was essential. This sandy coast seemed to alter at will. If attention were not constant the price could be high.

The water was roiled. He could not read depth changes from water color. Though substantial sand shifts were unlikely on this shallow slope toward Mexico, short of a hurricane, he prudently stayed a little farther off-shore. His thoughts strayed, as they had before, to the Pratt place.

Bill tapped on the door.

"Not ready to fall asleep are you, Captain?"

"Near enough. Funny how that sun will put you in a trance sometimes."

"All that slow wave motion and glitter—just like waving a pocket watch in front of your eyes."

Both men stared forward, through the rather smeared window panes, and below them, the much brighter open space bisected by the window prop. "Don't notice how dirty these windows get until they're open. Half the time I've been fogged in, it likely was only the dirty panes!"

"Last time they were painted, looks like they thought the glass needed touching up."

"That's been awhile back."

"Yeah. She'll win no beauty contest."

The run boat led a rugged life. Ungainly and box-like at best, it was more important to maintain its mechanical integrity than to worry over-much about its appearance. In constant motion six days a week, often before daybreak and after dark, there was little time or inclination to do more than the minimum scraping and caulking in port. The crew had their work cut out—a dozen or more stops a day and long miles between stops. Jim kept the decks swabbed clear of fish slime—far slicker than ice could be. But the action of three-hundred pound chunks of ice loaded off and on ship, metal baskets chain-hoisted and loaded with fish, or a chute rattling aboard to direct the catch to the hold—apart from the daily tread of three men and the constant abrasion of the elements, fair and foul—all conspired to destroy the boat's paint and polish.

"Speaking of beauty contest losers, I heard tell something about you. I'm told Jim's mama brought you into this world, Bill."

"She tell you that?"

"No. Didn't talk with her much. Old George mentioned it."

"Funny he'd know it. Or remember." Bill leaned against the wall. "Yeah, she midwifed both us boys. The old man was off converting the heathen both times."

"Preacher-man, huh?"

"Yeah." Bill's face twisted like he'd planned to spit, but realized he was indoors. "He preached. He didn't always practice."

"What d'you mean?"

"He sheared more sheep than he led. Including my Ma. You ain't heard the story?"

"No, never came up."

"Well, let's just say he had the makings of another family on the side, until Mama got wind of it."

"Uproar, huh."

"Do tell. He tried talking his way outta it, but Mama didn't care to have him around after she found out. He'd dragged her as far down as she would go. She started out acting like a cornered wildcat, and then threw him out—chucked his clothes in the yard. When he came around to try to talk to her she just picked up the shotgun and said 'Git.' He did."

"What happened?"

"She died that winter. Pneumonia."

"So you lived with him?"

"Nah. He always had to travel. Selling sometime. Flashing his smile. Couldn't thump his Bible no more, but he made up for it with a bottle. Lost at sea when I was fourteen. Probably fell over drunk as a lord."

"You and Sam raised by kin, or alone?"

"Alone."

Captain Murdock shook his head. The boat purred along, hardly needing his hand on the wheel.

"I'm afraid those Pratt kids are about to lose their mama."

"Don't sound good." Bill shifted his position. "Her sister stay and raise them, you think?"

Murdock looked dubious. "She might. But doubt she'd stay on the island. Don't know if Charles'd let them go."

"She's a schoolmarm."

"Yeah."

"That boy looked able."

"Maybe so. But it's four . . . well five kids. He isn't as old as you were, either. I have my doubts they'd manage."

They were silent, thinking. Bill stood, saying, "I'll have to agree with you." He stretched. "Better go check on my engine. Might be leaking some oil. We should have plenty of daylight left this evening if I need to work on her?"

Bill doubted his engine in some way every trip. The captain believed he couldn't be happy before he inspected each square inch of the engine each layover evening. He assented, saying, "We should be a couple hours early. Plenty of time."

Bill returned to the engine room. The captain returned to his thoughts.

That night after dinner when Bill was satisfied with the operation of his equipment belowdecks, the three men relaxed around the small table. Jim had a small smudge burning in a bucket of sand just outside a cheese-cloth curtain shielding the door. A small pile of black mangrove branches lay beside the bucket to replenish the fire when it burned low. Despite that doubled protection, the men switched mosquitoes off frequently, brushing them away with a palm frond or simply slapping them.

Talk had burned out some time before, and a pack of cards lay forgotten on the table. Each man was at ease with his own thoughts, allowing his body to recharge after the lengthy day.

Bill reached over and blew out the lamp, and individually but unconsciously each man's pensive gaze lengthened, focused outside the darkened room through the now-grayed windows. The air was still. Sounds were few. The water had an oily sheen. It lifted and subsided occasionally, in sluggish response to what might be storms and ships dozens of miles away. Twice a night-heron squawked as it flew past the boat. Perhaps it was the same bird, passing and returning. It did not expect the boat in its flight path, and the squawk was a protest or curse making it clear this was his territory and he wanted no intruders.

Murdock quietly lifted his glass in a salute to the bird and finished its contents in a swallow, followed by a short, involuntary shudder as the liquor burned down. He set the glass down firmly on the table. It seemed to ring like the ship's bell, a signal for movement. The other men rose, and Jim went out to the smudge, adding a number of sticks to the smoke. They were all soon asleep.

According to the doctor, Felicity weighed about seven pounds. She was asleep in Emily's arms, having satisfied her demanding stomach a few minutes earlier. Ida had concocted a corn syrup and evaporated milk mix, and the women fed it to the baby with a twist of cloth that she sucked eagerly. Her blue eyes were hidden behind coquina-shell eyelids now, and a soft fuzz of reddish hair gleamed in the lamplight. She glowed, with skin like a China doll, perfectly formed and healthy.

The labor had not been long—five or six hours. But it left everyone exhausted—perhaps more so than Amy herself. She seemed to rally, to gather forces for her ordeal, and throughout the labor seldom cried out or wavered in pain, although it was clearly horrendous. Her determination to meet her challenge showed every moment of the long afternoon. Her burns tore and began to bleed, her suffering had to be monstrous. But she had somehow confined that with her resolve. Finally in late afternoon, the baby arrived.

"How is she?" Amy demanded when the doctor announced her sex.

"She is beautiful, just like her mother," he replied, bringing the crying girl to where Amy could see.

"Yes, . . . yes, baby girl. Yes," she crooned, touching her. The baby fastened on Amy's finger with her hand. "Yes, darling, everything's fine, it's all done, shh, love, shh. I know your name, Felicity. My happiness, my Felicity."

Amy smiled and nodded at Charles. "As you are." He bent over her. They kissed with tears on their faces.

"Do you remember," Amy whispered to him, "I told you our baby wouldn't be born in a rainstorm?" She waved her arm vaguely toward the window where the late-afternoon sun was bright.

Charles didn't look. "Yes, I remember," he said, his eyes intent on her face.

She sighed, almost more contentment than exhaustion, and more distantly said, "Love her, Charles, don't blame her."

He shook his head, "Sh . . . don't talk like that. You'll be putting ribbons in her pigtails in no time." She was drifting away from their conversation, not listening to his urgent words.

The doctor put his hand on Charles' shoulder, saying, "Let her rest now, and Ida and I will make her more comfortable. Go see your daughter now." He swabbed Amy's arm as Charles slowly got up, and gave her an injection.

Charles, dismissed, went to the door. He looked back at his unconscious wife being washed and arranged as carefully as a corpse. He went into the kitchen where the older children surrounded Emily and the baby. They giggled and cooed at her, a bee-hive of energy. He couldn't bear their chatter. He escaped outside.

The doctor came into the kitchen and sat, watching Emily and the sleeping baby. Ida poured and brought him a cup of coffee, which he took with a smile of thanks.

"I've tried to talk to Charles," he said.

Emily looked up from the baby's face.

"He won't listen to me."

She nodded.

"I expect you know what I'm going to say," he continued. "You're a level-headed girl, you're facing hard facts here."

Emily's shoulders slumped and she returned her gaze to Felicity. "I don't think I want to hear this any more than Charles," she replied softly.

Ida got up and reached out for the baby, after squeezing Emily's shoulder in reassurance. Reluctantly Emily surrendered the child to the black woman's arms, resting her hand a moment on Ida's elbow. As Ida left the room, Emily poured a cup of coffee for herself, and sat down with her shoulders squared, preparing for the doctor's words.

"Emily, you know your sister as well as anyone. She's a determined girl, that's obvious."

Emily blinked in agreement.

"That's the only reason she's still with us—determination. Anyone else, well . . ." he sighed and drank from his cup.

"I think she was determined to have this baby, to see that through. You heard what she said this afternoon. She's accomplished her goal, and I suspect she'll slip away quickly now."

Emily set down her cup. She could not swallow.

"There just isn't anything left in her system, no more resources to draw on. Now that the baby's here, she is relaxing. She won't be fighting any more. At least we can ease the pain now, so she won't be so uncomfortable. But I don't expect her to stay more than a couple of days."

He looked at Emily. Tears ran down her face, but her chin was up. She looked back.

"I know this doesn't surprise you," he continued. "But I don't think Charles is prepared at all. I don't know about the children."

"Will she be conscious?"

"For a little while. But if you want the children to see her, to talk to her a little, do it soon, tomorrow morning. Her mind will start drifting. She'll probably sleep away."

Emily bit her lip.

"What about medicine?"

"We can make her comfortable now. I'll leave a syringe and teach you. Also pain pills. I worry about Charles—I'll leave something for you both if it's needed. Ida's planning on staying, of course, and she's a good nurse. But you know that.

"You'll have to think beyond her death, Emily. Will you stay here? You have other responsibilities. What will Charles do? What will happen with these five children? It is a lot to contend with. I know you're strong, but it is easy to get overwhelmed. Take care of yourself just as carefully as you care for that baby. It's important—if not for you, it's important as that baby's nurse."

He leaned back in the chair and studied her face.

"I don't mean to lecture you. But I've seen it happen too often. If you wear yourself out you do a disservice to everyone involved, not just yourself. Right now I know appealing to yourself means nothing. But recognize that five kids and Charles lean on you so take care for them."

He reached out and patted her limp hands. "I'm going to try to talk to Charles again. I don't know how successful it will be, but I'll keep trying. And don't ever hesitate to ask for help. The kids, neighbors, passing fishermen, whoever. When people are in trouble, it's easing for others to help where they can. Let them do it. Don't shut them out." He patted her hands again and left the room.

17

Charles was gone, again. Evan searched for him after he fed the pig and other animals. His father disappeared frequently—whenever he left Amy for a while he seemed to vanish from sight. This morning the doctor waited to be taken back to the fish-house, and his irritation showed.

Evan carried his case to the boat. "Perhaps I'd better take you over—the run boat might come a little early."

"I think you'll have to. I believe your father's avoiding talking to me, Evan. I'll just say goodbye to Emily."

He went into the house. Emily had been busy with the baby and two younger children. She had taken all three to see Amy individually during the morning. The emotional strain showed on everyone. Nell had been especially difficult, since at age five she was old enough to feel the tension and able to sense the changes in her mother. She had gotten upset and ran from the room. Emily did not look forward to the older children's visits.

It had exhausted Amy to focus her attention on the children. Now she slept.

In the yard Ida Jewel scrubbed every linen and stitch of clothing she could find in the house, taking advantage of the cleared skies and of Evan's water-hauling and fire-building. The yard looked like a spring cleaning in progress. It reminded Evan of the day before Aunt Emily had arrived—sheets spread across bushes and lines filled. The little washerwoman had none of his copper-haired mother's sparkle and bounce. Though Ida Jewel's wash sparkled, the woman trudged, curiously bent from years of carrying yoked buckets of water and lifting wads of dripping wash on a length of broomstick. She attacked her job steadily and thoroughly, not wasting a moment for sighing or mopping her sweaty face. She poked at boiling wash and moved it through successive rinse and bluing tubs until she had it subdued by cleanliness. Only then did she spread the garments out to meet the sun and breeze. Already she had folded a pile of crackling clean dry laundry into neat stacks, to be returned inside the house, in drawers, on shelves and in closets.

Her example seemed to galvanize the others—at least some of them. Katie had dusted and swept the front room this morning. Ned and Nellie had helped.

Last night Ida served the first meal the family'd sat down to since the fire. Ida had handed Kate a paring knife and pan of potatoes, and she delegated Nellie to set the table. It almost became a festive meal with the brand-new baby in Aunt Emily's arms. Ida crowded the table with two big plates of biscuits, ham, potatoes, cornbread, canned peaches, jellies, and gravy.

Ida gave Charles and Emily no chance to demur. They sat at her direction, as did the children and the doctor.

At first the group paused silently, staring at the food. Nell took a biscuit, and bit it with the tentativeness of a field mouse. The rich smell of ham gravy and the molasses-dribbled ham touched Evan's days-hollow stomach. Suddenly he knew how starved he was, and followed by the others, he filled his plate, and then refilled it. By the time Ida's raisin-bread pudding reached the table, chattering was almost normal among the children, Emily and Ida smiled occasionally, and the doctor leaned back with a satisfied sigh. Only Charles ate little, and kept his eyes low.

After dinner the girls washed dishes while Ida told them tales about their mother and aunt when they were children. She had the girls giggling helplessly over the dishwater while she never changed her expression. Ida even crooned some lullabies when the baby fussed for its dinner. Her matter-of-fact appearance jogged the family into a semblance of life. Each child fastened on her concrete normalcy like a sunflower would follow the sun across the sky. The doctor ministered to Amy's physical need. Ida Jewel addressed deeper wounds.

Sam had rowed to the dock near dark, and managed to eat three ham and biscuit sandwiches as well as pudding. Ostensibly he came to borrow some tools. But his mind was on Amy's condition and the baby's arrival. He walked down the beach a little ways talking with the doctor before he returned to the fish-house.

Now, as Evan brought Doc to the fish-house this morning, Sam could be seen rummaging through some lumber. When he heard the skiff coming, he shaded his eyes to see who approached, and waited companionably to moor the skiff alongside.

Evan handed up Doc's case as the older man scrambled awkwardly onto the deck.

"I guess I'll always be a landlubber," he said, as Sam gave him the support of his strong arm. "Thanks." He looked down into Evan's skiff, saying, "It's not easy, boy. But have faith. Lean on each other." He stepped back from the edge, straightening. The boy raised a hand in silent acknowledgment, for an instant covering his worry-pinched face as though he warded off an imagined blow.

Evan turned the boat toward home, and the men followed him with their eyes. Evan huddled in the tiny space in the stern with the stick drawn protectively across his midsection. Small as the boy appeared in the skiff, the moving boat was tinier yet on the bay. The men exchanged mute glances.

***

There were fish in the hold, and the promise of more. Murdock spotted two crews stop-netting as he made his way north. The second crew had a number of birds wheeling above it. Tide was near its low. They had penned the fish, propping the corklines high out of the water with stakes, to deny the fish a chance to jump over the net and go free. The penned area boiled with panicked fish, in contrast to the smoother surrounding water. That smoother water was dotted with bobbing pelicans intently looking on as though they were spectators at a great play. The six men had three large skiffs they were filling with fish for the run to the ice house.

"Looks like a fair catch."

The captain started. Bill had sneaked up behind him without his noticing.

"Should be a pleased bunch when they get it loaded."

Bill nodded. "Worked on a crew some years back where we netted over 30,000 pounds in one haul like that." He waved in the general direction of the busy fishermen. "We worked from about mid-morning almost until the next morning loading those fish. I've got the scars to prove it." He extended his oak-like padded hands toward the captain. Lines and gouges ran everywhere. Gouges from fish that had finned his hands in their fight to escape capture. Lines indicating rope burns from hauling or setting nets. Some of the lines were black. The tarred net had left permanent tattoos.

"Got too old—or too smart—for that."

"Stand in that water all day tossing little fish in the skiff, you don't get hot and sweaty." The captain baited him.

"Hmpf." Bill snorted, and shifted a wad of tobacco in his mouth. "Don't believe that. How you think this bay got salty? That's fisherman sweat, that's all. And you'd be pleased to sweat on the boat once you mucked around that soft bottom tossing fish in the skiff a few hours. Especially in the middle of the night, tide rising and God knows what swimming round your legs, stirring up the phosphor. You begin to think you're growing fins yourself."

Murdock seemed to be looking down the bowl of his pipe, smiling faintly as he listened. "Look at those pelicans come," he muttered.

"They get thick when they see a meal set up. See the way they're guarding? A mullet jumps that net he'll be down their gullet before he knows he's free. Them birds'll reach over the corkline trying to grab a fish from the pocket. 'Course that scares the fish away from the net so he don't jump over, too."

"So that means you tolerate them."

"Sure. They'd rather dine on the little fish, so . . . Sometimes they're a pain though. Sometimes they're so thick you hafta stop tossing fish long enough to toss pelicans out the way."

Murdock laughed.

"It's true. But they learn. They ain't dumb. They know what the crew's doing and don't get too greedy. They know who's boss. Least the older ones do. The babies are the ones what give you the biggest trouble. The brown ones."

"I believe they'd steal you blind if you'd let them."

"Oh yeah, bet on it. You don't leave them alone with the goods. But they do know how much they'll get away with and no more."

"Ocean-going raccoons."

Bill laughed. "And don't think the coons wouldn't be right there if they could reach the nets. You've seen them out rummaging in the mud on strong lows. I wonder who'd win in a tug-of-war between a coon and pelican?"

"I'd bet on the coon."

"Yeah. He'd get the fish. Brother Pelican probably give him a knock in payment though. The coon would steal pelican chicks if he could. So no love lost, I'd bet."

The cloudy green Gulf water would soon be running in, mixing with the bay's browner hue. Rain run-off had changed the early summer water clarity to a thick obstinate hue that bested all attempts to see bottom through it. It was as though a curtain had been drawn to hide the beginnings of the new summer growth—plants, crabs, and fish. Privacy was needed. Like birds in a leafy forest, water creatures moved securely in the opaque water, in contrast to the spring clarity. Not as beautiful to look at, it nevertheless was immeasurably richer for them.

The captain felt a sadness just the same when that ephemeral turquoise and violet season ended with tongues of brown extending from every river and creek along the coast. Those delicate color variations reminded him of the reefs and Gulf Stream in the Keys. The bay colors signaled water depths and sea grass beds, sand and mud bottoms, unlike the keys where coral knobs lay in wait beside a fierce, flowing, river in the sea. The bay's colors were softer and more benevolent.

There had been years when the elusive water clarity had not appeared, times when the spring winds were followed too closely by summer's rains. He missed that serene amicable season when it didn't occur. It was an un-solicited friendly smile, a boost to his spirit. For this year, now, that season was irretrievably gone.

***

Mrs. Stanhope had arrived at the manicured hotel grounds at dusk, and watched the remains of the sunset across the water before she went into the lobby. The carved woods, crystal chandeliers, and rugs were unchanged from her last visit years ago. The hotel seemed ageless, and comforted her with its familiarity.

The desk clerk's smile of welcome was warm. As she checked in, she mentioned her request of a hired boat.

He was dubious. "I know you wanted that, Ma'am, but most of the guides have gone to fishing or left for the summer, now."

"I don't want a guide, just transportation to my daughter's place down the harbor. It's a lengthy trip—the Pratt place."

The clerk's eyes opened wide. "The Pratt's." He glanced behind him as though searching for help. Then he squared around to her again with an audible breath. "Ma'am, Mrs. Pratt is your daughter?"

"Yes. Do you know her?"

"No, well yes. I mean I know of the lady. Does she know you're arriving?"

"Well no. It was an impulse I must say. But she is about to give birth, and . . ."

"Oh, yes Ma'am. I mean, excuse me Ma'am, yes we know the baby's coming soon. Ah . . . Doc . . . Dr. Haliburton went down on the fish run boat this morning, Ma'am."

"They called for the doctor? Is there a problem you know of?" Mrs. Stanhope half-leaned across the desk.

The clerk's eyes grew wider still and his stammering intensified. "Oh, no Ma'am. Ah, ah, ah, not a baby problem, I, I, don't believe Ma'am." He reminded Mrs. Stanhope of a newly-caged bird, struggling to get out.

"There must be a problem to summon the doctor from town. What is it?" she demanded. She was a foot smaller than the clerk. He recognized her imperious tone of authority, and any thought of hiding the story from her evaporated. He wilted.

"I don't really know anything, Ma'am." he tried.

"Tell me what you've heard." Her voice plainly indicated his duty.

He sighed. "Well, Ma'am. I understand there was an accident of some kind. Mrs. Pratt got burned some, and it worried them—her about to have the baby and all . . ."

"How badly burned?" she interrupted. The clerk looked at her hands, gripping white on the desk. An impulse, quickly curbed, sprung in him to pat those fear-filled hands. He raised his eyes to hers. Her eyes held fear and anger.

"I don't know, Ma'am," he said sadly.

"Emily's there," she said, as to herself.

"Her sister, yes Ma'am. And Miss Ida Jewel went down with the doctor, too. She's . . ."

"Ida!" Mrs. Stanhope's face flared joy. "Oh, it's been so long . . ." she looked, stricken, at the nervous clerk. "But if Ida saw fit to go it's certainly not a good sign. She hates boats, and it's been years since the girls have seen her."

The clerk squirmed.

"I must have a boat tomorrow morning."

"I will do my best, Ma'am. But, the run boat will be back tomorrow—guess Doc's coming on it—he has other patients here in town. Might I suggest talking with him tomorrow evening and then riding down on the run boat next morning?"

"I can't sit here twenty-four hours knowing Amy's in trouble."

"Yes, Ma'am." He sighed. "But finding a boat won't be easy. I'll do my best, but if it takes the morning, well, the run boat would still be faster. There won't be any fast boats around. It'll be a long ride in a skiff, and I don't know if they'd start out in the afternoon. It'd mean much of the way in the dark, Ma'am."

She looked down her nose at him, actually down her nose, he marveled, distracted. "Sir, I am not fearful of the night!"

He gulped. "Oh no Ma'am. But travelling on the water at night—the fishermen aren't gonna chance your skin or theirs in . . . Pardon me, Ma'am." He halted, blushing hotly. "Ma'am, this time of year a thunderstorm or the bugs could addle you. It isn't worth the risk, when the run boat would get you there in a few hours. I know it looks calm out there, but we just had a bad storm. More could . . ."

"You are right of course, I've some knowledge of the water, young man, and I understand what you are trying to say. But if you can find a boat early enough to leave tomorrow . . .?"

"I'll see to it myself, Mrs. Stanhope. Soon as it's daylight, I promise you."

"Thank you." She reached over and touched his hand.

Again he blushed. "Ma'am, you should get some rest—all that train ride and now the boat ride to look forward to. The dining room is closed. But I can send for something, should you require it?"

"Thank you, no. Just the room for now, please."

As he handed her the key, he shyly said, "I do hope that it is all right with your daughter, Mrs. Stanhope." He turned away immediately, and called the boy to the counter. She followed him up an ornate staircase to her room.

There she sat, alone in her hotel room. She was tired. The fear, though, was stronger.

18

Late the next afternoon Mrs. Stanhope walked to the city dock. As the desk clerk had feared, no transportation was available today, though he had found one boat which would take her tomorrow if she wanted. The clerk strongly recommended the run boat, complimenting its captain as a gentleman who had already given much help to Amy. Mrs. Stanhope's image of fishermen made her doubt that assessment. Yet Charles was well-enough mannered, if not typical of the breed, she mused. And the clerk had been right about the boats.

She stood straight under a tin roof on poles. It offered little shade. A sea-breeze blew up-river, rattling the corrugated tin in the space between its nails and supporting framework. A dock worker eyed her resolute stand, then continued his work without any attempt to approach. Others called directions at the far end of the dock as boxcars were loaded with crates. Their voices sounded like gull cries far out on the harbor. The sun slid lower. Mrs. Stanhope opened her umbrella for shade and continued to stand.

It was nearly two hours later when the bulky white boat appeared out of the sun. She didn't move until it eased to its berth. A Negro slung lines to the dock to moor the run boat, and came ashore to secure them. Perhaps that impelled her forward. No other movement occurred on-board.

"Is this the run boat carrying Dr. Haliburton?" she said to the Negro's back.

He turned. "Yes, Ma'am. He's aboard. 'Spec' he'll be ashore in a moment."

"Thank you."

He started to turn away, then did not. He stared curiously at her.

"Beggin' your pardon, Ma'am, but you do look familiar—it isn't Mrs. Stanhope by chance, is it Ma'am?"

"Why, yes. But . . ."

Mullet Jim grinned. "I thought so!" he declared. "I'm Miz Ida's Jim, Ma'am. Don't know that you'd remember, but . . ."

"Of course! But you were only a boy!"

Jim grinned again. "Yes'm. But no more." He sobered. "You here 'cause of Miz Amy."

"Yes. But I just learned last night what has happened. What do you know, Jim?"

He shook his head. "M–a'am, I don't wanna be the one to tell you, but it don't soun' good. Let me take you to the Doc—he's talking to the captain right now. You gonna come on board tomorrow?"

"If it's alright with Captain . . . Murdock?"

"Yes'm. Murdock. C'mon this way." He laid a plank to the boat from the dock and in a moment they had reached the wheelhouse.

The men's voices carried from inside.

"Sam wants me to get some fresh-milled pine—said he felt it should be a clean lumbered box when it comes time, so I'll go down and roust Beemon afterhours, have Jim bring it aboard for the morning run. I expect it'll be needed in a day or two if what you . . ." The voice stopped in mid-sentence as Jim and Mrs. Stanhope came in.

"Ma'am." The men rose, almost in unison, looking puzzled.

"Cap'n, Doc, this is Miz Pratt's mama, Miz Stanhope. Captain Murdock, Dr. Haliburton." Jim stood back as the white-haired woman gravely shook hands with each man.

"I know this is an intrusion. But I arrived last night, thinking to surprise the girls and have received an enormous shock instead."

The men murmured and the captain offered her a chair.

"Thank you, no. Captain, would it be possible for me to ride to my daughter's with your boat tomorrow? The desk clerk did find one skiff which I could take if it's too large an imposition, but I'm told it will take many hours longer, and . . ."

"Madam, I am at your service. I cannot imagine why you should suffer that length of a ride in an open skiff. Certainly—come aboard at dawn."

She smiled at him. "I do appreciate that. Thank you."

"You want medical details from me, Mrs. Stanhope. I haven't yet dined. Let me take you to your hotel and we can talk over dinner while Captain Murdock sees to his vessel." The doctor gave her his arm, and with another nod of thanks to the captain and Jim, they left.

The few blocks back to the hotel seemed very long for Carrie Stanhope. The doctor didn't seem inclined to small talk, and her only thoughts were like a heartbeat, echoing Amy, Amy, Amy. She drew a breath to ask a half-dozen times, and each time stifled it. He's deciding how to tell me. She's gone.

He held open the lobby door. As they crossed to the dining room the desk clerk greeted them, looking at both intently.

At the doctor's request they were seated at a quiet table.

"I wish I could offer you some sherry, Mrs. Stanhope," he said as their waiter left.

"Will I need it, doctor?" she managed to say calmly.

"Oh, I am sorry!" He gripped her hand for reassurance. "She is alive, Mrs. Stanhope. And you have a healthy new granddaughter. Amy named her Felicity."

Mrs. Stanhope, relieved, settled in her chair.

"But I can't deceive you. Your daughter's condition is precarious. I can't promise you will see her alive. It is very close." He leaned toward her. "I feel you're made from the same cloth those two women down there are. I can see where their backbone came from. I won't try to misrepresent the facts.

"Amy's burns cover—well I estimate forty percent of her body. Her head, torso, arm, other scattered areas. That means an extremely delicate situation for anyone. Add to that her pregnancy. The trauma of the birth was important, but almost incidental compared to the drain on her body processes that maintaining the baby in utero had been. The body fluids are disrupted by burns—it's akin to a bucket of water which has developed a leak. The larger the burns, of course, the more severe the drain. The baby being totally dependent on the mother has also in a sense drained her. I was very relieved at the infant's robust health. It was not a certain thing in this case. In normal conditions it would scarcely be noticed, but in Amy's case, where the outflow from her 'bucket' is greater than the inflow, the baby is a grave complication.

"Luckily she had been a very healthy woman . . ."

Mrs. Stanhope heard "had been" echo in her head

". . . and pregnancy has been uneventful—not difficult—for her. This baby's delivery was not especially traumatic in length or complications, except for that overriding if external one—these burns. A normal birth depletes body fluids. Amy has none to spare. We are attempting to force fluids into her. And with the baby safely delivered, we can ease her pain more satisfactorily.

"At this point you might think that with the birth behind her, she might rebuild more easily. But her fire is banked very low, and what fuel we can get to it isn't sufficient to keep her flame even at that level. It declines with each moment." Dr. Haliburton paused to examine Mrs. Stanhope's face. Her eyes were intent. She nodded tightly, mutely urging him to continue.

"You've heard of people who supposedly collapsed of heartbreak, or who have died when they discovered a wife or husband had succumbed."

She nodded again.

"People often scoff at that—claim its coincidence. But there is some reality in it. The mind is an awesome piece of machinery. On a battlefield a man can will himself on, though mortally wounded, to protect another. Your daughter has this quality. She had determined that her baby would be born. It was her goal. Once she arrived, Amy could relax. I don't mean to imply that Amy has given up—is now 'ready to die'. But in her mind she has won her battle. She's at peace with herself. It will be easier to slide away, despite her family, which she cares about enormously. Does this make any sense to you?"

"I am thinking about when my husband Franklin died. It was so sudden, so unexpected. But I had an impression—like what you describe—that he had accomplished what was important to him. That he was satisfied. I believe it was more difficult for us than for him."

He nodded.

"And afterwards. I remember I was in a trance. It would have taken very little for me to have lain down to die as well."

"Exactly. Then you understand what I mean. The energy she needs is not there. Even if her physical condition were excellent. And it is not."

Carrie realized she had twisted her napkin into a rope. She spread it out, smoothing it over her lap.

"You are saying there is no real hope."

"I believe she has little time. I think she has accepted that. Her husband has not."

"Charles."

"He will be devastated, to judge by his reactions today. If you arrive in time, it will probably animate her. I want you to understand though, that it won't last."

"I won't give up on her, doctor."

"Absolutely. I just don't want false hope to build, you understand." He peered at her closely.

"I wish I were there now."

He nodded. "But you are closer than you'd have been otherwise. Now, please, eat something. You haven't touched your food."

Paradoxically, having heard the worst from Dr. Haliburton, Carrie Stanhope found that sleep came easily. A note from Captain Murdock (in a finely-written hand) reiterated the dawn departure and indicated he would meet her in the lobby to escort her aboard. Another thing the desk clerk was right about . . . She thought about her twin daughters, their differing pain . . . grandchildren . . . Ida . . . Franklin . . . She remembered nothing until the maid's knock on her door awakened her in the dark of early morning. She quickly dressed and closed her valises, coming down the stairs just as Captain Murdock entered the lobby.

***

Sam paced nervously along the fish-house deck. He was used to wider horizons. Here fishermen came to him, but he usually did the traveling. He thought about fishing, perhaps stopping by at the house to see how things were. He had heard nothing for twenty-four hours. It gnawed at him, though he knew it meant the situation remained quiet at the house. They didn't need him adding to a death watch. But time was passing so slowly!

The clock had slowed for Evan too. Katie had spent a half hour with Amy while he and his Aunt Emily sat at the table in the kitchen. Although she hesitated at the door, she bravely went in with her aunt. Emily left her with her mother after a few moments, when it was clear that mother and daughter could cope. Katie eventually came out softly, saying Amy had fallen asleep. She seemed calm although her eyes were reddened. She didn't seem inclined to talk. Emily gave her a cloth to wash her face.

Katie pressed the wet cloth to her face, then lowered it to say, "You don't look alike at all, any more, Aunt Emily." That forced tears from Emily. She embraced Kate.

Evan went to the porch. Ida sat on the porch steps with Nell. The dog lay behind them. In the house Evan could hear his aunt preparing the baby's milk. His father appeared from the far side of the house. Evan's mother had changed these last four days. But Charles' appearance was at least as dramatic. His clothing seemed a size too large for him and his beard had grown past stubble. It approached scruffy.

He walked past Ida and the children as though they did not exist. Evan was sure Charles passed Emily and Kate the same way as he walked through the kitchen to his wife's sickroom.

"That man hasn't picked up his baby yet," Ida said. She was frowning back at Evan. "That baby's too little to carry his load. Don't he know?"

Evan couldn't find an answer for her. His father seemed a stranger. She turned back, shaking her head and still muttering. Evan walked to the far end of the porch and watched as two hens scurried under the house near a clump of periwinkles. On impulse he hopped off the porch and broke off several stems of blooms, both pink and white. A porcelain vase, sent by Nana Stanhope, sat in the front room. He took the flowers and vase to the kitchen, where Emily fed Felicity, and filled the fancy vase with flowers and water.

Emily looked up at him. She said nothing. The vase had always been off-limits.

A short time later Charles came out. "She wants to see you." he said to Evan. He didn't look at Emily or the baby.

Evan took the vase in with him.

Charles stood in the dirt yard, his back to the house. Nothing seemed changed, looking toward the bay. Everyone had written his wife off. He could not accept that. The children shouldn't see her ill. Charles had somehow lost control. He had no say. It was not his house. One woman ran the house while another minded the children and Amy. Two, to replace her.

He should be grateful. But dammit! He shoved his fists in his trouser pockets.

A part of it was that he just couldn't look at Emily since the accident. To his eyes, she had become a mocking gargoyle of her twin. Hadn't she come here to help? How could she have let this happen? No, that wasn't . . . he shook his head to clear it. Worse, he knew Amy felt his revulsion. She always knew his feelings. He had caught a look in her eyes, more than once, which shamed him. Its memory embarrassed him now. But he could not control it. He had lost touch with his household. And now the boy was in there, saying good-bye to his mother. At her request! If she wouldn't fight it, what could he do? Charles rocked back and forth on his feet. He could not accept it. Would not.

A skiff rowed into the bayou. His skiff. It was Sam, and someone else. There was no end to the stream of people. All curious, poking. Why can't they just leave him alone? Sam too. Not fair. Sam gave up his time for him. Hell, they all have. Not at all fair. But still, Charles wanted to be alone with Amy. Not housing a collection of . . . Was that another woman in that skiff? Jesus! White-haired, even. Some old dame. No. Not . . . it is . . . how the hell did she . . . He strode down the dock, taking Sam's line for him.

Carrie Stanhope had been handed from Captain Murdock to Sam. She hadn't caught his full name. She stood on the deck while the boat people unloaded ice and the captain and this rough-looking Sam went over some papers. Then Jim unloaded some lumber and other oddments. Both he and the captain said good-bye, and the large boat left her on the little fish-house.

Sam had loaded her in his skiff and immediately rowed for the island. She had to admit, rough as he looked, he spoke and acted with politeness. Then, into the bayou, here came another ruffian, if possible even more disreputable in appearance.

"Mother Stanhope, how did you manage this?"

She looked at him in shock. This . . . man . . . was her son-in-law! It had been seven or eight years, but he was nearly unrecognizable! Had he aged so from life here? Or from the last few days? She finally managed to say his name.

"Charles."

He helped her to the dock and took her bags from Sam.

"How is she, Charles?" she asked.

"She's talking to Evan right now."

Having heard that, Sam pointed to his line, and when Charles released it, Sam headed out of the bayou. Charles and his mother-in-law walked toward the steps, where Ida now stood peering at the on-coming woman, shading her eyes with a muscled hand.

19

Amy had dozed off again. Evan, holding her hand, wasn't prepared to leave the room yet. They hadn't talked much. Amy seemed to fade away periodically. Her eyes would roll upward and her breathing would dim. Then she would return, eyes holding Evan's, and smile faintly, almost apologetically. Little needed to be said, beyond the assurances, the unnecessary assurances, of love. Evan had never seen the effects of severe burns before. He expected to be repulsed. Although one part of his mind was horrified, he hardly noticed her wounds on the important level of their communion now. Most of her waking time she looked at his face as though she were memorizing it. Occasionally she glanced at the picture he had brought from her dresser—an old photo of his grandparents. She rested her eyes on the vased periwinkles, and again watched her son.

When he offered her a drink, Amy seldom wanted it. Occasionally she sucked a sliver of ice, allowing it to melt in her mouth. It seemed to refresh her.

Her small hand was nearly fleshless. She seemed to have almost melted away.

"So proud of you, Evan." She was smiling at him, that soft smile that brought him near tears. He squeezed her fingers. She returned the pressure.

Evan could hear excited voices from the kitchen. Amy looked at her son with a quizzical expression.

The door opened and Charles came in. He came to the bedside and bent over Amy.

"Darling. You'll not believe who Sam just brought to the dock."

She turned her head slightly, toward him.

"Your mother is here, Amy."

Amy gasped in surprise and started to lift up before sinking back as the pain hiding behind the morphine flicked at her.

"How . . ."

"She just decided to come. She didn't know about this until she got here. Just knew she wanted to see you."

Her smile made her delight clear.

"Go get your grandmother, boy," Charles growled at Evan. He pulled the rocker close to Amy's side.

Evan hesitated, then deliberately squeezed around his father and bent over to kiss his mother. They looked carefully at each other again. "I love you, Mama," he whispered. She squeezed his hand. Her eyes were wet. He kissed her again and went to the door, then looked back. She was following him with her eyes. They smiled again.

Evan closed the door, and immediately his eyes went to the small white-haired woman holding Felicity. She was exquisite, delicate and strong at the same time. His mother would have looked like this at her age, Evan suddenly realized. It hurt him for that instant to look at his grandmother, though he hadn't felt that way looking at Amy's damaged face and body a moment ago.

"Nana?" He hadn't realized he'd spoken.

She looked at the boy, his shoulders braced against an invisible load. She impulsively put out a hand, and he found himself hugging this strange woman fiercely.

"Mama wants to see you," he said. "She's awake."

His grandmother stood up. She was scarcely taller than he. She gave the baby to Ida, whose grin was startling against her dark, and usually unsmiling, face. Still wordless she laid her hand against Evan's cheek and went in to her daughter.

Thunderheads had built inland along a line parallel to the coast. They would have shown the captain where to find land if the boat had been out of sight of the shore. Sometimes one of those thunderheads could slide west, heading toward the Gulf like a truant schoolboy. The captain doubted that would happen today. The sea breeze was steady. It kept unruly clouds corralled over the Everglades. Clouds were like thoughts. They formed so insidiously the sky would be nearly choked with them before one became aware of their appearance. He wished for a sea breeze in his mind as effective as the one on the water today.

Without volition he looked west. A sea-breeze could bring clouds too, not merely keep them at bay.

Lydie loomed in his thoughts. She never retreated far below his conscious horizon. Sometimes she filled his sky, other times she yielded to more short-lived concerns. Lydie and clouds, he smiled to himself. Fluffy, rose-tinted by sun's rise or set. Hurricane. Silver-lined. Grey all-day-long overcast. Gauzy streamers of mare's tails spangled with stars. Neat methodical lines of identical dumpling clouds marching low across the morning. Yes, Lydie was all of that.

But there were more parallels with Lydie and Amy Pratt than with any clouds. Fancies were getting to him. The woman dying on her island had accepted and rounded out her life according to Dr. Haliburton. *She's about Lydie's age,* he thought. *All that time she should have ahead of her. Family to care for, loving husband.* Then a niggling voice in his mind wondered, *why not now? Hasn't she touched the heights? Could she improve on the family's love with time? Love wasn't measurable. It didn't matter how long it lasted. It wasn't two cups a day for thirty years. It just was. Is. Maybe it would only go downhill. Isn't she going out on top? Didn't Lydie? No!*

The boat shuddered slightly in its course as he struck the wheel. Jim, relaxing at the stern, saw the jog in the wake stretching behind the boat. *Cap'n's nodding off* he thought to himself.

No. She had so much to live for. Children one day. Each other.

Yeah, the little voice mocked, for you. She should have lived for YOU. Selfish bastard aren't you?

No. She had so much to give, to live for.

Sure—to give. To live for, it mocked. She cheated you. She died, so you weren't her idol any more. Just another tragic face. Think about her! Lots of people die. She had it better than most. Love, comfort . . .

Yeah. Comfort. Died really comfortable.

How do you know? She went to sleep. Easy. Lot more comfortable than you struggling in that rowboat off-shore. She knew you were taking care of her.

The captain snorted. *Some care.*

You didn't succeed. But you did your . . .

. . . best? Never! She died. I let her die.

She died. You didn't kill her. She died knowing you were trying, knowing you loved her. If you were in her position would you fault yourself—if you switched roles?

No answer? You might be an idol—can't see it myself—but you sure are no god. You're blaming yourself. But she wouldn't have. Still just being selfish. Big tragic load of guilt. Make you feel special, does it? You're not special. Just look at that Pratt family.

Murdock sighed.

Yeah. Look at them. Look at someone else. Talk about pain. All those kids. Family. You any better than Charles? You know why you're all tied up in knots? Because she died? No. Because you're mad at her for dying on you! You're chewing yourself up and spitting it out because you're mad at her for dying, and mad at yourself for feeling that way. So you figure you're a worthless . . .

"No!" He shouted aloud.

"Yes, you did."

"Huh." He spun toward the voice, disoriented.

"You went right by the pass!" Jim was laughing.

"What?"

"George's stop. Carlos Pass, Cap'n." Jim spoke emphatically, puzzled, as though he were shouting at Bill in the engine room over all its noise.

"I thought you just realized. You didn't turn in at the pass. Saw it go by from the stern and came to tell ya."

"Christamighty!" He sounded disgusted as he spun the wheel on a big clockwise turn toward the west. "Asleep for sure, Jim."

"Yassir," he laughed.

They both heard Bill's voice. "What the hell's happening here? We turning into a Gulf cruise ship? Or a merry-go-round?"

Mullet Jim retreated from the wheelhouse. He noticed the captain's face had reddened under his black unruly hair. He walked toward Bill, whose head peered from the engine room like a baby bird looking for mamma's return. Jim's face crinkled in a grin as he went.

Carrie Stanhope had been standing by Amy's bed for most of an hour. Although her feet had begun to complain, she made no move to sit in the chair Emily moved beside the bed. She merely shifted a little for relief. Amy hadn't released her hand yet, though from time to time she'd faded into a light sleep. Many years ago, Carrie had been summoned to her grandmother's bedside. Perhaps she had been Evan's age. When she'd gone into the room, her grandmother had been elevated by pillows. Her long white hair had been combed out, the counterpane was folded back evenly and laid across her upper body, and her hands were neatly folded on top of the pane. Nothing of that old memory resembled Amy's room. Nothing but the face. Perhaps skull was a better term. The skull dominated the bed, announced its presence in the room. Any hope Carrie had brought to Amy's room died on the instant she glimpsed that skull.

Yet Amy was animated and happy to have her there. It was a healing process for both women. Emily came in and out. Charles sat quietly on the other side of the bed. He watched his wife.

The silence rested on the room lightly. Outside the chirp of a pair of cardinals sounded. From Carrie's vantage she saw them flick along the tree margin occasionally. Amy slipped into her doze again, eyes not closed entirely, but rolled back under the lids. Her jaw sank open. Her breath caught in a snore, and then exhaled. Carrie found it distressing to look at her unconscious face. Her eyes followed down the covers to their entwined hands. She was staring at them, nearly trance-like, when Amy's hand moved to squeeze her own. Carrie looked at Amy's face to see once again her gentle smile as she looked at her mother. They did not speak.

After a moment Amy turned her eyes toward Charles. He had leaned back against the rocker, and was staring, though not seeing, through the window. His head, turned away from the bed, lay against the rocker back as though he hadn't the energy to support it. His open eyes looked like dry dead pebbles. He was unaware of Amy's look. Desolation was in every line of his posture. Carrie's eyes went from the motionless man back to her daughter. Amy had forgotten her mother. The wife was utterly nakedly alone, watching her husband with a yearning sadness that prickled Carrie's eyelids. A moment later Amy turned back, looking within. Charles became aware she was awake. A cardinal flashed again, chipped.

Carrie made the discovery she had stopped breathing. The image was seared in her memory. Amy's inaudible message of love, of desire to ease pain, and the inability to lift that pain from her husband, had rooted Carrie. She felt an immediate and profound sense of loss and emptiness, almost an anger, in the recognition that she had for so many years shielded herself from the unreserved love she'd just seen, cheated herself of that, until nearly too late.

Emily came in the room with Felicity. Carrie felt light-headed. In the motion created by the baby's entrance, she managed to sit down.

The growing moon was sinking close to the trees. Evan watched its slow slip towards the Gulf. It was about ten o'clock. The younger children were asleep. Some of the adults too. Charles had gone out on one of his walks. Evan had thought he was sleepy. But as soon as he lay down, his eyes refused to close. So he watched the moon, which was grown to nearly half-size, and pillowed his head on his arms as he leaned against the windowsill.

The breeze brought a peppery sharp smell tonight—unlike the normal night air. Some nasty night-flower that attracted bats? He didn't remember smelling it before.

His father stepped out of the shadows of the trees below him. Evan had not heard him. He seemed to walk without purpose, hands forced deep in pockets. Evan thought about going out to him, but his father clearly wanted to be alone.

He could hear his grandmother saying good-night to Ida. They had been sitting up talking about years ago. The house was settling down for the night. His father stood in the moonlight. Occasionally he disappeared, walking around the house to return to this quiet back. Evan realized he was waiting for the family to sleep before he re-entered the house.

Evan's legs were cramped under him. He had crouched at the window well over an hour—the moon had expanded and reddened as it reached the horizon, its distorted light sporadically showing through the trees.

Charles walked around the house again. Then Evan heard his quiet step on the porch and the barely-heard "scree" of the spring holding the screened door shut. He went into Amy's room. Evan felt he even heard the sigh of the cane rocker in the dark as Charles took up his vigil again.

Evan turned himself, sitting on the floor a moment to allow the 'pins-and-needles' in his legs to dissipate. It was time to sleep too.

He had pulled a sheet up over his face and squirmed into a comfortable position when it seemed as though a siren went off under him, a wavering sound that rose and rattled, disorienting. He sat up, confused, and realized at last that it came from downstairs. He stumbled for the stairs, and saw the women burst out of the front room in their nightgowns.

He followed them to his mother's door, and when it opened he grasped that the sound was his father, wailing. Ida and Emily went to Charles, pulling at his arms, while Carrie, with the light, bent calmly over Amy's body. She looked back at Evan and motioned him to take the light. He drew back.

"She's at peace, son. Please."

When Evan reluctantly took the lamp, he knew his grandmother was not as calm as she seemed. Her fingers trembled cold against his. But she turned to her daughter and straightened her, closing the eyes. She kissed Amy's face and drew the sheet neatly over it. She continued to stand beside the bed, her shadow crossing the hardly perceptible shape Amy's body made under the sheet. After a moment Evan lowered the light. The change of the shadows roused Carrie. She turned back toward the boy and they wrapped arms around each other, reaching across the missing generation.

20

The family sat quietly at the kitchen table at midnight. Ida Jewel had made coffee and set out some cake. This had been ignored. No one had spoken for some time.

"I want for y'all to go to bed. Take them pills the Doc left and go. Ain't no use in sitting up all night." Ida stood by the stove, arms crossed.

"Too much needs doing, Ida."

"What needs doing is my job. Not yours. It won't be the first time, and you know I'll take care of her right. Cain't do nothing but prepare her until daylight. Then Sam'll help me."

"You leave her be! Don't touch her!"

Ida looked startled and a little insulted.

"Charles."

"No!" he ignited. "I don't want it!" He slammed his hand on the table, spilling his cup. No one moved.

"Charles Pratt." Carrie's voice was low, but his head jerked around, surprised.

"She was your wife. But also my daughter. And you will allow her proper respect. I insist."

"I don't want her dead," he cried out.

Carrie covered her face with her hands. Then she got up and hugged his head to her body. "Nor do I, Charles, nor do I."

After a few minutes Ida pointedly set the vial of pills on the table. "Take these, go lay down on the boy's bed," she said to Charles. "You're spent. You ain't slept in a bed since the beginning a'this. G'on now." She nodded at him.

He picked up the pills and set them down.

"G'on," she insisted. "It's over. Nothing you can do. Take'm."

"All right," he said finally. He went up the stairs.

"And you too." Ida continued. "G'on back in there." She pointed to the front room.

"You need some help."

"No I don't. Rather be alone. Miz Amy, bless her, weighs nothing. Just g'on, please."

"I won't sleep."

"Rest then. Better I do this alone."

She shooed them.

"And you, boy. I got a chore for you, first. Sam put a wide board up on the porch for me. Bring that in here. And I need that jar of turpentine too. I got 'nuf water, I believe."

He knew what the board was for. Ida intended to lay his mother out on it. That the board had been brought to the porch in anticipation gave him an eerie feeling. Although they had known it would be needed.

But why turpentine? He didn't want to know.

"You go over there, lay down in my bed, boy." Ida pointed across the kitchen to the mattress dragged into a corner. "I'll handle the rest."

Evan lay down, but watched the black woman as she carried two ladder-back chairs into the bedroom. Then she maneuvered the unwieldy board through the door, waving him back when he started to rise to help. She took in towels, sheets, the turpentine, water, a washpan. Finally she carried in the lamp, and shut the door. Except for a glow from the stove and under the door, Evan was in the dark. The house was silent. To Evan's mind it listened. There was little to hear except an occasional floorboard creaking. Evan had an awful desire to creep to the door to see what was happening in the other room. But a deeper fear held him to the bed. Ida seemed to be a priestess in an unfathomable ritual. He feared her powers. It was sacrilegious to spy on a ceremony.

Evan woke to a light tap. Emily stood by the bedroom door. Ida opened it to her, then shut it behind her. As yet there was no semblance of morning, but Evan felt it could not be far away. A stair creaked. His father put a kettle on.

"Dad."

"Son." It was an acknowledgment. No more. Charles prepared to shave. It would be his first shave in five days.

"Shall I go get Sam?" Evan ventured.

"I'll go at dawn." He combed his hair. Then he went in the bedroom. Evan went upstairs to dress.

A half-hour past sunrise Evan had fed the animals, Ida the children. Carrie and Emily kept watch. Evan heard the boat return and went to the dock. The men had a pine casket which straddled the gunwales. Sam held onto it as Charles ran the boat. Instead of coming alongside Charles had to nose under the dock. Sam wrestled the box upward while Evan pulled from his end. They carried it to the porch, where Carrie held the screen open. Her eyes looked somewhat startled. Sam could see she had equated it with the lumber she'd traveled with yesterday.

When Sam and Evan reached the bedroom they set the casket on the floor. Sam approached Amy's body on the cooling board and lowered his head, lips moving in a prayer. She looked waxy to Evan. Ida had combed her hair to cover the burns, and the dress, long-sleeved and high-necked, covered most of the other burns. The cooling board seemed a precarious perch for the corpse. Evan noticed Sam had also shaved this morning. A nick on his cheek had barely stopped bleeding. Ida touched Evan's back and guided him out. Sam came out ten minutes later, carrying the board. Evan opened the screen for him and watched as Sam set it by some other lumber. It looked like any other board in the stack. Then Sam took a shovel and went up the hill.

"Evan."

He turned. Grandmother Stanhope had ushered everyone into the bedroom but him. He could hear the girls snuffling as they saw their mother.

By mid-morning they were prepared for the burial. A sledge Charles used to haul heavy things over the sand had been brought around for the casket. Charles insisted on nailing the coffin shut. The family waited outside. It took a half-hour before the first hammer-blow sounded in the house.

Sam and Charles pulled the sledge as the rest followed behind it. At the grave site, after each person had approached the coffin and prayers had again been said, Sam and Charles lowered the casket. Sam filled and covered the hole at the ridge crest. Continuing the control he'd displayed all day, Charles asked to be alone, and everyone returned to the house.

Evan did not go in. He leaned against the wall, feeling exhausted. Twelve hours ago she still lived. Now she was buried. Too short a time. He felt there should be black horses with feathered plumes, music played slowly in cathedrals, crepe billowing from the house and trees. This seemed hardly more momentous than burying a dead chicken. He felt cheated for her sake. The sun shone and a light breeze moved. No thunder and lightning stabbed the ground. Just another quiet summer day, like thousands of others. The day she died.

Sam came outside. He sat beside the boy. "Do you feel like going out to the fish-house now, or shall I bring the boat back later?"

Evan focused on him.

"Never mind, son. Later." Sam took the powerboat back to the fish-house.

That afternoon it returned without Sam. Captain Murdock had come to proffer his sympathies. He brought Jim as well. Charles hadn't returned from the ridge, so the captain went to him.

Emily asked Ida Jewel, "What about you? Do you want to get back today? I know you have other things to . . ."

"I'll wait till next trip, Miz Emily." She smiled at her son. "Jim can git along, and I know you can, but you need to get your breath here first."

"If you're sure, Ida?" Carrie smiled at her. "You're invaluable, as you know. But we could manage if you need to go."

Jim spoke up. "It's Saturday. We'd be bringing you back Tuesday then, Momma."

"That's fine. You tell Lily Anne I be back Tuesday night, son."

Charles and the captain came in. Murdock appeared to have lost an argument.

"I'm going out to the fish-house," Charles said, "let Sam get to town and home like he'd planned. I ain't staying here. We can talk later. Not now. Evan, you come so's you can bring the boat back and I'll keep the rowboat." He looked at the women.

"You just hafta understand I'm not gonna stay here or talk right now. I'll come back tomorrow or Monday night." As he made his speech Charles put some clothes in a towel and wrapped it in a bundle. He hurried out the door.

The captain looked at the three women. He shook his head. "Give him the room. He needs it right now. But I wouldn't let him get too alone. I'm worried about him, but he won't be ready to listen to anyone for awhile."

Charles returned Monday night. It was late enough in the evening that Emily had begun to think he would not come at all.

Katie had helped the women through the weekend, as they'd cleaned house. It seemed a necessary ritual, not so much to lay ghosts as to tire themselves and allow their bodies to rest at night. They waited to hear what Charles had in mind.

He wanted the women to take the children, to go to Michigan with all of them. The girls objected, Evan said no. Emily offered to stay at the house. Both Charles and his mother-in-law objected to that.

"I love my children. But I will not stay here in the house. I can't mother them and support them both. It isn't possible to stay in this place right now without seeing her. I need space. They need mothering, not neglect. I'll send money. But I can't take care of a baby or little ones. It's best for them."

"I'm staying." Evan had spoken.

"You're going, just like your mama'd planned."

"That was before. Somebody's gotta be here with you."

"I can do without a kid nurse-maiding me." Charles looked bad. His stubble had resurfaced. He'd been sleeping in his clothes. "I don't want them here," he emphasized to the women. The protests continued. Finally Charles jumped up and left. Evan followed him to the door.

"He went up the path," he reported.

Charles didn't return. The boat was still tied up a couple of hours later. The next time someone looked it had gone.

Evan took Ida to the fish-house the next day. It had been especially difficult for Katie to say bye to her—she hugged her several times. Those weren't the only hugs. Everyone in the family knew Ida had kept them from collapse.

Evan stayed with Ida Jewel until the run boat arrived from the south, but his father avoided him by simply walking away whenever approached. Evan felt like he'd lost both his parents, as though he'd been orphaned. He determined to talk to his father.

After saying a reluctant goodbye to Ida, Evan went to the office to try to talk to his father again. The door was shut. He knocked. His father ignored it. So he turned the door knob and pushed to open it. Charles had barred the door.

"Dad! Daddy?"

"Go home, Evan. Just go."

"Please, Dad . . ."

Charles crashed against the door, slamming the crack shut. Evan gasped, startled, then waited. Nothing happened. He knocked again. He was answered by something thrown at the door. He gave up and went back to the island, crying.

Instead of going in the house he walked to the ridge, visiting her grave. The breeze and showers had so nearly repaired the sugar sand that after three days it was difficult to see the precise location of the grave except for the whelk shells the children had laid along its margin. He looked at the other markers. He would carve her marker himself—use that cooling board. He couldn't imagine using it for ordinary lumber. He would start that tonight.

The tide was high. Sea oats rustled. Tonight the moon would be nearly full. Evan turned right at the path intersection, heading for the beach.

***

He walked north to the pass and back but that had been the wrong direction. Too short. He wasn't yet walked out. So he kept on, walking in the surf line and watching the coquinas exposed by the wash re-bury themselves. The island stretched south for three miles. He seldom went that far. Perhaps he would today.

The sun was high and hot on his right cheek. It would shine in his eyes when he returned. There was little to see save gulls, but he wasn't looking anyway. He marched straight-line from one horizon-cape to the next as the island curved slowly eastward. Sometimes he marched on wet sand, sometimes dry. Sometimes in the water foaming around his bare feet. When he came to a downed tree he stepped over it. It was all the same to him.

Clumps of seaweed wrack cluttered the beach. He stepped over those as well, if they happened to be in his way. Once he detoured around a long-dead jewfish that gulls flapped over. Buzzards waddled around it. Other fish, eyeless, littered the beach occasionally, as though waiting their turn with the scavenger birds.

He walked on. He was getting tired. He must be almost to the south pass. He'd rest there before coming back. He sneezed, and wiped his nose, realizing he'd been crying again without knowing it. He stopped while he wiped his eyes.

The wash edged at a mullet. Another dead fish. Everything seemed dead. He remembered his mother pointing out that you find what you look for on the beach. Walk the beach to look for scallops while someone else looks for fighting conchs. Both of you will walk over the same stretch of sand and see only what each person is specifically looking for. It seemed crazy, but he had tried it time and again. That was the way it worked. Now, Mama, he thought, I'm finding dead things. What does that say, Mama?

Abruptly he started walking again. More gulls circled in the distance. And buzzards too. Something big. Certainly not another jewfish? He slowly grew closer. Not a fish. But what? The sun gilded it, hiding its shape from Evan's eyes.

Finally he stood over it, sick at heart. This sea thing had not washed ashore dead. It came to give life and had been murdered. Evan looked down at the remains of a loggerhead turtle. Her shell was crushed and shattered, the head lolled in the wash, attached by a few inches of skin. But why? She hadn't been butchered, taken for meat. No need to kill her for the eggs. She had been attacked—but who could fear a lumbering turtle? It was insane.

He could see the tracks the turtle'd made to and from her nest. She'd been returning to the sea when this happened. He followed the track toward the nest and saw the jumble in the sand where the struggle had taken place. Indistinct footprints.

Something glinted, nearly buried. When he uncovered it, his breath caught in his throat. He stared at his father's belt knife. It was stained . . . with turtle blood? Evan had seen it on Charles' belt last night. He looked over at the turtle again, and up to its nest area. He went back to the shattered turtle. Only then did Evan see the old wound—the double bite carved from its shell.

He remembered his father telling Emily and himself that that was Amy's turtle, first of the season. Amy's lucky turtle. He shuddered. In his mind he could see his dad walking down this night beach and seeing the turtle start off its nest. After depositing its eggs, it headed seaward once more. Evan could feel the anger, the rage, that the turtle should endure while his mother lay buried like those eggs. But buried without hope of re-emergence. He felt the knife blows raining on this turtle that dared to continue its life, felt his father snap and kill, felt him run back down the beach in horror.

As Evan ran.

After two weeks they gave in. All but Evan. He insisted on staying with Charles, and the women found it hard to argue watching the wreck the man had become. Charles refused all comfort or talk. But Evan was adamant. Maybe once it was only the two of them, once time passed, it would be easier. Certainly Charles couldn't be left alone. Evan's Grandmother objected most strenuously—Evan was only eleven. He should not be taking charge of his own father. But the practical necessity of it finally won her over. Telegrams were dispatched by the captain, and the day came when they left the island to father and son.

***

The trip to Punta Gorda was rough. The weather was squally, the water choppy. The children were as upset as the weather. Emily and her mother had their hands full.

At one point the captain came to Emily. "Have you seen something like this before?"

She looked out on the sound. They rode through a floating mass of dead fish, silvery on maroon-colored water. The smell stung her nose and eyes.

"What is it?"

"Red tide. This's a bad patch. I've seen other spots the last couple of weeks, but mostly in the Gulf. Seems to be spreading."

They looked at the acres of fish. Most of the floating fish were small.

"This is awful. I'd heard of it but never saw it."

"It happens mostly in summer or fall, when you'd be gone. This is early for it."

"Bad for business."

"It could be. But fish will avoid it. See how we're running out of the patch now?" The water gradually changed color, and the skin of fish floated behind them. "Long as it doesn't blanket the whole area it will be OK. Most of the fish can escape it. The shellfish though, that's a different story. Don't go eating any clams or oysters now. They can't duck this stuff."

"Would it hurt us?"

"It could make you sick, eating them. The smell of red tide alone can make you sick, if it's bad enough. I wouldn't go swimming in it. But no, mostly it makes you sneeze and cough."

"I wouldn't swim in dead fish, you can be sure!"

He laughed. "Old timers claim it cleans out the area every few years. Makes banner crabbing—they have a feast."

"You've just put me off crabs for good!"

"It's nasty while it lasts. No fun if a batch concentrates around a fish-house. Hard to breathe. But most creatures just leave till it's over. Including people, it gets that bad."

"I hope it goes away. I don't see any value to it."

"Be hard to, I agree. Unless you're a crab." He laughed as she made a face and went back to the family. He realized he would regret leaving them at the hotel tonight. Even though he'd see Emily in the fall, when she returned to teach in Florida. If she returned. As soon as he thought that little word, he erased it from his thoughts.

21

August had ended. The rain of early summer had diminished to humidity and heat. They met an occasional violent thunderstorm on the run, but most of the coast they traveled through baked under shimmering humid airless days. The smell of dead and decaying fish hung ominously like a rainless cloud and permeated their clothing and food. The meals they ate, the water they drank, the tobacco Captain Murdock smoked, all had been flavored by that pungent spice. They ate little, drank while willing themselves not to taste the liquid, and in the worst-hit parts of their run, squeezed their streaming eyes to slits against the breeze. Bill said his eyes felt like he had rubbed them with cut onions. The red tide moved farther up into the creeks and rivers on the flood-tide as fresh water outflow declined. Leaves looked dejected and hang-dog on the trees. Their shade looked promising only from the distance. Close to, the mangroves' humid darkness was crowded with sand flies and mosquitoes delighted to welcome a warm body.

Flies abounded. They persisted in lighting on the men's faces. The men slapped them away vigorously as they visualized the flies maggotizing the dead fish that hung moon-tide-high in the mangrove roots. Every drop of sweat rolling down their face felt like a fat crawling maggot. The water, where it was free from red tide, remained unappetizing. Warmer than horse piss, to quote the sour Jake at Bull Bay. He didn't exaggerate either, thought the captain. The men, short-tempered, seldom spoke except for necessary commands.

September promised no relief. Jim watched the barometer religiously. But no hurricanes loomed. Murdock would almost welcome one, if only to blow this miserable weather away.

He heard thunder rumbling over the Gulf. It sounded as irritated and short-tempered as he felt. The squall it heralded was nearly hidden in the hazy whiteness of the sky. No magnificent storm would swell from that. Any disturbance from such a sky would be as petty and vicious as a kicked dog, and as dangerous. But not cleansing, not glorious, not refreshing. It would leave the land still thirsty, even if the rain ran in torrents. He sighed and wiped his face once more with the rag he had hung around his neck. It had been saturated for the past hour with his mopped sweat.

Last night in the islands, he had spent his worst night ever aboard this boat. Maybe that's part of the trouble, he thought—needing sleep. The temperature had never dropped. It was eighty-five degrees at midnight. No storms approached, but sullen lightning flickered much of the night. If a storm had gotten closer, it might have stirred some small amount of clean air.

Instead the heat lay motionless on the water. Biting night fliers were at their peak. At least he hoped that was their peak. He doubted they could crowd many more insects into the same square inch. It must be their peak.

Sand flies could drive a man insane. The captain was sure of that. One on one, a mosquito or deerfly produced more pain, but the blanket of sand flies was infinite and impossible to get away from. They thickened his eyelashes, climbed down the strands of his hair like monkeys shinnying down coconut palms, and tortured with a burning itch that did not stop when he smashed the life out of them. They became trapped in the sheen of sweat on a suffering man. The pain they inflicted radiated like flames from burning matches dipped to oil.

At the first brush with them, he would resolve not to allow such an insignificant thing defeat him. But only a moment or so of the onslaught would make him turn tail and run for whatever cover he could find. He breathed them, feeling them in his throat, burning his nose. They fell on his clothing in showers. The worst was that they kept coming. The only escape was to roll up in blankets, and still millions nestled in with him. Every one had to have its blood feeding before it would calm. For hours after his skin would burn from the bites. Temperatures inside the blanket were sufficient to cook bread. The heat exhaustion could kill.

He would rub the intolerable stings, often tugging an opening in the blanket. He would feel the delicious cool piercing air, which instantly filled with the flying sparks of pain. They penetrated mosquito netting as though it were gill netting. In the morning the floor was dusted black with the multitude of bodies, and even at midday he could stir some quiet corner and dislodge dozens which would vent their displeasure with bites of reprimand.

Murdock had heard that the Indians covered themselves with mud to protect against the bugs. If he'd been in easy reach of it, he would have been tempted to try that remedy. He suspected though, that the sand flies were the mud. That mud was their daylight camouflage.

The sand flies were fierce, the night hot and still, the smell of red tide strong in the air. Sleep had been impossible. And the mosquitoes! The stories of mosquitoes bleeding a calf dry overnight were not tall tales to him, or to anyone in the swampy Everglades sloughs and prairies overnight. No exaggeration exceeded that reality.

Mullet and redfish were thick, if the expanding pods of red tide could be avoided. It promised to be a banner year for the company, which loaded five refrigerator boxcars of iced fish from three run boats last week. All the fishhouses were busy. Even Charles Pratt had little time to think about his tragedy. Not that, the captain thought, he was thinking any more. Pratt moved and worked as needed, but it seemed no one existed behind his likeness. The boy had tried coaxing him to the house without success. Then Evan moved to the fish-house to sleep, going to the island to care for his animals and chickens, and to tend a garden planted by his mother. Charles didn't seem to notice what the boy did, or see the lean and haunted look he wore. Perhaps because it mirrored the father's. Murdock sensed no communication had occurred between them.

The boy wrote to Michigan regularly. Letters had come to Charles at first, but had been ignored. Now they were addressed to Evan. Before it had gotten so busy the captain took Evan on the boat overnight, to show him the route. They had both enjoyed it. Evan had talked some, telling Murdock about the mutilated turtle, and about the marker he'd carved, which had been ripped out of the ground and thrown to the beach. Evan returned it. Charles had not disturbed it again, or ever mentioned it.

Captain Murdock looked grim when he heard. The situation wasn't one for a boy, not even a level-headed one. When winter came, Evan would go to school. Perhaps he could persevere until then. It wouldn't be easy. But growing up too young was common on this edge of civilization.

George's stop was in sight. The captain would be glad when this day was done. He felt as wrung out as the rag he had hung around his neck.

The open water around George's fish-house had so far remained clear of the red tide. Fishhawk Bay, and even the little "Moonshine Bayou", had also remained clear. Murdock remarked on it as the two men did paper-work.

George replied, "There's a good reason. Sam'n me, we're upright, clean-livin' righteous folk. When you lead a proper life, well then . . ." He trailed off his sentence, grinning elfishly at the captain's snort.

"Speaking of clean living. That righteous moonshiner neighbor of yours bring anything for me yet?"

"H'ain't seen him for a couple of days. Which means he's cooking, sleeping, or dead."

"He's likely to be the last, he doesn't get to me soon!" He sniffed the pungent air. "Don't know how you'd ever get a clue if he'd croaked, the way this tide stinks."

"Want some coffee?"

"Hell, no. You changing the subject?"

"Ice it, you like it that way? Or I got a half-case of Coke." George continued as if the captain had not spoken.

He shook his head in defeat. "Y'know, I think I'll take you up on that pop. Don't usually like it, but sounds good today."

George smiled. "Since Sam's product's lost in shipment?"

"Ha. It's hot as the hinges out there, George. Also smelly and noisy as hell I reckon," he continued as both men started at a flash of lightning and its near-simultaneous thunderclap. "We like to got carried away last night. Now these little storms carrying on around us. When I get home tonight I'm gonna eat, take an hour's soak in my tub, drink a pint of something hard, and sleep until tomorrow afternoon. The rest of the world can go hang."

"It Saturday already?"

"Damn right it is, and none too soon." He finished with the receipts just as Sam appeared in the doorway. "Sure hope you brought more'n your ugly face, Sam!"

"Brought some nice fat reds for you, Cap." Sam turned to George. "Can we weigh them in right quick?"

George went out, followed by the other two. Sam climbed down into his skiff and then guided the iron basket to the skiff's center. He threw the reds in, nearly filling the basket. George cranked it to the dock via the A-frame tripod, and weighed in the fish. He went back to the office, shouting at Jim to take those "sorry reds of Sam's" so they wouldn't smell up his fishhouse. He left the other two smiling.

"You looking for this, Cap?" Sam lifted his burlap sack toward Murdock, who hefted it with a grin.

"Only good thing happened all day, Sam."

"Don't feature running north this afternoon." Sam nodded toward the slate-colored sky.

"Probably lose Jim pretty quick."

Sam nodded.

"How's it going at the Pratt's?"

"They're both quiet. Think the boy's about worn out."

"Suggest him coming here for a visit. I'm thinking about going hunting soon. Maybe he'd like that. He could sure as hell stand looking at something else 'sides Pratt's gloomy face a while."

"That sounds fine. When should I say?"

"Time doesn't matter. Ain't the hunting—just the getting away. If he comes next pass that's fine. Not for a couple weeks. Just as fine."

"Sam, I wouldn't be surprised that's just what that boy needs. Great idea."

George brought the final receipt to the captain, and the run boat headed out again.

The clouds were thick ahead, but Murdock felt perkier than he had all day. He suddenly realized he'd never gotten that pop George'd offered. "Helluva note," he muttered out loud, smiling. He knew it wasn't just the thought of having the sack-full of shine that brightened his day. He had been worried about that Pratt kid. Evan would enjoy a hike in the 'Glades.

They had managed to miss the worst of the storms shifting around them. As the captain had suspected, Evan's face lit up at the prospect of a hunting trip. Charles even seemed to be pleased by the idea, though he quickly refused when Evan suggested he come along too. He emphatically said no when they persisted. They set a time in two weeks, so Sam wouldn't feel rushed. Charles ordered some shells from town, so Evan would have a shotgun, and Evan left before the run boat did, eager to bring the guns from the house for cleaning and to choose the right one for the hunt. The captain left there with his fingers mentally crossed.

Before long it was obvious they couldn't avoid stormy weather before reaching town. The skyline to the north was solidly black and thunder became louder and heavier in the background. They had been picking their way up the channel, hoping to reach deep water before the storm broke over them. The run boat was still in a tricky, shallow section of the bay when they had to heave to for the duration. The boat, more than two-thirds full with fish, ran deep. Visibility barely extended the length of the boat. Progress was impossible. Hail mixed with the torrents of rain. Although wind gusted and pushed at the superstructure, the anchor held. The men donned their oilskins to protect against the sting of the deluge. Lightning struck the water directly ahead, searing their eyeballs with its wide afterimage. Seconds later, it struck again, in the same spot. The captain counted eight strikes, all shaped alike and in the same place. Other, more distant strikes, were diffused by the rain's filter to constant flickering counterpoints. The choppy water chattered at the hull. From time to time the inundation would lift in one direction or another, like a dancer's whirling skirts, to allow a brief glimpse of a dark island or shore floating between sea and sky.

Jim had frozen during the repeated lightning bolts. When he moved it was to disappear into the engine room.

At the height of the storm the captain noticed a small dragonfly which clung to the lee side of the wheelhouse. It hung on gamely while gusts of wind fluttered and tore at its wings. When he looked again it was gone, blown away to fall into the water exhausted.

In a quarter hour the determined storm had eased enough that Murdock could track the boat swing by watching the smudge of the nearest island. The bay surface close to the island had frothed to the same ashy color as the sky. Nearer to the boat it darkened to almost the same steel grey as the island. Waves raged with foaming crests and darker troughs. The island seemed to hover above the horizon line, an illusion compounded by the storm hiding most of the island with streamers of rain.

An oyster bank suddenly loomed as the boat swung. They had obviously been missing it each swing by no more than twenty feet. The anchor need not slip much to pound the hull on those knife-like clusters. The current pushed the boat toward the bar. They would have to power away just right to avoid being pushed into those muddy oysters, and to stay in the narrow twisting channel while the wind and current tried to force them in different directions. When the rain had settled to a steady downpour, the captain looked in the engine room.

"Bill, Jim, I'm gonna need you both for lookouts. We got a good chance to break this tub open and scatter dead fish here to China." He peered into the darkness.

"Say when for the power, Cap. Jim, you with us?"

A corner stirred finally. "'Zit over?" Jim's voice was pitched higher than normal.

"Just lots of rain now, lightning's moved off."

"You sure, Cap'n?"

"I wouldn't lie about it, Jim. I think it's OK now. C'mon up." He stepped back from the entry. "Power up Bill. Let's get outta here."

While the men stood lookout, Captain Murdock ran the boat up to the anchor while Jim cranked it aboard as fast as he got slack. When it let go of the bottom, the boat revved forward, turning into the channel while fighting slippage back against the bar. Murdock thought he felt the side graze the oysters as the boat gained momentum. Bill signaled OK from his lookout, and then stuck his head in the wheelhouse to say, "Nearly on, Captain. We didn't have any spare."

"Good thing there wasn't one more oyster out there. At least it's not so dark ahead now. Guess we've seen the worst for today."

"Hope so—I know Jim does!" Bill laughed as he bent into the rain, heading back to his engine room.

22

Evan had everything he needed in the boat for his trip with Sam. He had fed the chickens and gathered eggs. Lightning, the dog, would go with him. He had fed the cat and pigs earlier, and his father had promised to take care of the animals while Evan was away. That reassured Evan, because he knew his father's word was good. Charles seldom came to the island, but Evan knew he would honor a promise to care for the livestock.

Evan then walked to the graves, followed by the dog. That trip had become almost a ritual the past two months. Later he went into the quiet house. It would be a couple of weeks before he returned to the place. Since he started sleeping at the fish-house the little house had an unused feel. Dust had appeared, settling lightly on floors, stairs, and furniture. The mantle clock had stopped. He had not thought to wind it. He peered into the various rooms and the loft, simply because he had not checked them for weeks. The utter stillness of each room, unchanged since he'd last looked in them, was unpleasant. The house had died.

He hesitated before going into his parents' bedroom, although he knew his grandmother and aunt had left it as neat and tidy as the other rooms. Nothing trumpeted that his mother had died on that smoothly-made bed. Her rocker, slightly dusty, sat quietly by the windows.

The kitchen was the only room that felt at all alive, though no wood had been burned in the stove since the family went to Michigan. The wood basket was full. So was the water bucket. When Evan looked at its surface, dust-scummed and moving with mosquito larvae, he hurriedly dumped it outside. The essential kitchen equipment had gradually travelled to the fish-house, and little remained here.

He sat at the table, letting his eyes go around the room. After a minute he sighed and got up, ready to leave. His hand slid wetly along the table. He realized with disgust that the dust was actually green mold.

A washpan on the porch still contained a bar of lye soap. He wet a rag, soaped it, and scrubbed the tabletop clean, hoping that would prevent the mold from growing again. He went upstairs and slightly cracked open his bedroom window. His Mama had frequently done the same thing, telling him it made a chimney out of the house. He didn't understand what that meant, but it did clear the smoke out of the kitchen if something had burned. He felt the draft when he came back to the kitchen.

"C'mon Lightning, let's go!" he called to the yellow dog. "In the boat, boy. Lie down, now." As he left the little harbor some red-tide-smothered mullet bobbed in his wake.

Every day the red tide became more wide-spread. Fish catches had declined markedly in the last week and prospects for improving seemed gloomy. The discolored water, with cork-like dead fish bobbing in much of it, had spread. The peppery smell travelled inland and upriver as sea winds persisted, keeping the usual afternoon storms bottled up well inland. Two fishhouses in the Ten Thousand Islands had shut down to await better times. Fishermen had left and the men running the fishhouses saw no reason to bear the stink, so they went to Naples for the duration. When Jake heard that, he nodded and said, "She'll get worse, you know. Before it clears. Might be the run boat'll shut down altogether a while."

"You think it'll get that far?"

"Could. Has before. It's a plague, like. You remember the locusts in the Bible?"

Captain Murdock nodded.

"Well. Oncet they ate all the greens, they moved on. This red tide, it's worsen that. Cuz it's not eating, just destroying. It can kill ever'thing in the water, but once it's all dead, it still hangs on. It don't always leave. It can hang on all summer, it has a mind to."

"That's sure an encouraging thought, Jake."

"Oh, it'll leave finally. Wind break it up, hurricane, or cold weather. Eventually. But it's beyond me why she starts OR why she stops." He seemed to take much satisfaction in that pronouncement.

"If it hangs on for long it'd be a disaster."

"Yes and no. While she's here it is. But next season, fish'd be back. They move back in once the water's clean. Would take longer for the oysters and clams than the fish. They'd hafta start from babies."

"Yeah. Well I've never seen such a big outbreak before. This one's plenty too big for me already."

"No argument with that. Nothing you can do, either." I watch this stuff here, and it seems like ever' tide change it thickens. No fresh sea water or rain slopping in to thin it out. The water keeps on evaporating in the sun and we just get worse 'n' worse."

"It's off shore far as I can see, all the way down the coast, Jake."

"Yep. Hafta be. And that don't omen well, Captain."

"I guess you're right, Jake."

By the time the *Jeanette* reached the Pratt place, Jim had tied a kerchief over his mouth and nose to attempt to filter the smell. His eyes and nose were running, and he sneezed constantly. The red tide had become the major topic of conversation at every stop. Except with Evan. He was too full of his upcoming adventure.

"You'll go over to feed the animals?" Evan worried at his father.

"Said I'd take care of them, boy. Now stop acting like you're my father!"

Evan colored, but smiled too. "I left a couple windows cracked open so the air'd move in the house."

Charles said nothing to that. Murdock's impression was that Charles had no intention of going to the house. He'd care for those animals. The house, though, was no longer a part of his world.

Evan got his things settled on board, and called the dog. Lightning wasn't interested in boarding. He didn't like the vibration underfoot from the heavy-duty engine. Evan tied the dog to the rail, and left him to whine piteously.

"I'm gonna miss you, Dad. Sure would like you to come."

Charles looked at his eldest child. "You have a fine time tramping around with Sam. He'll show you a lot of things. I'm just not ready for it."

"I don't want you to be alone."

"Captain here'll be by every day. I can take care of myself. Really, Evan!" He slapped his boy's bottom and said. "G'on now, Captain's ready to leave. Can't be holding him up."

Evan started aboard, then turned back to give Charles a blind, fierce hug before he jumped back on board. He watched the fish-house recede as they eased toward the main channel. Charles continued to stand on the deck, hand raised in farewell. He looked very small.

Evan went into the wheelhouse with Captain Murdock. They ran south off-shore of a long sandy beach. The day was bright and hot, and the boat provided its own breeze, heavy with its odors. If you squinted just right, the red tide and dead fish disappeared, and it was lovely.

Lightning had finally resigned himself to being on the boat. Perhaps looking at the water convinced him, perhaps the vibration of the working engine was more comfortable then when it idled at the dock.

Evan watched the island pass. "Almost there," he smiled at the captain.

"You remember, huh?"

"Yup."

"Must be age."

"What?"

"You remembering after one pass. I went right on by it awhile back. Never even knew it."

"In a storm."

"No. Day was pretty as today. Jim had to come tell me."

Evan's look was incredulous.

"Honestly. You ask him—he'd be delighted to laugh at my expense."

"How'd you do that?"

"Just daydreaming. It'll happen before you know it." He hesitated. "Something to keep in mind out there in the woods."

Evan laughed.

"I'm serious now, boy. You be sure you keep track of where you are. Sam's a good woodsman. But he could lose you, or get hurt too. So you pay attention right from the start. Where you are and what Sam does. That's the way you learn."

"Yes, sir."

"OK, OK, lecture over." The *Jeanette* turned into the pass. Evan went out and knelt with the dog to concentrate on the fish-house approach. He had watched the boat close in on their dock hundreds of times without ever tiring of the grace with which the two structures, floating and fixed, came together.

The process was less familiar, but more illuminating from the boat. As the captain eased forward or reversed, Evan felt each shift kick within the deck and heard the whine as the prop reversed. He could feel the current pushing them toward the fish-house, and realized that Captain Murdock had maneuvered the boat to press against that current almost as hard as the water pushed against the boat. The net effect settled the run boat against the fish-house as lightly as a leaf floating onto his porch.

Evan was profoundly impressed. A boat captain was someone other men looked up to. But it had never looked like a hard job. Well, maybe in bad weather . . . but help was on board. In the feel of the boat's docking movements, though, Evan had a sense of the overlapping judgments and decisions that went into what looked so effortless. He had no doubt that a different tide or breeze would be accounted for just as easily. The respect the captain received evolved because of what he knew and did. For Evan that regard rose as he realized what the captain accomplished was hidden to ordinary view. Evan looked toward the wheelhouse with a delighted smile. Murdock smiled back, and saluted the boy. No one seemed to notice how extraordinary the docking had been. But Evan guessed that was the point. Jim disappeared into his fish room. George and the captain exchanged a few words and walked to the office. Evan untied Lightning, who immediately leaped onto the deck, relieved to be free of the monster boat. He carted his belongings over while Jim set up to hoist ice blocks to the fish-house.

Evan now saw that Jim, the captain, and Bill were parts of a whole. They relied on each other to carry out separate pieces of the same overall job. Jim's hardest work was at dockside, the captain's at sea. Captain Murdock's was mental, Jim's physical. Bill's job combined both. The skipper was the brain, Jim the legs, and Bill the guts of the boat. They needed each other and weren't whole unless all three worked together. A team.

Evan realized in that moment how Charles had been torn out of his world by Amy's suffering and tragic death. Her death was not just a wound for him, but a dismemberment. They had been a smooth-working team just as the men on the boat were: Charles, the body, and Amy the heart. The insight was frightening. Evan had an impulse to hurry back home. Yet he knew he couldn't help Charles any more than Charles had been able to help Amy.

George was in his office out of the sun. Lightning immediately sat under the old man's damaged hand, hinting at his desire to be petted. He was obliged.

"Looks like this pup's grown into a fine dog," George said. "What's his name?"

"Yessir, he has. Lightning, his name is."

"Lightning, huh." The dog moved when he heard his name, moving his body under the man's temporarily stilled hand. "That mean he's fast?"

Evan laughed. "Least getting to the food, he is."

"No fool then."

"Yes, sir."

"Sam's dog's his brother, you know."

"I didn't."

"Yup. Good dog for hunting. 'Spec' Lightning here'll enjoy a ramble in the woods too. They look like twins, the dogs."

Evan's face twitched. "Oh, yeah?" he said.

George could have kicked himself. Not thinking, he thought to himself. *I gotta yap about twins right away. Senile old bastard.* "You going off to school this winter I understand." He awkwardly changed the subject. But Evan wasn't too interested in that gambit, so after a few more words they fell silent.

"Sam'll be here anytime. He had some business to clear up first." Sam was cleaning his still, but George wasn't going to advertise that to the kid, even if Evan knew Sam made shine. The still was an intensely private thing for Sam. He and George had been neighbors, and more importantly, friends for over fifteen years. They had fished together all over the back bays. But Sam had never taken George to his still.

George had a shrewd guess as to its general location. If he had to find it—say Sam had gotten hurt—he probably could. And Sam was aware of that. But he would never look for it, or ask, unless that necessary time should come. He doubted it ever would. Sam was young and strong, unlike George.

Lightning tensed under his hand. "He heard the boat," George said. The mosquito-ey whine became more evident. A few minutes later Sam threw Evan his line.

"Pass down your stuff boy. Might as well get going." As Evan went for his things, Sam passed two heavy sacks up to George.

Sam continued, "Think I timed this trip just right. Damn tide's up through the whole bay. Fish are starting to stink good. Inland's where I want to be!"

"Captain said he never ran out of it coming down," George replied.

"Don't you set here in this stuff, it gets too thick. Ride on up to Punta Gorda."

"I might at that. I get to breathing hard in it," George promised.

"I'm taking the dog. Cat'll have a feast on the beach, and the chickens too. So just go, don't fool around. Leave me a note here. OK?"

"I will, Sam, if it gets any worse."

Evan came back and passed down his things.

"Ready or not, kid, let's do it!" Sam grinned at him.

Lightning yipped once getting into the skiff, but he'd travelled in small boats enough times. He soon settled as the boat headed for Sam's place.

***

Of the children, Katie had had the worst time adjusting to Michigan. But even she soon acclimated. Aunt Emily, Nana, and Rosa, Nana's housekeeper, all seemed to have either activities or chores on tap, and meeting the dozens of children in her neighborhood also kept her busy. Two girls who lived nearby were particular friends now. Being with others her own age was new to her. Michigan was such a different world. The funny thing was that these new friends seemed to feel she was the one who had led an exotic life.

School had started for both Kate and Nell. Kate thought it was strange that although Evan had planned to attend school they had started first. Her teacher had been uncertain at first of Kate's abilities, but as Aunt Emily predicted, a couple of reading and spelling sessions had convinced her that

Kate belonged with her peers, notwithstanding the lack of previous formal schooling.

It had begun to seem to her like Florida was a dream—a movie on a distant screen. She missed her parents' presence, and especially felt lost without Evan around. But so much happened here that thinking about Mama and Florida got limited to the time she went to bed before she fell asleep. She had distractions all around her—school and friends, shopping for warm winter clothing, watching the color-filled leaves change.

Like the day the family made a trip to Lake Michigan. They had built a roaring fire on the beach and stayed late watching the crackling flames. The water, even in August, was too cold for them to swim in, as used to the warm Gulf as they were. So they spent most of their day chasing each other up the amazing mountains of sand, and rolling and sliding down the dunes.

When she helped collect some driftwood for the fire, Kate found some interestingly-marked and colored pebbles, and they spent time gathering them as though they were seashells on the beach at home. Kate and Nell built a castle studded with the stones. Even though the water looked like the ocean, rolling past the horizon, the lake couldn't destroy their castle with a high tide overnight. Eventually the wind or rain might level it, but the structure would stay a while. Kate found that comforting.

23

Sam shook Evan awake hours before sunrise. Evan leaped up, and before long the man and boy had loaded the skiff. When Sam started the engine, Evan crowded into the bow with the dogs. The noses of all three pointed eagerly forward.

Evan found it exciting to move through the moon-dark bays. The stars seemed like drops of water glowing on the sky surface—brilliant but diffused spots of light in the humid windless darkness. White-bellied dead fish shone in similar water constellations, but the boat wake rocked their patterns so that fish twinkled in a way stars failed to do.

Sam turned south after reaching the bay at Carlos Pass. Evan could easily see the pass, defined by the blacker fingers of the islands to either side. George's distant fish-house was another dark shape on the water.

With the exception of the boat's wake rolling white behind them and the constant buzz of the motor, the world remained still and silent. Evan burrowed down, only his eyes above the gunwale, warming himself with the dogs' bodies. The damp pre-dawn air chilled him as it flowed over the boat. The water sang by his ears in a long one-note lullaby, sh-h-h. As his body warmed, his eyes threatened to close. He had to force himself to stay awake.

The number of small islands and keys increased. Ahead of the boat the sooty line of land seemed to detach islets which floated past them like black clouds wind-torn from a storm. Where open water and sky had been separated by that narrow dark streak Evan saw its darkness gradually expand and blot out the lighter sea and sky. He had a sense of falling into a hole, a dizzy feeling that an immense shadow was surrounding and enveloping him. The skiff continued to press forward as the solid land dissolved around it. He felt a kinship with Alice, falling to her meeting with the March Hare.

The boat slowed. As Evan turned to look back at Sam he realized the sky to his left had begun a faint graying. Sam turned the boat toward the still-hidden sun, and a river opened through the mist of mangroves, a wide silvered swath pointing to the east.

By the time dawn had truly begun coloring the sky, leaving an iridescent reflection on the width of river, Evan could see that most of the red tide had been left behind them.

As the sun sent its first light downriver, directly into Evan's eyes, a big white egret lifted from a branch and slowly flapped across the skiff's bow, banking through the peach light to land in a shallow, reedy spot that promised him breakfast. The river breathed a cloud of rising dew, contained by the shrubby banks and stained by the sun's rise. The elegant bird passed through the color, touched by a tint of its glory. Beads of moisture gathered on both dogs' coats, and Evan saw how the fabric of his shirt softened and grew limp as it too absorbed the dampness.

He no longer could look ahead—the sun's glare was too fierce. Sam stood as they continued upriver, steering the boat when necessary with a nudge of his knee against the stick. Evan had to giggle—Sam stood waist-deep in mist. To a sleepy bird he must be quite a sight—half a man floating upstream against the current, while his lower half, including the skiff, Evan and the dogs, remained nearly invisible.

Many birds moved now, flying in lines toward their favorite feeding spots or poking in the mud of the river edge. They passed cabbage palms, a cluster of coconut palms near a clearing, mangroves, wax myrtle, and other bushes, both wild and cultivated. Sam spotted a guava that had dropped some early-ripened fruit on the ground, and stopped a moment to pick a few. A wide patch of reeds filled the north bank for several hundred feet. A mist hovered in the grasses—lighter than the river's blanket. As they passed Evan saw a little creek nearly smothered by the reeds that entered the river there.

Looking back behind Sam, Evan noticed that every tree and bird was sharply delineated by the low sun. Each brilliant green leaf, sun-painted, seemed crisp and fresh, each bird feather visible. As the sun climbed the mist sank and thinned under the weight of the day.

"The best part of the day, I believe."

Evan nodded. "Sure is beautiful."

"'Course, you catch me with a full-moon rise, or new-moon set, or storm building, I might say the same thing. We'll be going under the bridge shortly here."

Evan turned upriver again, eager to see. "Can I get out?"

"Sure, you want to. Nothing to look at but an ole wood bridge and a cow-path road, but you're welcome to it."

Soon he nosed the skiff into the bank just below the bridge. The dogs beat Evan ashore, scrambling up the marshy slope for a short run. Evan walked across the bridge and peered both ways. He couldn't see anything but grass and trees, and some indistinct tire-marks in the sand. He hung over the rail, looking down at Sam, who munched guavas as he relaxed in the bow.

"D'you know this river's real narrow on the other side of the bridge?"

"Yep. Been this way afore."

Evan colored. Of course he knew. Sam rinsed his hands in the river and wiped his mouth with a wet hand.

"There's a reason for that. You figger it out."

Evan frowned at him. "Does it get deep instead?"

Sam drew his mouth down in a pout of appreciation. "Not a bad idea. It might, some. Get's rocky, and the current moves faster."

"OK. I think I see. The river runs fast so it's narrow. So this side is slow so it's wide?"

"Partly so. But why wouldn't it still run fast? Same water. Why's it slow down here?"

"Flat?"

"Yeah, but it's pretty flat up there too. No mountains inland."

Evan was stumped. "Don't know."

"Think about where it goes."

"The river? To the bay."

"Right. And sometimes the bay's empty and the river water can run right in fast as she wants. But sometimes . . ."

Evan was grinning. ". . . sometimes she's full and the river's gotta wait. So it backs up!"

"You're getting the idea. River keeps running all the time, but it's easier to empty at low-tide. Past a certain point that tide can't affect the river-water anymore."

"And that's here!"

"Yep. Other side the bridge you can drink the water and be pretty sure it's always fresh, not salt mixed in."

"So when they built the bridge it stopped the saltwater here."

"Hell, no. You got your cart in front of the horse. Guarantee you no spindly-legged bridge'd ever stop any water flow what wanted to go some-wheres else. Think about it, if you were building a bridge would you rather build a long one downstream or a short one further up?"

Evan colored again. "Sure, they put it where she narrowed. Pretty dumb of me."

"No. Figuring out the why of something can be mysterious. Now, I'd say dumb if you stood on the bank and started building downstream after looking it over upstream. Besides the Indians had a log bridge or a crossing place here years before any fancy one-lane wood bridge got built. They were the ones figgered it out. We just followed their lead.

"C'mon, Lightning, 'Kane. Time to go!" He waved Evan back to the boat as the dogs returned, bounding high through the wet coarse grasses.

When the *Jeanette* reached the Pratt's fish-house, Captain Murdock was inclined to chat. Charles seemed chipper, joking with the crew. Though it surprised Murdock, he was pleased to see the change. They relaxed in the office after the paperwork had been tallied.

"George said he'll be coming back to town with me next trip. The tide's giving him sneezing spells and the fishermen all quit."

"No reason for him to suffer through that stuff."

"Think management's considering curtailing the runs until the tide clears. They were talking about once a week run just to keep an eye on things. They aren't bringing in any catch to speak of right now," the captain said.

"I could see that coming."

Captain Murdock nodded agreement.

"So think about packing out for awhile. Couple of weeks in town would be a nice change. You're welcome to hole up at my place, you're a mind to."

Charles looked his surprise.

"'Preciate that." He looked around. "I'll hafta think about it. Lots of things around here and ashore that need doing though."

"No doubt most of it can wait. No reason to sit here, the company shuts down a bit."

As the run boat pulled away Charles seemed to be watching, but a closer look showed he was deep in thought.

George went to Sam's house to check on everything before he left for Punta Gorda. The red tide had spread impressively. The wine-colored water and birds cawing over prize tidbits brought back his most persistent nightmare, the day at the shark factory when he had lost most of his hand. The shark factory. Now that had been a place, he mused. You needed a strong stomach to work there on a still summer afternoon. The ammonia smell of dead shark and the struggle to skin the sandpaper hide off those rubbery, toothed, monsters. The nightmare though was the time that half-skinned big old hammerhead shark suddenly come to life under his knife blade. It was so quick he didn't have time to be scared. He suddenly had only one finger and his thumb. He had screamed and jumped back, and the shark thrashed into the water, still attached to the chain hoist by its tail. Although it ran the chain all the way out, it couldn't get free. It jerked and whipped the water just off the landing while George stood screaming and holding what was left of his left hand. He was nearly as crazed as the shark, but finally the other men got him pinned down to wrap up the mangled hand. Nobody cared to deal with the shark, or even get near the wildly jerking chain. The hoist looked in danger of being pulled right out of its cement base. One false movement near that chain could have a person decapitated quicker and cleaner than the shark had removed the portion of George's hand.

It didn't take long before the half-skinned, bloody shark's thrashing had attracted dozens of his brothers and other kin-folk. With typical family manners, they proceeded to make that hammerhead's final moments a lasting memory for everyone onshore. They started ripping at the momentarily revived shark. The hanging skin and exposed gory flesh excited their bloodlust until they dove blindly for chunks of flesh. The hammerhead disintegrated rapidly. Probably a blessing for him, George later thought, knowing how painful it must be having saltwater in a wound of that magnitude. The chain slowed its wild dance. The water was roiled and red as the feeding frenzy only precipitated more frenzy. Sharks, half-eaten themselves, tore chunks from other sharks. More continued to come, to eat and be eaten. Belly-up victims floated free of the maelstrom only to become a separate little whirlpool of terror. Bloody spume washed ashore along with pieces of the vanquished.

Birds screamed and circled, eager for their portion, but were unable to deal with the storm as it raged. A bolder few landed on shore to pick at the strings of remains drifting in. Most circled impatiently, scolding.

The men on shore stood dumbfounded. Even George had been mesmerized, watching the death throes of what seemed to be hundreds of sharks. The more religious of the group muttered prayers, or incantations, to ward off the horror. They saw it, smelled it, heard it. Still they couldn't believe what their senses told them.

Finally the red water calmed and the birds spiraled lower, grabbing fragments of meat. As abundant as the refuse was, still they fought over choice pieces. Insanity wasn't limited to sharks—only its volume, not the intensity had muted.

But the men ignored the gulls. Supporting George, they trooped up the beach to their palm-thatch sleeping quarters, and cleaned and bandaged the nearly surgical wound that had started the frenzy in the bay. No one spoke. Eyes met and heads shook slowly in amazement.

That afternoon had been his last to clean a shark. He wanted nothing ever to do with them again. But he could not stay away from the water. Eventually he returned, not to fish, but to be around fishermen, and especially to be where the wind blew freely across the water.

George left a note on Sam's table warning that the run boat would run south only on Mondays and return the next day. Sam would be away for a while anyway and expected that to happen.

The run boat had barely begun up the coast when George's eyes were burning and tearing. He retreated to the wheelhouse, sneezing and wiping his face.

"How bad's this damn stuff in town?" he demanded.

"Nothing like out here. You can smell it though, some dead fish floating. But you get away from the waterfront and it's not real bad."

"This's the worst tide I've ever seen—and I've been through a raft of them. You won't believe it, but it's God's truth. Yesterday I motored in to Sam's place, checking on it before I left, and I passed a dead sea cow—grounded on an oyster bar in the bay. All swole up. And all kinds of fish—tarpon to pinfish. There's a creek out the north end looked as clear and pretty . . . til I looked on the bottom. Couldn't see sand at all—just covered with silver jennies. Looked like giant scales covering the bottom." George shook his head. "Goddam waste of fish."

"Wish I knew why it happens."

"Ha. Who knows? Everbody guesses. Too much rain. Not enough rain. Hurricanes. No hurricanes. Too hot. Too windy . . ."

"Jake says it's a plague."

George grinned, his wrinkle face mobile.

"Jake might be right. But seems God keeps repeating the same plague here then. Mebbe the Ole Man just gets cross sometimes, takes it out on this little corner of the world.

"One reason I've heard. This place is so full of con men and outlaws run outta other places some think it's the entry-way to Hell. This here red tide's what happens evertime the devil opens his gate for another load of sinners—little bit of his poison escapes and kills off all the sea-creatures, even with the ocean diluting it."

The captain laughed. "I like that one. Mebbe you should try that on Jake."

"That sour old reprobate would accuse me of blaspheming or something."

"Speaking of sour. Charlie Pratt's starting to perk up some. Acts like he's getting some purpose back."

"You don't say." George rubbed his face. "That's interesting. What purpose?"

"Huh?" The captain frowned. "Oh. Well, I don't know, really. He said he had lots to do around the place, straightening up and all. Seemed on track, not like he's been."

"That's good to hear. Seems strange he snaps out of it when the kid goes away." George scratched his thin scalp and repeated slowly, "But it's good to hear."

"How long Sam and the boy going to be out?"

"Oh, a week, ten days mebbe. They'll be doing a grand tour, sounded like. Sam does his hunting, but I swear it ain't the reason he goes. I accuse him of going out to watch the grass grow, sometimes. He comes back fulla stories about finding this pond-apple swamp or that palm hammock. Sometimes he remembers to mention the deer or gators too."

Captain Murdock smiled. "Sounds like the boy'll have a fine time then. Poking around at their leisure."

George sneezed, and nodded in return.

By the time they'd reached Charles's fish-house George had been sound asleep in the chair for an hour or more. He woke up to an empty cabin and soon found his way over to Charles's office. The captain was leaned back in his chair puffing silently on his pipe. Both men looked up as George came in.

"Hey, George, you're a sight for sore eyes," Charles laughed. "Pull up a chair there."

"Thanks, I think," George retorted. "You coming up to town with us?"

Captain Murdock stirred. "Can't convince him he should."

"Not this time anyway. Mebbe next trip."

"What's so pressing now?"

"Oh, just odds and ends. I want to have things all cleared up before I walk off, you know?"

"Shoot, it'll wait on you. Y'ain't going away ferever. Never know'd you to worry about dust in corners, Charlie."

"Well." Charles seemed to struggle for an excuse. Finally he said, "I'd not be able to enjoy myself with chores undone. I've let them hang long enough."

George snorted.

Captain Murdock said, "A week's a long time now."

"Yeah. It's okay. I've got plenny of supplies and as you can see more chickens than fish." He waved toward the half-dozen gutted birds he had pressed on the captain earlier. "Let me get my house in order here while Evan's away and I got time on my hands."

"OK. But I expect you to head north next week. Even if Sam and Evan come back early they'll head up overland no doubt."

Charles nodded. George appeared to be staring at the little window. He got up abruptly and went out without a word. Captain Murdock looked at Charles. Both men shrugged and smiled slightly as they, too, rose.

George, in his chair in the wheelhouse, didn't look at the other men as the run boat prepared to leave.

Standing in the sun at the corner of the place, Charles stood until the boat had gone long out of sight. Then, as though coming awake, he climbed into his skiff and sped for the island.

24

Near dusk, Sam cooked a pair of rabbits that he'd earlier shot. He spitted them on sticks over the small campfire and the meat roasted as they set up camp. They were within the brown interior of a palm hammock, strewn with crackling dead fronds. Evan had piled some firewood nearby and sat leaning against the bole of a tree, letting his tired legs rest.

"I think if a rattlesnake crawled over me right now I'd hardly move."

Sam laughed. "You'll sleep good tonight." He added some small sticks to the fire. "Actually, if a snake crawled over you sitting still'd be your best bet."

"Whew. Could you?"

"Mebbe. Never tried. Don't care to, either."

"Dad told stories about snakes crawling in the blankets at night."

"I've heard that too. But they're only looking to stay warm. Ain't cold enough for that here and now."

"Sure glad to hear that!"

The palm hammock they set up camp in was one of several they'd passed today. This one covered a large extent of higher ground, a dry island in the wet flatland they had tramped across. They had set up near its eastern edge, and Evan could look out over another wide grassy prairie similar to what they'd walked through much of the day. At first glance it looked like any field. The grass hid water under its waving leaves. Evan could not remember a time when he did not know that the Everglades was water and grass. But knowing it and walking through it were two different things. He had developed a respect for that land today.

Sometimes the water was only a couple of inches deep over a smooth rocky bottom, but sometimes it was hip-deep over bottomless soupy mud. Evan had quickly learned the value of going far out of his way to avoid those deeper spots.

The first few steps into a muddy, deep bog he had to force back his fears of an alligator or some other creature grabbing and dragging at his legs. He followed Sam's confident strides, motivated more strongly by the desire not to be left behind than by curiosity about what may be ahead. He had asked Sam if he weren't afraid of something attacking. Sam's claim that the woods creatures were more fearful of them than the reverse had eased Evan's mind. But he couldn't entirely relax with that thought whenever a sudden scurry in the grass startled him. Gradually, as the day passed, he grew less jumpy at unexpected movements and sounds. Sam pointed out alligator holes—small ponds surrounded by green reeds and flags which signaled a change in water depth. What had seemed like an endless stretch of sameness became a multitude of subtle differences as Sam pointed out details. He showed Evan deer browse-marks on ground orchids and pointed at a cabbage palm shredded by claws of a black bear. A raccoon feast on turtle eggs or the passing of a mouse could be distinctly read on the slick jellied mud lying gray-black in low spots. They explored a number of hammocks, crossing animals trails on clear, dry-shod paths that ran (to Evan's sorrow) largely perpendicular to Sam's line of march. But the sunny flowered prairies with occasional stunted trees and rock bottoms washed with water were a joy to splash across. After one crossing through a gator hole "for the experience" Sam avoided the bogs whenever possible.

With an exception. Their approach to a large strand disturbed and lifted a flock of ibis from its roost. Once they'd entered the perimeter of stunted grey cypress, Sam halted in the knee-deep water near a small dry mound. He pointed at a long dead tree, half-fallen in the water.

"We can hang our things here. Easier walking without it and we'll come back out this way." He ordered the dogs to stay as well.

There appeared to be a trail winding through the trees where under-brush and fallen branches were absent, unlike most of the visible terrain. Walking through it was a strange sensation. The water grew steadily deeper, and Evan had the illusion he walked in a creek with banks to either side. He felt a periodic urge to climb out. But the "banks" were only brush and the water as deep within it as where he waded. Water flowed around him as he slowly pressed forward, stepping over moss-slick logs and cautiously around rough limestone outcroppings. Sam warned him about most of the underwater hazards. The sun was high, so Evan could see into the water fairly well.

As the water deepened and the current strengthened, vegetation be-came greener and leafier. He saw more trees than sky. Their variety in-creased.

Sam stopped in a hip-deep glen and waited for Evan to catch up.

"Stand still a bit. Do you see the water movement?"

Evan watched a leaf float by.

"Drink from where it's coming from," Sam continued, as he leaned over and cupped some swamp-water to his mouth. "It's fine as well-water," he assured the boy. "Try it."

When Evan tasted it he had to agree.

"Cypress water's good as can be," Sam said.

It felt pleasant standing still in the moving water. Despite the heat of the day, it was cool under the tree canopy. Ahead of them, the woods opened out, stretching to either side only to meet again at the far side of a tear-drop-shaped pond. A purple haze of pickerel-weed softened the rank greenness surrounding the central, open part of the pool. The pond re-flected the blue sky—the dark pupil within the green iris of an unwinking eye. White flecked the vegetation. Water lilies floated like paper flowers, and arrowroot bloomed. A small egret sat on a branch while a larger one perched on a log. A bent cattail leaf moved and reflected a glitter of sunlight. As they stood quietly, Evan gradually saw other birds, picking them out as they tilted a head or shifted. Their purpled grays and blues hid them admirably in the tangle of trunks and branches.

Sam touched Evan's shoulder and pointed left. About twenty yards away on the weedy margin of the pond, a duckweed-covered alligator floated perpendicular to them. Even as his breath hissed in pleasure, Evan was aware of surprise that although he stood in the same water as that powerful creature, he had no fear. The low hedge of brush between them was no barrier. But he knew instinctively that he was unthreatened.

Evan breathed quietly, Mama'd love this.

Sam rested his hand on the back of the boy's neck and squeezed it.

They stood there for an enchanted time. Their small movements in the water did not reflect in the pond. When the alligator moved toward the open center of the pond he too failed to stir the syrup-like water. Birds landed, and left. A drying anhinga with wings outstretched began to groom her feathers. She folded her wings carefully into place. They could almost hear the creak of each joint folding.

Evan followed the ever-rising flight circles of some soaring birds with his eyes.

"Vultures. Couple hawks. Even an ironhead." Sam said.

Evan looked a question.

"Wood ibis."

He nodded in recognition. A crash beyond the trees startled him. It was followed by a number of others, each farther away.

Sam smiled at him. "Deer. Probly wasn't sure of danger til he heard my voice. Then he knew he didn't want any part of us."

The deer had drawn the attention of the resting birds as well. They seemed wary, nervous, after they heard the alarmed deer's flight.

"Well, son, had enough?"

"Do we hafta go already?"

Sam grinned. "If there was some way to hang in these shrubby trees, I'd be tempted to try. Sure would like to eavesdrop on this place all through the night and early morning. But . . . "

"Where ARE we going to camp?"

"Oh, it's still a couple of wet miles. And we need to find some supper too, unless you hid a cow in your pack. So let's get moving now."

Sam circled back to their packs via a different creek run. The dogs greeted them happily. As they went Sam showed Evan air plants and orchids—some that were nothing but roots spider-webbed to trees.

"Flowering time this is something to see," Sam told him. "Wintertime's the best."

As they left the central part of the strand they speeded up. The water grew steadily shallower and vegetation thinned out. Sam nodded at the sun as he adjusted his load.

"Better put those hiking feet in gear now, boy. We want a dry spot to sleep tonight."

In the few moments Evan had been resting near the campfire, he realized darkness had become nearly complete under the palms. The prairie still held some yellow monochrome light. One thundercloud, nearly over the horizon, reflected sunset color, which simultaneously rose up the cloud and dimmed as he watched. He sighed in contentment and turned his attention to the fire, focusing on the roasting meat.

"That's sure smelling good!"

"Ain't it though. Got the best spice in the world on it."

"What's that?" Evan expected to hear about a special Indian cooking secret.

Sam grinned into the fire. "Well, a hungry belly a'course!" he laughed.

"I got that spice sure enough," Evan retorted.

Dinner was quickly eaten, and Sam's fry bread mopped up the last drops on their plates. The well-polished bones went to the dogs, although they had already feasted. Sam and Evan sipped mugs of coffee as they watched the flames.

Evan's eyes were drifting shut when the owl hooted. It seemed almost overhead, startling in its unexpectedness. The raspy, querulous sound penetrated to Evan's bones.

"Gee!"

"Listen."

The answer was ghostly, faint in the distance. Their owl sounded again. A call came from a different point, and when their owl answered it his voice had moved. The buzzy-ness of the cry had evaporated with the distance and its haunting quality became overwhelming. Evan sighed.

"Couldn't hear him move at all."

"Wouldn't be an owl if you could hear him."

"Mmm."

The day had been warm, but Evan's blanket felt pleasant wrapped around him. He stretched out near the fire. Sam still moved around. He would soon be sleeping on the other side of the fire.

Evan closed his eyes. He listened for the owls, but only heard the low background of frogs and insects. The fire hissed and crackled like a friend whispering secrets, and he slid easily toward sleep.

A breeze rattled through the palms. A tree branch rubbed against a neighboring trunk, causing a creaking nearby. Sam laid a thick log over the fire, startling and crushing the nearly-asleep embers left from dinner. Then he rolled up in his blanket as well. Evan heard all these sounds without opening his eyes to check on what was happening. The large log had darkened the camp—that he could tell from behind closed eyes. One of the dogs whined in his sleep and Sam sighed heavily as he settled in.

"G'night, Sam."

"Thought you were asleep already. G'night, Evan."

Evan opened his heavy eyes long enough to see firelight reflecting from the palms' trunks, and to glimpse the moon-washed prairie beyond. It looked so bay-like he wouldn't have been startled if a sail had loomed over its whitened surface. His eyes dropped shut and he sank into sleep.

25

Bill walked around the *Jeanette*, scanning the mahogany water for signs of life. The boat's wake animated clumps and rafts of dead fish, but here in mid-bay even the birds were gone. Scavengers had eaten until they could hold no more. Now they scarcely moved from their roosts.

As he passed the wheelhouse he heard the captain whistling. Bill frowned in surprise. *Never heard him do that before*, he thought, and muttered, "First time for everything." Seems a strange time to be happy, though, with a Gulf-full of dead fish when your living depends on them.

It had been a while since the captain had been in one of his black moods, come to think about it. Maybe whatever was eating at him had been pushed aside by all the uproar this summer—Mrs. Pratt dying and all the confusion with the kids and other relatives. And Charles Pratt. *That's a man with the world on his shoulders*, he thought. Seems like the captain really got involved in their troubles. Spent a lot of time talking to Charlie. Bill had never seen any similarity between the men before. Strange, the way they'd grown together. Could be the skipper'd kept Charlie from some real bad moves. That turtle killing the boy'd found, that had an ominous look about it. It had worried Captain Murdock a lot, Bill remembered. Curious though how much Charles Pratt now reminded him of the captain—at least the captain of up to the last few months. One a family man, the other a loner. Now both loners.

But maybe the captain's interest in the Pratts extends to Miss Emily, Bill smiled to himself. *Cap'n seemed impressed with that little red-head. Maybe he won't be a loner much longer.*

"Something tickling your funnybone out there in the water?" Captain Murdock's voice boomed at Bill's shoulder, and Bill started visibly.

Bill didn't have the temerity to tell the man what he'd been thinking.

"Just woolgathering, Captain Murdock. You sneak up on a fella like that, you're likely to be running this boat alone—cause me to jump overboard from fright!"

"You sure looked like you were carrying on a conversation or something in that head of yours, Bill. Figured you wanted to share it."

"If I was, you scared it plumb out of me!" He changed the subject. "Been watching this nasty water the last half hour and ain't seen the first mullet jump or bird fly. Besides Charlie Pratt, I doubt there's a live thing between here and Romano."

"Looks that way. And we'll drag him outta here this trip. We'll bring him aboard for the ride down if he'll come. Plenty of room."

Mullet Jim had stayed at home this trip. There was no need to take ice south, and no fish to bring north. The run boat was all but empty today. It floated higher than either man was accustomed to. This would be a fast trip. The stops would be no more than quick inspections like the ones they'd completed earlier today.

But Charles wouldn't be dragged once they reached his place. "You're early," he complained. "Besides I got chores to finish over there on the island—getting the pig rounded up. Damn thing escaped on me yesterday. I'll catch you on the return."

Captain Murdock argued, but finally agreed to that.

"Understand though, we'll be here mid-morning. I'm not planning to stop back at the other fishhouses after checking them out going down. You be ready for me!"

"I promise. You can see I've been busy around here. I'll catch that pig and be all ready for you."

The captain looked at the office. Things had been cleared away, and three boxes stood under the window. One had clothing and sheets folded into it, the other two were sealed.

"Looks like you're moving out for good, not just a couple of weeks."

"Well . . ." Charles hesitated, "seemed like a good excuse to clean up proper. These two boxes I'm sending up to the kids—things they should have. You'll make sure they're mailed, now?" Charles scrutinized the captain.

"I'll let you do it, in town tomorrow afternoon."

Charles' eyes widened. "Well, yes, I keep forgetting tomorrow I'll be . . ."

"Well don't forget it in the morning—see you then," the captain interrupted.

The afternoon had been uneventful. In the week they'd been away, no storms had blown off roofs, no rogue waves smashed docks. Before long they were moored for the night. Early in the morning the run boat would chug north off the coast, the weather being so quiet, until it had to cut inshore to pick up Charles. It shouldn't be much past noon when they would tie up in town. No one on board the boat would miss the smell of death on the water.

***

The ten days in the woods had stretched to over two weeks. Evan had lost count of the number—he was surer of the downpours that passed over them—seven, or maybe eight. Some days the storms skipped by instead of soaking them; but every day the clouds grew from the horizon like unfolding genies from a lamp. It became a game to choose which innocuous puff would become the storm of the day, marshalling the other clouds into its command. The ones he picked usually faded. Sam picked winners much of the time. But gradually Evan learned the look of a storm, and before too long he could tell whether it was heading their way and how quickly it might arrive.

One night early in the trip when the moon was just past full, they broke camp at 3 AM to walk until dawn along a ridge of moonstruck pines.

The night walk made Evan nervous at first. That memory of his first wade through the swamp came back strongly. But the damp silver air and Sam's utter silence calmed him. The woods seemed charmed, as though nothing could ever harm him. When the sky began to show color he felt almost cheated, unready for the night to end.

That morning Sam cooked hotcakes after sunrise. They ate until they could eat no more, and then slept until the sun woke them near noon. Sam peered at the sky and announced they would camp where they were, so they built a palmetto frond lean-to and crawled under its protection just in time to miss a soaking.

As the rain drummed on the leaves, Sam again slept. Evan watched the ground absorb the splattering rain. Several ants sheltered on the underside of a dead leaf. He watched awhile, and then turned the leaf over. The panicked ants scattered—some flushed off their leaf by runnels of rainwater, others escaping under their own power. Ashamed, Evan replaced the leaf over the few ants he could see still struggling. But they ignored the shelter that had just betrayed them, burrowing into safer havens.

The palmettos quivered and rattled as the water flowed off. A whole troupe of bears could have passed, clanging cymbals. Evan wouldn't have known. But bears would hole up and sleep just like Sam, waiting for the rain to end.

Evan could smell the rain and the earth. Other aromas too—too faint to identify, though the dogs' noses knew them. Their nostrils moved—awake, though the dogs slept. Evan closed his eyes as well to better drink in the fragrance of the woods.

Evan saw that they were gradually working back to the west now. Sam had not said anything about returning home, but it seemed a sign to the boy. The terrain had reverted to swamp. They had left the pine, prairie and sawgrass of recent days.

"We'll be there tonight," Sam waved toward a clump of royal palms which towered in the distance.

"An old cabin. Sleep inside for a change," he joked.

"I like sleeping out."

"Yeah, you've hung in real good, son. Think you'll make a woodsman one day."

"I could stay out here forever!"

Sam laughed. "Yeah. But the world waits. Maybe the fish are running again."

"We ate fish here."

"Doubt the run boat would be willing to work through the swamp here to haul out whatever we could catch to sell. I fancy you're trying to persuade me to stay here, boy."

Evan giggled. "Guess I don't wanna go yet."

"I never do. But there's a time when the flour and bullets run low. We stay too long they start worrying that some wild cat or gator ate us. Then because they worried they don't want us to go again. They get to imagining. That's dangerous, imagining. What's real out here would as leave let you be. But the imaginings, they can go on forever, get more dangerous with every day. Can't ever let that get ahead of you."

They walked steadily on as the dogs crashed through the tangle surrounding them. In the swamp the dogs stayed close. But in the open spots they ran like the rabbits they loved to chase. No matter how distant a tree line the prairie would have, the dogs rushed to explore it for all of its new and exciting scents. When Sam entered the next strand the dogs would magically be foraging within several feet of them.

"Whose cabin is it, Sam?"

"Belonged to an old man I knew years ago. He's gone now, but the cabin's good for a little while longer. It just belongs to the woods."

"We really have to leave?"

"'Fraid so. We'll spend a couple of nights at the cabin first. But then to home."

They walked without talking for some time.

"Are you going to school this year then?"

"I guess so. Dad wants me to. He wants me to go to Michigan too." Evan whipped the cypress trunks they waded past with a frayed rope end he'd been toting over his shoulder. "I don't think he wants me around any."

"He's got a lot on his mind."

"He's doing nothing! Not fishing, not working, nothing!"

"Don't judge the outside, Evan. He's all tore up. You know how you feel. It's worse for him."

"Captain said that. And I guess it's right, Sam. But I lost Mama too. So did Katie and the rest."

"Yes. I'm not saying children feel a thing less. I've been there, son. Lost both parents. But bad as it was, losing a wife—a woman you've made a life with—has to be harder. Parents, they bring you in the world. They hope to teach you the right direction. But then sooner or later you're on your own."

He squinted as they passed through a spear of sunlight reflecting on the swamp surface. A cypress tree had fallen. The crash had torn a hole in the overhead canopy. The edges of the hole in the forest roof bled vines which had lost their support and ripped away when the big tree fell. Sam and Evan worked around the remains of the collapse. The tree's foliage was still green. Perhaps the fall had rerooted the cypress in the muck of the treacherous swamp bottom. One of Sam's feet would sink without stopping while the next foot encountered buried branches or roots that it slipped on. Sometimes those roots broke under his weight just as he lifted his other foot to go forward. Other times a web of the limbs would snap around his ankle as though he had put his foot into a bear trap.

Sam cursed under his breath as he slipped yet again. He caught himself, but not before he skidded belt-deep into slimy mud. Then he saw the cottonmouth lying on a branch just above the one he'd grabbed. Its muddy unblinking eyes gave Sam a shot of adrenaline that made him leap backwards, bruising his backside and completing his soaking. Evan started to laugh, but then saw the snake and backed up too. The snake moved just enough to keep them in sight. Not enough to allow them to think it was at all afraid. Its swamp-water eyes telegraphed that this was its place. Not theirs.

"The damn thing knows I can't shoot it. Look at it stare. If I had a machete I'd separate it from its body right like that!"

"My gun's dry." Evan started to swing it around.

"No! Not in here where you'd be ricocheting shot all over. Forget it. He'll stay right there I think. Let's just work around careful, like. And watch for others!"

The dogs waited ahead, curious as to why they were so slow. Sam moved along warily watching each branch and being cautious about what he came near or touched. Evan imitated his every move.

The swamp shallowed and became more walkable after a while. Sam said, as though he had been talking all along,

"Your folks teach you the right direction, but they keep letting go, backing off—make you do things on your own. They know someday you will leave.

"But when a man has settled down like your father, he expects to go on to the old folks home or whatever with his woman. It's a shock to have his life turned upsidedown. If one of them gets sick, the other expects to see it coming. This kind of thing, he's not ready for it."

"But he acts sometimes like he hates me—like I did it."

"No. He don't hate you. Tell me, you ever kick your dog when your mama yelled at you for something? Or a tree trunk or whatever was handy?"

Embarrassed, Evan nodded.

"Felt stupid? Felt real bad to take it out on that poor hound?"

"Yeah."

"But you still had to do it. And that dog, he'd come lick your face and tell you it's all right, but you can't stand it. You, that rotten kid that kicked him, and he's forgiving you. So you shove him away again. Poor damn dog don't understand why you stopped loving him. He thinks he must have done something pretty awful."

"So I'm like that dumb dog?"

"Yeah, a little. But the point is, remember how you felt. Bad enough kicking the dog, but having to face the hound knowing he loves you in spite of it—having to face what you know you are, that's the real bitch . . . uh, well. Your father knows he's acting bad, disappointing you. Knowing that makes it harder to pull out of it, really. Does that make any sense?"

Evan had his eyes on Lightning, up ahead. "I push Lightning away, he just goes for a run or chases some chickens, and then comes on back when I'm feeling better."

Sam grinned. "Right. Smart dog. He just comes back like it's all okay, time to get on."

"Yeah." Evan was quiet for several hundred yards. "Is that what this is?"

"What?"

"This hunt. We out chasing chickens a while?"

Sam smiled again. "I guess there's something in that. But don't expect to come home and it's all better. You'll need to keep it up a long while before your daddy can shake this."

"I know. Lightning comes and sticks his head on my knee, and I shove him away. So he brings me a stick to throw."

"And finally you chuck it to get him out of your hair, and pretty soon you're having fun with the dog, want to or not. Things shake back to normal."

Evan laughed.

"Remember, son. That dog just keeps coming back. You chase him fifty times, fifty-one you might not. He don't remember all those other times, just the one when you scratch his ears again."

They had reached the royal palms. They towered overhead, straight-trunked. In the clearing below them, the same grey as the palm boles, was a tiny cabin with an attached porch.

The dogs, though, ignored the house, sniffing in the muddy path leading to it instead. Lightning's hair had raised, and he growled.

"Zat so, boy?" questioned Sam. He bent over the dogs. "Look here, Evan, fresh tracks."

The boy looked at the slick black mud. Cat tracks. Wild cat. Panther?

"Old man screamer. Here last night, I'd judge." He straightened and glanced at the intent boy. "He may visit us tonight."

Setting up camp on the cabin floor seemed strange. Evan almost suggested sleeping outside, but the possible presence of the cat deterred him. After supper they sat on the stairs watching the sun set in the tangle beyond the palm grove. Somehow, with the house behind them, Evan didn't feel as sleepy as he usually did when dusk fell. Instead of wrapping in his blanket and snoozing, he listened to the creakings in the swamp as Sam hummed softly to himself. The dogs slept at their feet.

"Roof overhead tonight. Guess that explains the clear sky," Sam said.

"Ummm. Hasn't even threatened today."

The first stars showed. Evan noticed that when he focused on one, another would soon appear, until he lost count.

Suddenly Kane, Sam's dog, jerked up his head, listening. Then Evan heard the whispery patter. He looked behind him on the porch. A white-bellied big-eyed mouse, poised for escape, eyed Evan curiously. Its whiskers in the dusk-dim light seemed enormous, and quivered almost, Evan thought, like its heartbeat pulsed in them.

"Sam," he whispered.

The older man turned with the care Evan's voice asked for.

"Looking for crumbs. Aren't you?" Sam extended a cautious finger, and the mouse skittered backward several feet, and squeaked. After a moment it moved a little forward as Evan scarcely breathed. He could barely see the creature, except for its white belly.

Then Kane stood, looking onto the porch. As Evan watched, the mouse disappeared like sand through a crack.

In that short time night had fallen. Stars were distinct. The woods were a solid black broken by paler sky, the palms' feathered fronds high above the rest.

Evan's dog thrust its head in his lap, and sighed.

"OK, boy," he petted the dog. "OK."

Later, when they finally lay down to sleep, Evan still felt wide awake. The room was so dark the window and door stood out clearly. The old fireplace, beginning to shift, had separated from its wall in one spot, letting some light in. He focused on the crack, seeing an occasional star pass by, and listening to soft rustling in the other room—the mouse, or its kin?

He hadn't slept, he thought, but the scream brought him up as the dogs backed and their toenails skittered on the floor.

Sam's command came, low but demanding. The dogs held themselves still, jittery, as the man went to the window. Evan saw he had a shotgun in hand.

Once more the wild cat sounded. Evan's arms goosebumped. The creature wasn't far away. Long moments passed and nothing happened. Evan's eyes drooped at the same time that he felt grateful to have a solid wall at his back.

"Lay back down, son, I doubt he'll be back."

"I want to see him."

"That'd be a bit of luck. He knows we're here, and the dogs. 'Spect he'll yell again, he reaches the far side of the slough, just to let us know."

Evan lay down and was asleep as the wild cat called in his dream.

26

When Evan woke, it was to the sound of Sam's gun. Evan had slept later than usual, not waking with the sunrise as he had all the other days. This morning he was under a roof. Although it was still below the trees, the sun had definitely risen. Evan guessed that breakfast would be rabbit.

After the meal, Sam stretched.

"Two choices. We can stay here until tomorrow morning, and head for the boat. Be home by nightfall, I'd guess. Or, we could leave the boat near the rail bridge downstream, and flag down the train tomorrow. We'd get to Punta Gorda in the afternoon. I figure everyone'll be up there by now, so going back to the bay'd probably be a waste of time. Your choice though."

Evan's face shone. "The train'll pick us up?"

"Sure they will. The conductor won't be thrilled with our dogs and smelly selves, but they bend the rules when things are slack. They've stopped for me in worse shape, and we'll have time to clean up a bit anyway. Think you'd like that?"

"I sure would!"

"Settled then. Can't oversleep though, like today."

"Oh, I won't!" Evan assured him.

The day was Evan's own. Sam intended to sit on the porch and watch the sun cross the entire sky, he said. Kane lay down beside Sam where he leaned against a porch post.

It was too early for the woods. The boy and his dog headed for the prairie which opened south of the cabin. He pushed through dew-damp grass and watched the morning light glitter on the spiderwebs.

The idea of a train ride was exciting. It would be his first. Evan discovered that that prospect made the idea of leaving the woods less painful. But he might not have another opportunity to explore. He intended to use his day, big cat or no big cat.

His nervousness was gone, replaced by a watchful assessment of his surroundings. He had absorbed much under Sam's eye, and now moved quietly with a sure step. He wandered south through cypress heads and pine hammocks, marshes and meadows. He saw signs of other creatures, berrying plants, birds, and the sky. Once he found a rounded-smooth limestone rock, and stretched out on it to feel the sun bake into him. Just like a gopher snake.

He had no goal, no pressing thoughts. He saw last year's growth, died back and tangled with the vigorous shoots of the summer. Where a tree had fallen, vines wrapped it and reached for other, standing trees. Cabbage palm trunks sprouted ferns and figs where their fanned leaves had grown. Everything grew tangled with its neighbor—a part of its neighbor. Bushes intruded into the prairie, water onto ground. Nothing seemed to have a place permanently its own. The mosses on the cypress seemed eager to travel as well. It excited him to move through this restless land.

When the sun was nearly overhead he stopped. He was in an open brushy prairie. A palm strand paralleled it to the east. To the south the same vista seemed to go on for miles. Somewhere down there was a new road, the Tamiami Trail, and beyond it, mangroves and tidal bays. He felt that he could walk on forever.

Evan had a sense of reluctance about turning back. He stood alone and unprovisioned. He had to return to the cabin and Sam. But that act of facing north was an ending. Once he turned, he knew he would continue north, to Sam, to Punta Gorda, to Michigan.

As he paused, facing south, looking down at his feet, he watched the soft dark mud ooze up around his boots. It glistened in the sun, and when he raised his foot he stepped carefully to the side to preserve his bootprints. Although he had to return, his prints would remain, like the panther's. His presence would be marked, and known. He turned north and walked parallel to his trail.

***

As the *Jeanette* turned into the channel leading to Pratt's fish-house, Captain Murdock could see Charles, true to his word, drag out the second box he planned to mail. He bent over them a moment and went into the fishroom, waving a greeting to the still-distant boat as he disappeared within.

The captain concentrated on his piloting as Bill went to the lines, preparing to toss them to Charles when they neared the dock. Charles' motorboat was tied to a piling, prop in the water. Bill frowned in irritation. Charles still had to stow that before leaving. Uncharacteristic of him. He looked to be all ready with those boxes sitting out to come aboard. Probably forgotten the boat completely.

They were nearly at the mooring.

"Hey, Charlie, come catch the lines!" Bill bellowed. Murdock shifted the engine into neutral, and the noise diminished to an underlying burble. The fishhouse door remained shut. Charles didn't yell back.

The tide was easing the boat away from the dock. The captain shifted back into gear to counter it. Bill shrugged back toward the wheelhouse and leaped on deck, tying up. As he fastened the second line, Murdock came on deck.

"Hey, Charlie!"

Silence lengthened.

Murdock jumped onto the dock. Bill felt the shudder under his feet as the solid man landed.

"What the hell is he doing?" the captain frowned. He lifted the latch on the door and entering, said, "Why aren't you out there giving a hand,

Pratt?" He stood in the doorway. Bill couldn't hear Pratt's reply. Murdock leaned against the doorframe. He seemed to deflate, as though he were a balloon with a slow leak. He grasped the frame and turned outward. His face was pale and angry.

Bill was transfixed by the reaction. "What did he say?" He couldn't imagine why Charles Pratt would insult the captain without a reason.

"He didn't say anything." A clipped finality echoed in his words. "He's blown his head off."

Bill gaped at Captain Murdock as though expecting him to continue talking. The words hadn't developed meaning yet.

"Bring me that bottle." The captain nodded beyond Bill. He turned and saw that Charles had left some rum sitting on the boxes destined for his children. When Bill picked it up he also brought the note folded below the jar. He handed the rum toMurdock, who drank a deep swallow of the contents without a wince, eyes closed. When he opened them, they found the paper in Bill's hand.

"Last will and testament?" he queried bitterly. He took the paper and leaned tiredly against the building.

"Go shut her down. We'll be here a while, Bill." Murdock set the rum down and slid his backbone down the frame of the door to sit alongside it. He recognized the bottle. It was what remained of the rum he had given Charles before Amy died three months ago.

He unfolded the note, but Bill could see he wasn't reading it. Instead, he stared out across the bay. Bill had seen that defeated look before. It chilled him.

He kept his eyes on Captain Murdock a moment, then slowly went to the fishhouse door.

"There's no doubt." The Captain had closed his eyes again. "Or help."

"Well . . ."

"I know." He waved his arm listlessly. "Go on. You're half-way prepared anyway."

Bill opened the door slowly. He closed it faster, and turned away.

After a few minutes he said, "I thought he was getting over it."

"Me too. But George . . . last week George told me to watch it, that it looked like Charlie had made a decision. He suspected him, that old man. And he was on the nose."

"I'll shut down the engine." Bill went aboard.

The silence of the stopped engine opened the captain's eyes again. He shook the note's folds out and read:

> Dear Captain Murdock:
>
> I'm deeply sorry to do this to you. I wish there was a better way. But you can understand the things I'm facing. Tell my children how deeply I love them. I just can't make it without their mother. Try to make them understand. I only want to be next to her.
>
> Charles E. Pratt
>
> P.S. I built a box. It's in the office. The hole's half-dug, waiting next to Amy. Thank you.

Captain Murdock pictured his wife Lydie's grave. It had meant nothing to him. For him, she had not been present there. He had left Lydie on that island where they'd picnicked, in that sunny dell with leaves drifting down. There, Lydie could be felt. Not at the cemetery. *But I didn't bury her*, he thought. This island and Amy would be inseparable for Charles Pratt. Our women were both islands for us—refuge from this uncaring sea. He rubbed his face with both hands, and rose. He would think about it later, try to make sense of it. For now he would do what Pratt needed, what he had asked Murdock for. I'll take care of it, *Charlie. For you, and for myself as well.*

The sun hung above the island when the two men cast off. It would be nearly dark when they reached town. Captain Murdock remained very silent—even his footfalls seemed muted. Bill had no desire to talk.

His mind replayed the day in disjointed segments. Burying a man wasn't new to Bill. Even a man in his prime. Not on the edge of the wilderness. But he knew this would be one burial he would long remember.

They had brought the coffin out onto the deck. Charles Pratt had prepared well. He had planned it to the last detail. He had left sheets to shroud his body, a hammer and nails for the lid. Everything was ready. Charlie, too, had buried men. And his wife.

The coffin was painted pine. The wood had been used before—Charlie had caulked nail-holes before the fresh paint had gone on. Bill spread a sheet across the box, and they exchanged a glance before entering the fish-house. Each man took an arm and leg, bringing the body out feet-first so as not to look at the missing face any more than necessary. They fitted it into the box and Captain Murdock covered the head and shoulders with the sheet. Then it wasn't so bad, laying the limbs straight and folding the sheet neatly. He tilted the lid briefly so Bill could see its inner side. It was the cooling board, in which Evan had carved his mother's name and dates. Charles' body would face that eternally. Without haste or ceremony, the captain aligned the lid and nailed it down.

"Put his parcels aboard in case of a shower, Bill. Then we'll take him ashore." The captain went into the office, but it was tidy. The only room needing attention would be the fish room. Even in that, Pratt had thought ahead. Murdock waited on deck for Bill, and they carefully positioned the coffin across the skiff's bow, lowering it with the A-frame hoist meant to haul dead fish onto the deck.

The captain expected the sled that waited at the dock; the deceased had been thorough. The house, though, was the surprise. Only the foundation blocks and fallen chimney remained. Charles Pratt had burned it to the ground.

They left the coffin on the dock and wandered across the charred, littered ground. Bill pointed. Weeds had begun to spring up—probably seeds the chickens had missed scratching up.

"Last week?" Bill questioned.

"At least."

They walked around, kicking up an occasional chunk of metal that had partly survived the blaze.

Bill reached down to pick up a blue and white tea-cup, child-size, that was partly buried. He brushed crusted sand and soot from it with his hand and after looking at it blankly, slipped it into his shirt pocket.

The underbrush at the edge of the yard seemed poised to roll across the clearing. Captain Murdock, near its margin, disturbed a roosting hen who scolded him sharply.

"Where's the pig?" Bill asked.

"I'd check that barrel on the dock," Captain Murdock replied. "He meant us to take it off as we left."

Bill nodded agreement. "Probably been in the barrel a week, or two, as well."

Returning, they loaded the coffin on the sledge.

"Need a spade," said Bill.

"It'll be there."

As it was, and ropes for lowering. Charles had cut a joint head marker. It had both their names and the lone year date which they shared. It would span the hole Bill finished digging, and Amy's place beside it. All the graves had been recently tended and cleaned. They lowered the box and stood silently over it, each man thinking his own thoughts. Bill raised his eyes to the horizon, where the clouds seemed to be forming an anvil well off-shore. It was a beautiful day, but the stench of dead things crowded every breath. Bill suddenly wanted to be far away. The captain started shoveling sand into the hole. They traded off until it was filled, and tamped the mound tight and smooth. When they were satisfied they returned to the dock. The fish room still waited.

That was the worst. Jellied globs hung unexpectedly on the rough walls. Blood was spattered across the floor. The captain chased Bill out.

"Lower the chute and pump up some water for me. I'll deal with this."

Bill protested, but weakly. The glistening chunks of brain matter had unnerved him. He did as he was told.

Finally the captain came out with the broom. Bill kept his eyes from it. Captain Murdock swished it in the bay several times, and the water around it darkened, and then cleared. He pulled it up and looked at it a moment. Then he flung it violently into the water.

"Start the engine," he said.

27

When they got off the train in town, Jim was one of the first people Sam and Evan saw. Evan overflowed with all they'd seen and done. Jim grinned at his enthusiasm.

"You better be careful. You might git crazy as Sam here, sounds like. Why anyone wants to tramp around in a swamp he don't have to, beats me," he kidded.

"*Jeanette's* due in this afternoon," he told Sam. "And your daddy should be coming in on it, Evan."

"We'll be there at the dock, once we shed our dogs and gear at Bill's. C'mon Evan, you'll want to get a good look at that dock. The train-cars pull right out on it, by all the packing sheds."

Evan was first to see the run boat. Sam was inside a shed with some other men. The sun glared downriver, making it hard to look west. But from a distance Evan knew the old boat well. "Here she comes!" he exclaimed.

The captain knew instantly that the excited, sun-washed boy was Evan, well before he was close enough to see his smile and shining eyes. He cursed under his breath, and as his boat eased toward her mooring, he watched its shadow cut across the boy's form.

Shadows. He brought more shadows. But as the boat moved into the slip, the shadow also moved, leaving the boy in sun again. As the captain watched, the shadows on the water changed and diminished. The men mooring the vessel still moved in darkness, but Captain Murdock in his wheelhouse, and Evan on the dock, stood in the sunlight.

Strange that such a small spot of darkness could dominate even briefly, the immensity in which it happened to move. He thought of the red tide. Its touch, too, was ephemeral. Already it was dissolving in the Gulf water as though it had never been.

He stood straight, severe, alone in his wheelhouse. But he was no longer lonely, no longer eaten by the canker of his destroyed dreams. The water held more shadows. There will always be shadows. But the sun created those dark places. He knew now he would not have given up his short time with his sun, his wife Lydie, to have avoided the ensuing dark.

He looked at the waiting boy. Beyond the shadows on the sea would be light, again.

Acknowledgments

In more than a half-century in Florida, I have been blessed by meeting and growing to know many people with long roots in this fascinating place, some well-known, others less public. All had stories and information to share, and their love for and exasperation with this fantastical wilderness has shown through. Additionally, I've had the pleasure and opportunity to interview numerous long-term residents and transcribe their oral histories and diaries, and have also read accounts of all sorts from residents and visitors with their wildly varying comments on Florida's wild places. They succeeded in passing their love for this area on. I thank them all.

Special thanks go to Charles LeBuff, a family friend of many years, who loves this place, the people and the wildlife (sometimes the same thing). Our sailboat cruises with Charles and Jean added so much to Jim and my lives. A prolific author, this book would not have seen print except for him. Over many years, my late friend Lucy Fryar shared in exploring remote rivers, creeks and bays by canoe with me. Insights from our many trips will always remain. My family has explored many wild places with me. Sharing and learning about these spots bind us always. And I can't count the times Jim has shaken his head and helped put the canoe in the water, waved good-bye, and then listened to the tales I've brought back. His support has been invaluable, over so many years.

—Betty Anholt
Sanibel Island
August, 2019

About the Author

Betty Anholt is a long-term student of Florida's natural and social history, and in particular, that of Southwest Florida and the islands. She has published five books, including *Sanibel's Story, Voices and Images from Calusa to Incorporation* and more recently, *Protecting Sanibel and Captiva Islands: The Conservation Story* with coauthor Charles LeBuff. Numerous articles, columns, and smaller pieces round out her writing legacy.

Born and raised in New Jersey, Betty traveled with her family throughout Florida as a child. After graduation from Rutgers University, Betty and Jim moved to Sanibel with their young family many years ago, and owned/operated two local businesses for much of that time. She has canoe-camped along several of Florida's rivers and streams, canoeing the Suwannee from the Okefenokee Swamp to the Gulf of Mexico at the Cedar Keys, and crossed the Everglades by paddle. Reading, exploring wild places, and music are preferred pastimes. Volunteer opportunities have included City of Sanibel committees, local organizations, and extensive work in archaeological work and research. Well-versed in island history and ecology, at the writing she works in reference and cataloguing at the Sanibel Public Library.

Made in the USA
Columbia, SC
05 September 2019